i

Bay's Bet

Louise Furley

Bay's Bet

ISBN: 979-8-9859963-4-0 (Paperback)
ISBN: 979-8-9859963-3-3 (eBook)

Cover art by: *Pixel Mischief Design*
Photo: *Courtesy of Shutterstock*

ALSO BY LOUISE FURLEY

Bay's Bet

Chapter One

"Well, Bullet? You find one you like for the night or is it too early?" Shouting over the grinding blender at the end of the bar, Roddy 'Punchy' Curtis, an agent at Evgeny, a privately owned military base, swigged the longneck he held between thumb and finger.

Banter and laughter flowed amiably around *Prontos*, the local tavern in the town of Doberman, Colorado.

The earsplitting whir of the blender mixing margaritas finally silenced, giving everyone within earshot relief.

Hunched over his beer, the corner of his mouth quirked in irritation, Commander Bayou 'Bullet' DaRocco grumbled, "Hell, Punch, you ever talk about anything else other than skirts? Why don't you try something different like sports, movies, fishing, hunting, motorcycles-"

Grunting, "Ugh, bro," Roddy furtively slew his pale green gaze to the side without turning his auburn-topped head, as if no one could tell he was checking out every female in the place.

He said to Bullet, "We had a tough few months in that fuckin' hellhole of a dusty desert and we deserve some female R and R. You should be hungrier 'n me because you just got back from Washington after months of top-secret intense debriefing, and the additional complex transfiguring of the latest mission."

1

Roddy's gaze slouched back to his commander, and friend, with a sly grin. "Unless you were dickin' one of the chick interrogators, eh?"

The sardonic roll of his eyes bouncing uselessly off Roddy, Bay DaRocco lifted his jaw at his empty beer when the bartender came nearby.

The barman nodded and turned to grab up a fresh frosty mug.

Tossing down a slug of beer, Roddy wiped the back of his ruddy hand across his mouth and said with a snicker, "The ones I've seen there all look like female Sylvester Stallones to me, but hey," he shrugged, "in the dark, they got the right parts, so who gives a shit?"

Down a few stools, a redhead also, but his was more orangey and springy, Fitzgerald Willis primped his hair trimmed short on the sides, and a bit longer on top in military style.

Fitz looked around the bar also searching out single females. His locks were tight coils while Roddy's were darker with looser waves.

Fitz said with a snigger, "You're always on a female R and R, Punchy, remember those Egyptian chicks we banged in Istanbul?"

His pale eyes lighting up in recall, Roddy raised his bottle in a toast and grinned. "Hell yeah, what a fucking night that was!"

Fitz agreed with a leer of reminiscence. "Yep. Out in the middle of damned nowhere and Bullet shows up with a half a dozen doe-eyed wenches in tow. You about shot your wad trying to get one of them away from clinging all over him and interested in you. They had their hands in that honey colored hair of his, and vying to catch the attention of those jade green eyes."

2

"Aw, screw you Freckled Fitz, what're you, a fuckin' poet? You sound like you're in love with the commander, you jackwad," Roddy groused.

Fitz slingshot a rude comeback and the two redheads commenced bickering.

Beside Bayou DaRocco sat his best friend, Jules Winston. Copying Bay, Jules was hunched over his beer, but he held a phone to his ear. He clicked off the cell and stuffed it in his pocket with a pleased smile.

"Ah," Bay guessed with a knowing smirk, "date?"

Nodding cheerfully, Jules grinned. "Yeah, tomorrow night. Yvette. Met her the other day. She had a flat tire. All I saw was long, long legs under a very short skirt and flying yellow hair." Jules added with a chuckle, "I don't even remember changing the flat."

"Good for you," Bay said and broke off as a group of young women entered the saloon in a small babbling clutch.

When on leave, the DAK agents hung out at Prontos along with most of the occupants of the base.

Bay was commander of DAK, a secret squad comprised of blackout members, a short-armed, classified side of the Evgeny Base. They executed off-the-record covert missions. The squad was so clandestine most of the population had no idea it existed.

Even the other inhabitants at the base were unaware of exactly what DAK was and had no knowledge of their missions. They only knew they were an elite team of something, like the SEALs, and knew to not get into beefs with them.

DAKs did not back down from provoked fights, and due to their extreme training, never lost one.

People only guessed at what DAK meant. Some said it was Dark Agent Knights, others said it was Deadly Assassin

Killers, but that was ridiculously redundant, so people guessed on, coming up with more dangerous, and more mysterious sounding acronyms.

All well over six feet and stacked with muscles built more from real combat than workouts, the agents had no problem attracting attention from interested parties.

As the leader, the most powerfully built, and most lethal member of the team, hence the tag Bullet, Bayou DaRocco barely registered the continuous female attention he drew. He gets what he wants when he wants it, the rest was just a tinnitus haze of annoying gnats.

Prontos, the rustic bar composed of light colored wood, with white oak walls and cedar flooring had billiards playing in the back, and darts off to the side. A jukebox boomed, though on the weekends local bands played, and there was room for dancing.

Several TV monitors spread up high across the wall behind the bar counter were tuned to different stations showcasing sports. They were on but the sound was muted.

Amber lighting made the bar just dark enough for a bit of mystery, but light enough you could see who you were going home with.

Seeing Bay's mouth part slightly and his eyes brighten, Jules followed his line of attention. It was on the group of females settling at a table.

Six young women altogether and they must have started their drinking somewhere else because they were boisterous and laughing.

Commenting, "A hen pack, Bay," Jules set his beer on the counter and poked his friend with his elbow. "A wise man knows enough not to get involved with one of those. You have to wait until a bird separates from the herd and then make your move."

"Flock. You're mixing up your veneries."

"Huh? My what?"

"Collective nouns."

At Jules' confused expression, Bay told him, "Collective animal nouns, you know, packs, flocks, herds, schools, etc."

"Uh, sure. Okay. Whatever." Jules glanced over at the women and shrugged. "It's just Farah, Jessica, Ella, Marianna, you know, the usual. Civilians, admin assistants, analysts, researchers, the only agent is Wanda."

Tilting his head slightly to Bay, Jules asked, "What's with the big eyes?"

When Bay didn't answer, he glanced over his shoulder again, then smiled. "Ah, the new one. You haven't met her. You've been gone for months, bro. She's here for classes and training in strategy and air intelligence." His gaze flickered briefly up to one of the TVs to catch the score.

"And?" Bay chugged half his beer, discreet scrutiny under hooded eyes traced across the room to the table of women.

"And what?" Jules smirked.

With an exasperated exhale, Bay said, "And, who the hell is she?"

Jules shook his head. He kept his black hair just a shade longer than the rest of the men, combed straight back. His black goatee was neat and trimmed. Irises so dark they appeared to be all black pupils twinkled at his friend and commander.

"She is, ah, wait, she has a fucking long first name," his lids lowered as he thought. "Yeah, it's something like Elizabeth, or, yeah, Elizavetta…ah, Stirling. Wanda said she had no patience to learn, much less say the girl's name so

5

she called her Livy, and," one shoulder rose as he took a sip, "it stuck."

Roddy craned his neck around Jules and snickered, "We call her Creamjeans."

Both tawny brows arched. "Creamjeans?" Bay repeated.

His laugh snarky, Roddy winked a light green eye and replied, "Yeah, even though she hides it with her hair pinned up tight with that thick hairband covering most of it, and those frumpy ugly clothes, those stupid tinted glasses, she exudes like this insane sensuality even when just sitting like a statue with her head down.

"Steams my eyeballs up every time she walks past, and what a fucking walk she has. It's nuts 'cause you can't see her figure, her hair, or her eyes, yet there's that something…"

Fitz agreed, "Yeah, statue, you got that right, a stone cold statue. A fucking iceberg, won't give a guy the time of day." He scowled into the beer his freckled hands were wrapped around.

"So cold an artic breeze follows in her wake." Sticking his face in his beer mug, Fitz muttered, "Probably has polar bears and penguins as freaking pets."

"Anyway," Roddy continued, "I'd like to stick my Eskimo into her igloo. We call her Creamjeans 'cause one look at the fine sway of her ass and a man practically creams his jeans wanting to-"

"Why don't you shut the fuck up you crass bastard," another agent scolded him as he joined the group, waving to the bartender for a drink.

Tucking a hand in his pocket, Von Green, as tall and strongly built as the rest of them, hid his pristine white teeth in the dirty look he shot the ruddy-skinned agent.

Von's sharp cheekbones and crescent eyes were from his Asian mother, and skin dark as coffee with a tiny dollop of cream from his African father. Hair in neat braids scrolled down his head and tied back in a band letting the braids trickle past his shoulders.

He wore his normal uniform of perfectly creased, expensive black slacks, starched black shirt and dark blue tie, his polished designer shoes cost more than four month's pay. He inclined his head to Bay and Jules in greeting.

While the men argued, Bay set his mug down and went to slide off his stool, Jules grabbed his arm. "You don't wanna try it, Bullet, every guy has hit on her. And I mean, every guy, and," he grinned, "I hear a few girls did too. Everyone wants to see what's beyond that plain, cold exterior.

"I think Irish O'Connor, you know, Nels, said there might be a blazing inferno beneath all that frump. That got everybody's juicy interest, you know, got their horndogs on. But, bro, she barely makes eyes contact when she shoots everyone down."

"Yep," Fitz said. Pastel blue eyes blurred from alcohol, he scratched a few freckled fingers through the red springs on his head. "Sweet Livy puts the sugar in the frost in frosting."

Roddy's grin turned loopy. "Yeah, she also puts the frost in frosty."

A clap of laughter barked, Roddy had only a few freckles, he wasn't covered with them like Fitz, they darkened on his ruddy face. He wiped the back of his hand over his nose, "Frosty, yeah, she's frigid cold like Frosty the Snowman."

"Nah, that's Frostine the Snowgirl," Fitz said and the two men chortled.

7

"Huh," Bay grunted, and paused in his step. "Stuck up conceited bitch? Waiting on the rich guy to come around to stick her claws into?" He slid his ass back on the stool; a huge bicep bulged as he picked his mug back up.

He wore his striped button down shirt tucked into black jeans, the long sleeves rolled up just below his elbows. One boot hit the floor, the other set on the stool rung.

"Not my type," Bay muttered. "Anyway, I don't get involved with the broads on the base," but his hooded gaze hadn't wavered from the new girl.

"No, she doesn't act like that. She just keeps to herself, bro. Doesn't speak to anyone, stares off blankly. What you can see of her eyes," Jules pondered, "they're like, uh, sounds like a cliché, but they're haunted, sad, and I don't know, scared maybe.

"There's a rumor, someone said they overheard Lieutenant Colonel Garrett Miles talking on the phone, and supposedly she had been in an…extraordinary, traumatic situation where she was in terrible danger, got hurt real bad."

He ruffled a hand over his sleek black hair. "Anyway, that's all we got. Whatever it was, it put her off men. So, don't get your balls shot down like the rest of us. Just go for, oh," Jules tipped his head in the direction of a busty blonde at the table, four of the six women were blonde. "You wanna get your rocks off, go for Marianna. You know she's got it bad for you, just stick it to her already."

Bay frowned at his friend, said with a curled lip, "Way too high maintenance, way too much plastic, and she has gecko hands. Marianna wants to grab ahold of me and keep me. You know I'm not a long term kind of man." He picked up his mug and slid off the stool to his feet.

"True that," Von agreed.

8

Bay's curled lip twisted. A shudder rolling across his wide shoulders, he said, "She rubs all over me like a cat in heat. I prefer a woman wait until invited before humping my damned leg."

Jules snorted, then choked on his drink with a laugh. "What about Jessica? Huge handful of tits, big ass, lotta guys dig it."

Bay grunted. "Sure. She hardly comes up for air rolling out from under one guy to the next. No thanks."

The bar was packed, but his objective clear, Bay's attention was still on the one group of women. He muttered under his breath, "I'm not into big asses, I like my women rounded, but not huge like a fucking donkey. I wanna fuck 'em, not ride 'em. They're supposed to ride me."

The guys laughed, Bay kept his head slanted towards the females under discussion.

Seeing his interest still on the new girl, Fitz said to Bay, "Yeah, go ahead and try it, Bullet," he snickered. "I bet a 50 spot you hit the wall of ice and skid flat on your face like the rest of us."

"I'm in with that," Roddy sniggered, "that's a bet we'll win. You might snag the ladies with that hard-assed tough face you got, but trust me, you will have zero chance of bagging her, Bullet."

Tossing back the rest of his beer, Bay set the empty mug on the bar and turned from his team.

"You've never hit on the local talent before," Von pointed out. "Why her?"

Bay shrugged without answering.

"Huh." Von considered his friend's low hooded lids over shrewd eyes subtly watching the girl, his jaw set but flexing. "I can see those grey cells firing, my friend. You're devising a plan. Share with us, oh Great Commander. Show us neophytes how it's done," Von chuckled, teasing.

The others waited with interest for Bay's response.

One wide, muscle-packed shoulder bumped, Bay responded coolly, "I have strategy, boys."

"Hey," Roddy slurred, he was halfway to trashed, "that oughta work. Livy's training is in strategy and intelligence."

Jules shook his head grimly. "I'm warning you, don't bother-" but Bay was already crossing the room.

He threaded around tables, he knew a lot of people there, many trained and worked at Evgeny. He smiled equably and nodded, said a few brief words here and there but kept moving.

When he reached the six women, he nodded at Farah and Ella, said to Wanda, "Hey, I heard you scored the big twenty-one on your last sniper trials. Congrats, girl, that's great."

Wanda twirled a long black braid around her hand and cocked her head up at him with a coy smile. "Yeah. I practiced like a son of a bitch, I dang well should have scored big. But," her gaze scrolled down the hard body of Commander DaRocco with approval, "no one yet has reached your high perfect score of 30."

She let her gaze drift back down and then up, an overture offering brow arched. Her mouth a suggestive curve, she purred, "Maybe you could give me some lessons some time. What do you say?"

Bay smiled with a relaxed shoulder bump. "Sure. Maybe next week when we have breaks."

"Bay, darling," Marianna clutched his arm. Running her long nails up through the hair on his rocky forearms, she simpered, "What about me? I could use some lessons too. How about-"

Shaking his head, "Uh huh," Bay grasped her wrist lifting her talons off him and said placidly, "you don't have a weapon's permit and you don't need sniper skills to type. So," he turned from her quickly before she could respond, "what's up with you, Jessica?"

"You, if you'd let me." Jessica's smile of greeting and offer were blatantly inviting, he just smiled benignly.

Bay acknowledged all of the women except the new girl. He never looked in her direction, or asked her name, or for an introduction.

Peripherally, he could see she never raised her eyes up to him, but he knew she still had to be aware he ignored her. Part of his strategy, make her think he wasn't interested.

With a cock to his head and a short grin, he tipped two fingers to his temple and said, "See you ladies around," and he strolled off to speak with another agent who just arrived.

Chapter Two

"Yikes, Livy, he sure cut you dead," Farah exclaimed, blinking dark espresso eyes. "I guess he only has it for blondes." She fluffed her frilly blonde curls that bounced around her collar.

The other women casually tossed around demeaning comments about Livy's plain looks.

Saying with false compassion, "Oh, well," Jessica glanced at Livy with her head tilted up, she looked down her nose at her. "It's sad you're so homely, I hope you aren't jealous of some of us. I'm sure there's a guy out there for you. Computer nerds aren't always that particular about a girl's looks, ya know? They're just grateful to get a date."

"Ha," Marianna snorted, "or you can check out some of the classes held for the blind students."

Shooting Marianna a look of reproach, "It's those clothes, Livy," Ella offered, "makes you look like you have the figure of a potato." Her platinum blonde hair was straight as an arrow and sharply cut straight across her shoulders with blunt bangs. The lowlighting in the bar made the platinum glow like a flashlight's beam.

"No doubt you probably would do a potato proud, lumpy and frumpy," Marianna sniffed.

"Honey," Wanda said helpfully to Livy, "your hair. I mean, really, what adult woman wears a wide hairband like that? It makes it hard to tell what color your hair is. I don't think you've had your hair down and no band since you set foot on the base."

She leaned in with a kind smile. "Really, not everyone can have bleached hair like these other girls, or the natural ebony of my gorgeous locks," she fingered her braid that flopped over one seriously toned shoulder. "But still-"

"Ack," Jessica coughed rudely. "You get that 'natural' color out of the same bottle we do, hon." Her nose still up in the air, she sniffed haughtily. "She's right," she sneered at Livy who never raised her head, "that is something you could at least try to do to improve those mediocre looks of yours."

Eying Livy with disdain, Marianna shook her head, "I don't think even a good style and color will help that plain Jane."

"Come on, Mari, you've seen her hair down in the locker room." Ella directed her kind smile to Livy. "She has the loveliest shade of oh, I'd call it rich hickory, with brilliant flaxen highlights. And, it is obviously really natural, unlike," she looked pointedly at Marianna's locks, "the rest of us. She-"

Blurting, "Um, please excuse me," Livy pushed her chair back and stood up, her cheeks reddened at being the object of dissection. "I'll, uh, be right back."

"Honey," Farah said to her, "I'll go to the ladies with you if you wait a sec-"

"No, thanks. I'm good." With a quick shake of her head, Livy rushed off before anyone could get up. She hurried

13

through the crowded noisy bar, head down lest she make eye contact with anyone.

She didn't let out her held breath until she reached the ladies room. She chose the restrooms furthest from the bar at the back of the building, down a rarely used hallway.

Closing the door, she leaned her back against it and took a deep breath. Then she bumped as someone pushed at the door. Reluctantly, she stood aside so the person could come in.

Ella Carmichael entered the room with a mollifying smile. "Hey, Livy, listen, they didn't mean any harm, really, we're all just catty being on a military type base with so much male meat, we're competitive." She followed Livy as she moved to stand in front of one of the mirrors in the pink and gold room.

"It's okay, Ella, truly, I don't care." Livy smoothed a few tendrils back that had escaped her bun and straightened the wide band, then adjusted the tinted glasses over her small, slightly upturned nose.

Ella moved up next to her and took a comb out of her purse. Stroking the comb not through but over her hair that barely moved like a platinum shield hanging straight to her slightly round shoulders, she studied herself in the mirror.

Reapplying the cat's eye liner over her hazel eyes that gave her a blonde Cleopatra look, Ella said, "It's just, you know, you keep to yourself, you're so quiet, like a little church mouse. Sure, you're kind of plain, but that hasn't stopped the men from hitting on you. Why don't you go out with one or two or," she twisted the wand back into the tube, "three, lighten up."

Not replying, Livy bent and splashed water on her face then tugged out a few paper towels to dry off.

14

With a short laugh, Ella said, "Well, at least that's one good thing about not wearing makeup, you don't have to worry about smearing and such. I do hate when, you know," she smiled at her reflection, tweaking the blunt cut bangs with her fingers, "you perspire when fooling around and your makeup runs."

She bit off a giggle, then sighed. "Or worrying about his comments in the morning, if of course he stays the night, that he doesn't recognize you from the bar the night before, 'cause your makeup is half gone."

Ella unbuttoned another button on her already partially unbuttoned blouse to expose more of a rather meager bust.

Just slightly plump, Ella sighed at her reflection. "I really have to get to that gym, you know, maybe if I drop some pounds my cheekbones will stand out more, maybe have some more definition to my face."

Tearing her eyes away from her reflection for a brief second, she glanced at Livy then back to herself. "Like you. Even with those enormous glasses hiding half your face, you can see you are fine-boned. Except for those round cheeks, your face is so delicate. Like all over, you are a small thing, aren't you? You always seem bigger because of those baggy clothes you wear."

Still not saying a word, Livy balled up the paper towels and tossed them in the trash.

Ella rattled on, "At least we got you out for a change. You've only gone out with us a few times since you came here. You know we females of the NOVA unit must stick together, hon."

At Livy's lack of response, she prattled on, "So, the men in the DAK squad are all pretty hot, big, buff and tough, but that Bullet," she laughed. "I mean Bay, Commander Bayou

DaRocco," she waved her hand like a fan at her suddenly heated face, "he is one fine hunka man-meat."

Sighing in rejected aspiration, she inclined her head to Livy and said vaguely puzzled, "It's strange that he didn't even look in your direction much less greet you.

"Normally he has such a keen notice of anything at all different on base, people or things. You can tell he's a combat guy, but they keep him and his agents very hush-hush. They only show up on the base when they have a new exotic training, or a big secret mission to plan."

At Livy's continued nonresponsive silence, Ella carried on, "Oh well," she shrugged. "You wouldn't be able to hold a man like that's attention for more than one quick fuck, uh," she broke off at the flush rushing Livy's round cheeks.

"I mean, he might give you one night at the least out of sympathy of being with a plain Jane. A pity fuck you know? But, shit, you should take it. Any girl on this base would jump at it. Guy like that's gotta rock in the sack."

She paused while pushing at her eyelashes to help them curl. "He is one rough looking man, not handsome, just, hmm," she thought about it. "Dangerous. He looks darkly dangerous. Deadly. Ahh," she groaned, waving at her face again. "But he is so big. Hell, his cock is already a nice bulge in those jeans, I bet when he's hard he-"

Saying quickly, "I'll see you back at the table," Livy turned and made for the door. Actually, she'd had more than enough of 'going out' to last a long while.

As she fled the room she could still hear Ella jabbering on about the commander's privates. Slipping her purse strap over her shoulder, Livy exited into a hall, and looked in both directions.

To the left was to return to the bar. To the right, she saw a door that likely led out the back way. Not desiring any more visiting, with catty women or rude commanders, she headed towards the door.

As she passed the men's room, the door opened. She hastened by even when the man coming out said something to her.

"Hey there, sweetheart."

When she kept going, he said, "Hey, wait up," and strode quickly down the hall after her.

When he reached Livy, he moved to step in front of her, blocking her exit. "Don't run off there, sweetness, let's talk a minute. I haven't met you before. You one of the party girls? I heard they flock the base." He bent his head to get a better view of her, but she lowered her face.

"What's your name, sweetness? I'm Duke Rashad, and you are?"

"If you'll excuse me, I need to uh, go." Livy tried to step around him but he moved to block her path.

Handsome in his classical looks and olive complexion, he frowned. "Hey now, sweetness, that's just kinda discourteous you know. When a guy introduces himself, it's polite to respond in kind, not brush him off."

Mumbling, "I don't mean to be rude, please," nearing the wall, keeping her head down Livy tried again to step around him. "But I need to go, please let me pass-"

He suddenly slammed a hand against the wall by her head.

Livy jumped, startled, then moved to go the other way but he slapped his palm on the other side of her fencing her in.

"Now," the cajoling pleasantness left his voice and it angrily sank low in a coarse abrade. "I said, it is impolite for you not to tell me your name. A dowdy thing like yourself should be grateful I'd give you the time of day."

He leaned in close and conspicuously sniffed at her. "But, hell, there is something about you that is… elegantly arousing, makes my nuts spasm."

Her back against the wall, Livy thrust her hands against his chest and shoved him, demanding, "Leave me alone-"

Obviously intoxicated, his dark brown eyes flaring, Duke dropped a hand and deliberately palmed his hardening erection, then, he reached up for her.

Saying, "Now then," he gripped her chin, raising it so she was forced to look at him. "First, a kiss, then your name. Actually, on second thought, I don't really give a shit what it is, I just want a little feel, see how that goes before we go further, eh?"

Livy struggled to free her jaw from his grasp but he was too strong. She hit at his arm that was fencing her in, he just laughed at her.

"Seriously, you can't hurt me, sweetness, now, give me what I want." Holding her chin, he lowered his mouth to hers muffling her scream, and moved his other hand to shove up her blouse.

Livy squirmed, punching at his arms, his chest, but he grabbed at her breasts and kissed her with bruising force.

The aggressive violence felt suddenly so familiar, Livy's throat compressed, she couldn't draw a breath, panic overwhelmed her, blinding her. Her brain a buzz of terror, she couldn't think.

God, please, she was back there, back there with that monster. The cold cement floor banging her spine, scraping her back as he dragged her, ripping her clothes off, forcing her face first on the table while grabbing the cuffs- the frantic, futile screams for her father to come help her bubbled up but she couldn't get them out-

"Fuck, sweetness," Duke muttered against her mouth. "I can't get a good feel with those heavy clothes and thick bra. Let me, I'll take you out to my car and show you what I got for you, babe. You're a tiny thing, ain't gonna put up too much of fight, eh? Be like carrying a fussing kitten."

He dropped his hand to reach between her thighs. "I'll bet you're tender and tight, and real sweet down there, huh?" Glassy eyes heavy with lust peered through dark wavy hair flopping in them, his leer raked from her chest down to her sex

His voice was different from her nightmare- Livy shook her head back and forth to clear it. Blinking crazily, no, she realized that she was not back in the blood-bathed cabin, but she was under attack.

"No!" she screamed pushing from him, but he grabbed her and shoved her hard back against the wall, banging her head and knocking the wind out of her.

He reached his hand to cup her sex over her jeans, growling, "You're coming with me-" and then he was gone.

The man who had stopped at their table, Commander something, had gripped the back of Duke's collar and with an enraged snarl, hurled him into the opposite wall.

Slamming into the wall, Duke shook the stars out of his head with a curse, then lunged at the commander with a furious roar, "You fucking bastard, I'll-"

Bay threw an uppercut so fast Duke never saw it coming.

As Duke reeled from the punch and Bay went to town on him, wailing his fists all over the other man.

Duke sunk to his knees with his arms up trying to protect his bloody head, but that didn't stop the maddened commander. Bay clutched his shirt holding him up and landed punch after punch, blood spattered at the wall and the hall carpet.

Gaining orientation, still pressed against the wall, Livy saw the commander pummeling the man that attacked her.

Blood sprayed everywhere as Duke grunted with each bone-breaking blow Bay landed. Duke's body was limp yet the commander kept hitting him, he was killing him.

Coming fully to her senses, Livy ran to them screeching, "Stop!" She grabbed at Bay's arm. His bicep so big she couldn't get two hands around it, she frantically clutched at him, shouting, "Stop before you kill him!"

A red haze of rage deafened Bay to her screams. Shoving her back, he kept punching the now unconscious man.

On his way to the restroom, Von Green heard Livy's screams and dashed down the hall.

Seeing the chaotic violent scene, he raced over, bent and grabbed Bay's arms tried to pull him back, calling out, "Bay, bro, enough, stop!" But Bay kept pounding on Duke.

Then Von barked with a loud snap, "Commander DaRocco, cease!"

His words broke through the blinding rage and Bay allowed Von to pull him off Duke.

Sweat darkening his temples, Bay's shoulders rounded like a boxer's, arms bowed. Bloodied fists crunched tight, his big chest heaving from his hard panting, he glared at the prone Duke.

"Motherfucker was practically raping her against the fucking wall, Von, he was going to force her into his car."

Blinking back more sweat dripping from a lock of hair hanging over an eye, he turned to Livy who had flattened herself back against the wall when Von had interjected.

"You," Bay snarled, pointing at her, "you got no sense getting between two brawling men?"

Her mouth dropped, then her brows drew down like daggers, she spouted angrily, "There weren't two brawling men, there was one man pulverizing another. I was trying to keep you from getting arrested for murder."

Dragging his arm across his sweating brow, Bay snapped, "You're welcome."

Red spots struck her rounded cheeks, Livy lowered her head in her habitual humbling stance. "I didn't ask for your help. I..." she sniffed back a tear daring to escape and mortify her further. "I had everything under...control," sniff.

The old nightmare still bashing around in her head, when she looked down at the bleeding battered man, she didn't see him, she saw poor Jenna lying there broken in a pool of blood.

Lifeless eyes staring up- Livy's own screams reverberating in her ears- she covered her face with one hand, the other pressed against the wall holding her up on shaky legs.

Aghast that she thought she could stop the huge Duke Rashad from abducting her, Bay spurted, "You had shit under-"

Announcing, "I'll be right back," Von ran into the restroom and came back out with handfuls of paper towels, he handed a few to Bay and the others to Livy.

Bay wiped the sweat from his face and the blood off his knuckles. Livy turned away and dabbed at her betraying eyes, willing herself not to cry.

Her head down, she said quietly, "I uh, need to go. Maybe Mr. Green you could help...uh, Duke there," she motioned to the man bleeding on the carpet, "to the hospital?"

"Honey," Von said softly, "you shouldn't drive. I mean," he glanced pointedly at her trembling fingers wringing each other, her chest panting with alarmed fright.

Tossing the towels in a bin by the door, boots akimbo, arms crossed over his chest, Bay told her, "You can't go, you need to wait for the MP's." He fished his phone out.

Eyes wide behind tinted glasses, Livy said quickly with agitation, "No, no police, don't call the police."

"What? The fucker- uh, asshole tried to rape and abduct you! You need to file a report, you-"

"No," she cut Bay off. "No. I am not filing a complaint. It's over, you, uh, punished him enough. I...need to just...go." She didn't need her name plastered in the news again, a victim again, the butt of pitied or malicious gossip again. The salacious sensationalism, *no*, she edged towards the exit door.

Bay strode to her, raking an angry hand through his light hair, dark shamrock eyes darkened further. "No," he stood between her and the door, his palms up. "You have to make a police report, and you sure as hell can't drive home in the condition you're in."

His piercing gaze grazed hard over her pale as snow face, her blouse pulled up ruffled and askew, loosened hair wisped around and down well past her shoulders.

His eyes narrowed peering through the tinted glasses. Even through the tint he could see the terror still radiating.

Bay was so big and threatening barking at her, Livy backed up with her hands raised to ward him off. "Please, don't hurt me," her voice wobbled hoarsely. She turned her head as if she thought he was going to strike her.

Stunned, Bay dropped his hands and took a step back from her. Incredulous at her insinuation, he boomed at Livy, "Hey, shit, woman, I'm not going to hit you, for fuck's sake, are you crazy?" Hell, he was twice her size, he could kill her with one punch.

Mollifying them, "Okay, okay," Von moved to the pair. Trying to diffuse the overwrought situation, his voice deep and soothing he said, "Let's stay calm here. Bullet, uh, Commander, she has the right to press charges or not, maybe after she thinks about it she can go to the police. Right honey?" His dark face shiny with the heat from everyone's tense emotions, he smiled kindly at Livy.

"Yes, I'll…go home and think about it. Please," she uttered in an almost inaudible voice gesturing for Bay to move out of her way.

Dragging his hands through his thick hair again, half of it spiked up from the motions, "Fine," Bay said, but didn't move for her to pass.

"You think about it. But you are not getting behind the wheel of a car. I have rank on this base, Miss, even over you as a civilian. I am a commander, you have to obey me. I will drive you home and-"

He broke off at the stiffening of her shoulders, her skin paled even further if possible, her eyes dropped to his knuckles still red from Duke's blood, she shivered.

Von looked from one to the other, then said to Bay, "Well, how about you get Jules or someone who can keep his mouth shut to help you with," he shot the prone Duke a sneer of contempt, "him, and I will take Miss Stirling home."

Bay frowned when he observed some of the quaking in her body lessen somewhat at his suggestion, for Von, not Bay to drive her, but still she shook her head.

"No, don't be ridiculous, I am fine. I need to go." She fumbled for her keys in her purse then swayed against the wall to keep herself steady on shaking legs.

"Woman, uh, Miss," Bay grasped her arm to steady her, and snatched her purse out of her hands.

"What are you doing? Give me my purse!" Livy's nerves tightened her vocal cords, her objection came out in a squeak.

Leaning her to the wall again so she could use it to brace herself, Bay released her arm and opened her purse ignoring her protestations.

He took out her keys and handed the purse back to her. She grabbed it and held it against her chest.

"Like I said, you are not driving. You can choose either me or Von here to take you home. I'll have someone bring your car around later." He and Von stared with inarguable stoic faces at her.

"I…but…" a whoosh of defeated air exhaled. "All right. Fine. If Mr.," her head lowered, "Green wouldn't mind driving me…" She didn't see the tightening of Bay's jaw.

Annoyed at her choice, Bay nodded once sharply. "All right then. I will see to Rashad here," he inclined his head to Livy, "and Von will take you home."

The two men shared a look.

Rage still coloring his face, looking down at Duke, Bay muttered, "I need to chat with the asshole when he wakes anyway, ask him if he knows what the word eunuch means."

Holding his arm out for Livy to take, Von smiled calmly at her. "Okay, I'll see that you get home all safe and sound." He said to Bay with a nod, "I'll see you at the wedding next week."

Livy cast a wary eye at him, then his arm, then to Bay, who was now staring at her with a dark glower.

She took the proffered arm, and Von walked her out the back door shooting Bay a wink as they left.

Chapter Three

Due to the incident, Bay could not ignore Livy like he planned. The few times they'd run into each other he tried to talk to her, but she just kept that frustrating head down and mumbled nonsense words as she hurried past him.

Jules, looking like he'd been to the gym, sweaty in shorts and tank top, crossed the grassy yard between buildings.

Bay's team of agents all had their own residences as did many of the others, but the new agents in training stayed in the beige barracks and ate at the mess on the base. The civilians training or working there had apartments off base.

Because they had a mission coming up, the DAK squad was at Evgeny every day for combat and weapons training, and planning.

"Wassup?" Jules greeted Bay. He walked with his hands holding the ends of the towel slung around his neck. His black hair damp with sweat made it look sleeker than ever.

"Not much, I'm headed to the chow hall for a burger. You coming?" Bay moved in stride beside his friend.

"Yeah, I need a shower and change, I'll meet you there."

They traipsed over the expanse of green lawn disregarding the signs posted that said 'Keep off the Grass.'

"So," Jules twisted and cranked his neck stretching the kinks out earned from his tough workout, said with a camaraderie smirk, "making any headway with the new honey?"

His bottom lip bunched into the top one, Bay didn't look at him, keeping his gaze in a continuous sweep of the compound as they walked. "No. She practically runs when she sees me coming. That fucking Rashad fucked up my strategy."

Flashing him a cheeky grin, Jules laughed. "And what was your strategy?" He pawed his goatee, combing it with his fingertips.

His big shoulders shrugging, Bay watched a team of new recruits running in a line with heavy packs on their backs, their muffled chants dancing on the wind behind them.

"I had planned to ignore her for a while, especially when she was with other people that I could talk to. You know," a tad sheepish, mouth pulled in, "you ignore a person, and like a dog, it gets their interest. If you go right to them they regard you with wary suspicion. But, ignore them, and they start coming around you to find out why you're doing it."

He shrugged again. "Then, when you subtly hit on them, it seems to them it was their idea to get together."

"Huh, I see. So, has this ever worked for you before?"

Tucking his hands in his pockets, Bay turned his head away to watch a delivery truck drive over the tarred driveway to the mess, the cargo rumbling and clanging as it humped over rocks and pot-holes.

"Works like I said with dogs, women, dunno." He looked back at his friend and grinned crookedly. "Never had to try it before. I could tell Livy Stirling was going to be a tough nut to crack so I came up with the plan."

"That's a lot of thinking just to get in a girl's pants," Jules noted, tugging on the towel, he moved it back and forth rubbing his neck. Dropping his head back, he arched his spine in a long stretch and yawned.

"If I just wanted in her pants I would let time pass until she got to know me, and know right up front I don't do relationships. They are too distracting when on missions. Then she would be well aware that when we hooked up it would be a one, maybe two-shot deal."

Jules' steps slowed, he stopped. Bay stopped too.

"What do you mean by if you just wanted in her pants? What else could you get from her?"

Tilting his head back, Bay perused the puffy clouds lazing in the blue sky. Lowering his head, he dragged a hand through his short hair that was growing long in the front.

Shrugging, he said, "I don't know. There's something, when I saw her in the bar, I just felt, hell, I can't explain it. And after that pig assaulted her, I could see her up close, at least as much as possible with those fucking glasses," his hands in his pockets he rolled his strong shoulders.

"I don't know. She doesn't look like a quick roll in the hay, one night stand kind of girl, and...hell, Jules, I don't know." He tugged on his full, yet harshly carved lips in mystified thought.

Jules studied his friend's perplexed expression, then started walking again. "So, what's the new strategy?"

"I don't know," Bay replied, striding beside him. "That Rashad asshole messed everything up. Every time she sees me now I'm sure she's reminded of it. I think she's embarrassed that she had to be rescued, and that's damned ridiculous.

"And, hell, I think she's a little afraid of me too after watching the beat down I gave Rashad. Cripes man, that's our job, to protect the innocents, the helpless women and children. But, if she won't give me the time of day I can't convince her of that. I guess I'll just move on, let her be." His tone was reluctant, but his mouth firmed in resolution.

They reached the lockers where Jules left his clothes and could shower. "Uh huh," Jules said, "not like you to give up on anything."

Bay crossed his arms. "Yeah, well, she's just a chick, they're a dime a dozen. Why should I put myself out when I don't have to? Pussy is easy and abundant here, that's if I wanted to shit where I work, which I don't."

Jules murmured, "Uh huh. So why did you go after Livy in the first place then?"

His elbow resting on an arm, Bay scratched his hard jaw shadowed with scrub. "Shit, I wish I could tell ya that she has some kind of mystical hex on me," he chuckled. Then, shaking his head ruefully, he said, "But no matter, I'm done with the hunt."

"Good, good." Jules smirked with a sly curl of his lip. "By the way, Livy hits the gym some nights after her classes. Her name is on a list for the women's self-defense lessons that start next month."

"Well, that's good for her, she obviously needs it. But, like I said, I'm done chasing her skirts." He shot his friend a grin. "I'm starving, come in when you're all pretty and clean."

The men parted company and Bay trod up every other of the four steps leading into the mess hall. Being lunchtime it was almost full. He headed straight for the food.

The mess was set up cafeteria style. Grabbing a tray and a plate, he moved along with the line setting a hamburger, fries, coleslaw, two pieces of chocolate cake, and two milks on his tray.

After getting his food, he stopped and added a soda to his tray. Glancing around for a seat, Bay noticed a few of his fellow agents in a clump around a round table.

Across the room he saw Marianna sitting with Farah and a few other women from the admin pool, waving crazily at him.

Pretending not to see her, he headed for a table that Von Green and Roddy and another agent, Chuck Houston, were at.

Then he spotted her.

Livy was at a small table by the window with her head in a book.

Already getting a slight clue to the mysterious woman, Bay figured she brought the book to lunch so she wouldn't have to socialize.

He went straight to her table, pulled out a chair, and deliberately set his tray down with a slight bang to make her look up.

Startled, she did, and did not hide her frown.

"This seat taken?" he asked with a cool smile.

Behind the tint, he saw her eyes go anxiously round. They looked some shade of blue but the dark glasses distorted the color and shape.

"Uh, no, I mean, maybe, uh, I mean yes." She watched him sit down while she stuttered trying to find an objection to him sitting with her. Then she out and out lied, "Yes, I am…expecting…someone, any minute, so, you, I mean you have friends you can go sit-"

Bay's jaw worked as he tried not to smile. She was a lousy liar. She stammered and her cheeks turned the most appealing pink. At least the part the huge dark glasses didn't hide.

Agreeing with her, "Okay," he dumped ketchup on his fries then lifted the hamburger bun and squirted more on the burger. "When he, she, gets here, I'll get up." Dropping the bun back on the burger, he took a giant bite of the hamburger.

Totally ignoring her shocked look at his nerve sitting at her table when she obviously did not want him there, he motioned to her book with his chin. Speaking while chewing, he asked, "Whatcha reading?"

She looked down at the book like she'd forgotten it was there, then up at him. "A...a book," she answered inanely, blinking confounded. An empty salad bowl and glass with only a few ice cubes in it were in front of her.

"Hmm." Bay picked up his soda draining half of it. "Sounds fascinating. Is it a trilogy? Titles something like 'Book One, Book Two and Book three?"

Livy sat like the ice sculpture she'd been called, just blinking at him. Her eyes fell to his tray, he'd gobbled down the burger already and now stuffed half the ketchup-laden fries in his mouth, they bulged out his cheek while he chewed.

His question was so ridiculous it garnered no real reply. Struggling for something to say, Livy coughed, murmured absurdly, "Uh, you have soda and...uh two milks?"

Nodding, he shoved in the rest of the fries, chewed rapidly then swallowed. "Yeah," he wiped his fingers on a napkin then reached for the fork. "I need a glass for each piece of cake."

He gestured to one of them and offered, "Would you like one? I see you didn't get yourself any dessert."

Again she looked down like she'd forgotten what she'd eaten. Staring at the empty salad bowl, she repeated redundantly, "No. I didn't get any."

"So?" he said, then waited, forcing her to look up at him. It took her a minute before she did.

"So…what?"

"So," he picked up one of the plates of cake, laid a spoon on it and set it in front of her. "Have some. Don't all women have some thing about chocolate?"

Like an owl, she blinked at the cake but didn't move to lift the spoon.

Slicing off a big piece of cake, he stuffed it in his mouth. Elbows on the table, he motioned to her with his fork, "Listen, Miss Stirling, um, Livy right?"

He waited for her to respond, she didn't. "The other night," he observed her cheeks flush pink again. "You know, there is nothing for you to be…ah, ashamed of, or embarrassed about, right?"

She stared at the cake, saying nothing.

Ah, like pulling teeth. "So, you're okay, did you see a doctor?" Bay bit down his impatience as it was several seconds before she spoke.

"N- no, I didn't need a doctor. Listen, Mr. um, Commander-"

"Bay," he said.

"Huh?"

"My name is Bay. Actually it's Bayou DaRocco. My parents met in Baton Rouge." His smile slightly lopsided, he'd had to explain his name his whole life. "So, you were saying?"

She took so long answering him he didn't think she was going to. He could see why they called her artic. She held herself rigid, did not smile, it was like she'd put up a wall of ice between them, around her.

"Commander," she ignored his frown. "I would prefer it if you didn't bring that night up ever again, and I ask that you don't tell anyone about it. Mr. Green said he wouldn't speak of it."

She continued, her eyes dropping, "And, I hear that man…Duke Rashad, uh, has left the hospital and has gone back home to Georgia or something. So, I'd like to put it behind me. Now, if you'll excuse me-" she went to stand up but Bay reached out a long leg and hooked her chair with his boot keeping it from moving back.

"Wait, don't run away, Livy, let's talk. Get to know one another a little." Now it was his turn to try to think of something to say. Contrary to what he'd told Jules about backing off, he desperately wanted to keep her there.

"So, uh, are you going to the wedding?" Bay knew he was a hard looking man, and she seemed so…fragile, he tried to soften his rugged jaw, force his harsh mouth into a smile.

He had lived a tough, ruthless, violent life, and has been told it showed in the hard glint in his hooded eyes. There was nothing he could do about his height or intimidating broad shoulders stocked with cords of muscles.

It took effort for him to tone down the tough shell that was him, if she stayed afraid of him, he'd get nowhere.

She didn't look afraid though at the moment, she looked irritated. "Commander…uh, DaRocco, there is no need for you to be polite and try to converse with me. I can see half the women in here trying to get your attention. I'm sure you would rather visit with one of them. Please feel free to leave."

Her voice was cold as ice, but it had a slight tremble to it. She put her palms on the edge of the table to push her chair back, but he still held it immobile.

Women always tried to get his attention, he hardly noticed it any more. Bay liked to do his own choosing, forward aggressive women were a turn off for him. Maybe that's what he found so fascinating about this shy girl sitting in front of him.

She was dainty as shit, and appeared as he'd thought before, quite fragile, which brought out his masculine protective side.

But, she had a backbone that was laced with sheer stubbornness, and that crazy kick-ass sensuality that was hard to put his finger on, and he wasn't the only one that felt it, saw it, whatever *it* was.

Plus, for some odd, inexplicable reason, he felt possessive of her. He had no right to, of course, but still…he did save her from Rashad…

Pushing aside his empty plates, he leaned over setting his forearms on the table, and folded his hands together. "Livy, I don't want to talk to anyone else, I want to talk to you." He could see the surprise flicker across her face.

His heavy ridged forehead furrowed, he jerked a calloused hand through his hair shoving a lock out of his eyes. "Why does that surprise you?"

Still pushing at the table, she lowered her head to hide her expression that he could so easily read.

Then, she raised her head, looked squarely at him, her voice firm, she stated, "Commander, I know what I look like. A man like you would not have any interest in a woman like me. I don't know if you're doing this because you feel sorry for me, or you think it's funny, you and your friends are having a big laugh over it. Whatever the reason, please give me a little respect and stop."

Sitting back in his chair, Bay's brows quirked, then lowered in a frown. "The hell you say, what do you mean by a man like me and a woman like you? What the hell does that-"

Livy held a hand up. "Stop. Please. I need to go." She pushed harder at the table but he stubbornly kept her trapped.

His back against his chair, Bay crossed burly arms covered with dark golden hair over his powerful chest. "You didn't answer my question. I asked you if you were going to the wedding."

"You mean Maggie and Carlos'?"

At his nod, rolling her eyes with a sigh, she said, "I have to. Maggie and Carlos were so adamant that everyone come. Maggie made me promise, and Carlos threatened me if I didn't go."

The corners of her mouth pulled down at the sides. Her tone glumly sarcastic, she said, "Maggie is forcing me to wear something of hers, according to her I have nothing appropriate to wear."

His brows flinched down, he sat forward. "What the hell did Carlos threaten you?"

A tiny smile curved her lips.

Bay felt his heart tickle. He'd already noticed what luscious lips she had, but when she smiled, even that tiny one, damn, he took a breath. "What?" he demanded.

She gave a little laugh. "Oh, he said something silly like if I didn't promise to come he would follow me around for a week singing at the top of his lungs." A hint of a giggle rolled out.

Bay felt his heart squeeze at the girlish sound. Damn, he'd do anything to hear it again and see that smile.

Livy said, "It wouldn't bother me so much, but I feared for the other people's annoyance, and," the smile disappeared, "I prefer not to have the attention. Now, if you will-"

Bay relaxed at her explanation but still didn't move, so she couldn't either. His eyes were glued to that lush mouth that looked even more delectable when she smiled.

"Commander, please let me go, I don't want to cause a scene."

"All right. But I need a promise." The side of his mouth lifted in a sneaky half smile.

Livy put her purse strap over her shoulder indicating she was leaving even if she had to cause a scene. Her eyes narrowed in suspicion behind the tinted glasses. "What, what are you talking about? Promise what?"

He leaned into her again over the table, bringing their faces closer together. "You promise to go to the wedding as my date and I will instantly release you."

She couldn't have looked more surprised, or angry. Sitting back to get some space between them, she whispered fiercely, "Commander, I will not be the butt of your jokes. I insist you let go of my chair immediately!" The pink fled her face leaving it ashen.

Now he looked surprised. "What the hell?"

Shaking his head adamantly, brushing back that one lock of hair that was determined to flop in his eye, he said as seriously sincere as he could, "Livy, I swear to you, I am not playing you. Just, one date, just go to the wedding with me and if you tell me afterwards to take a hike, I will, no arguments."

He reached out to take her hand, but pulled back at the consternation crinkling her face.

She stared at him, her knuckles now as white as her face from gripping the table. "I don't," she didn't know what to say. Then, "You're in the wedding, aren't you? Aren't you one of his uh, groomsmen?"

Bay's brows lurched down as he remembered, damn. "Yeah. I forgot." Sitting back, he crossed his arms over his chest, massive muscles pushed against the button-down shirt he wore.

He shook his head. "Doesn't matter, I can't sit with you in the church, but we can be together at the reception. What do you say?" He reached over the table and this time captured one of her hands before she could move them out of his reach into her lap.

She stared in confusion at his huge hard hand engulfing her small delicate one. It was a minute before she blinked and tugged at her hand, but he held onto it.

Gently stroking his thumb over her soft as shit skin, he coaxed, "Come with me. I'll be a perfect gentleman, I promise. I won't even try to kiss you or invite myself into your home after the party." He watched the emotions flutter across her face.

Her jaw stiffened with disbelief, then loosened with resignation, then stiffened in, he couldn't tell if it was anger or fear.

Then, as if a light bulb went off, her face faintly relaxed, a brief smile of comprehension lifted her lips. "Okay. I understand now. You feel like I need a big brother or something after what happened," her eyes fell, "the other night."

Through the tinted lenses, her eyes rolled back up to his, her head cocked to the side joining with a fleeting smile.

"You'll see that I am fine. There is nothing for you to worry about. I can understand as a commander at this base, you feel it's your duty to make sure that I, as a citizen of the compound am all right, after, uh, you know."

He wanted to slap himself in the forehead, motherfucker she was tough. She thought he felt he was only doing his duty to ensure she was all right after the attack. His mouth firmed, fine, if it got him near her, he'd use her platonic thoughts for now.

His mouth softened into a friendly, *brotherly*, smile. "Okay then, so you'll go." He gave her hand a gentle squeeze.

Lips parting in surprise, she said quickly, "Oh, no, no, I was saying I understand how you feel. But, really, I'm fine, I don't need any reassuring. Now, if you will-"

Shaking his head, he said decisively, "No, Livy, you're right. It is my duty, and uh, I wouldn't feel right if I didn't confirm for myself everything is okay with you. That you're not experiencing any residual, uh, fear, panic, or such."

He gave her small hand another light squeeze, his thumb still brushing her soft skin. "So, really, you would be doing me a big favor by going with me, right?"

Seeing his words ruminate in the flexing of her lips, before she could decline again, he said, "I'll pick you up at six. I have to be there early because I'm in the wedding party and I-" he broke off at her shaking head. "Come on, Livy, just go, lighten up some, huh?"

"I'm already going, Commander, and I will be driving myself." She tugged at her hand so suddenly he lost his grip of it.

Perturbed, brows lifted then lowered, he groused, "Really, Livy, if you're afraid for me to know where you live, I have access to all the personnel files. I can get that info with a snap."

He didn't tell her of course he's already reviewed her file. It was frustratingly thin. Only her orders stationing her at Evgeny Base, tax information, phone number and address.

There wasn't even a picture of her ID or driver's license in the file. It was like she had truly been born yesterday.

He said roughly, "I don't have my dates drive themselves." His voice was harsher than he meant it to be, he took a breath and softened it. "You're with me, that makes you my responsibility. I see you safely to the event and safely home," he concluded his statement with male smugness.

"No." Livy looked down at the table then determinedly up at him. "I will drive myself or not even go to the wedding. It's too late for Carlos to make good on his threat now anyway."

His dark green eyes widened at her obstinacy, then they narrowed. At least she had agreed to be his date. Sort of.

Nonetheless, he stated, "You have to go, you gave them your word." He let out a heavy sigh at her head shaking negatively. Damn she was fucking tough under that fine-spun packaging.

"Fine," he ground in surrender. "I will meet you at the reception. But you will be my date, there won't be any more arguing about it here, or at the wedding."

Forking his fingers roughly through his hair, he grumbled, "Woman, you are quite damned difficult, did you know that?" Hell, he felt like he'd fought a fucking battle, he was exhausted.

He leaned over towards her again, his eyes tapered, and warned, "But, mind you, if you fail to show, I will leave my friend's wedding to hunt you down, and that would hardly be fair to him or me, right?"

Perfectly arched brows rose at his threat. She put both hands back against the table, one of the perfect brows stayed arched. "I can't say that I've ever been *threatened* into a quasi-date before. It's..." she paused. "I guess it's nice that you take your duty seriously, but you're pretty high-handed about it."

His sigh beleaguered, Bay released her chair. "All right. I'll see you at-" she was already up and out of her chair. Book pressed tightly to her chest she hurried out of the mess.

He realized she had not actually agreed to be his date. Damn, he lowered his head shaking it, the girl was going to be a challenge.

Lifting his head with a faint smile, he thought, that's okay, nothing he liked better than a good challenge. Chasing a woman was a unique experience for him, at least since middle school. Even then he was the one that had done more of the running.

He glanced over and saw where Von, Roddy, Chuck, and now Jules were all grinning at him. They'd seen her practically fleeing from him. Great. An audience to his groveling.

Bay picked up the chocolate cake he'd offered Livy and made his way to his friends to endure their teasing.

Chapter Four

Bay was so annoyed with himself.

Hell, he was commander over an intensely secretive and elite Special Forces squad.

He'd brought down the worst of the worst felons, warlords, gangsters, dictators, on and on all over the world, and every one of them expressed fear of him. No matter how tough they were, he forced them to do as he ordered, he controlled them.

And here he was, dolled up in a tux, pacing back and forth in front of the church window that overlooked the parking lot, staring at his watch and getting more and more aggravated as every second ticked by and he didn't see that piece of shit ancient convertible VW Livy Stirling called a vehicle.

His stomach clenched, he couldn't believe he was so tense that she wasn't going to come.

Worse, she was turning him into a stalker. He didn't want to prowl outside her classrooms, so he had hit the gym every night trying to catch her there, but to no avail. Damned bitch.

He didn't know why he was this…disturbed over a woman that he basically didn't even know what she looked like under that disguise she wore. They'd barely conversed and that had been mostly acrimonious. Except that one rare split second when she had almost smiled.

As delicate as she seemed, she had a snap to her spine, and he had actually enjoyed talking with her albeit most of it was arguing, and her misunderstanding his intentions. Which was probably good. If she thought he truly wanted to date her, she'd likely run like a scared rabbit.

That small, feisty little female had him coming and going. Half of him wanted to protect the brittle young woman so afraid of something she closed herself off from the world, the other half wanted to tear off those bulky clothes and see what treasures were hidden underneath.

There was some kind of sensuousness to the way she moved, the way she held her head, and those lips, hell, he'd pictured them all night long, what he'd like to do to them, and what he'd like them to do to him. Fuck, he tugged at his collar; he was getting warm…and hard.

"Yo, Bullet," Chuck Houston stuck his head in the door. "Jules told me to get you, says it's time."

One last look out the window, gusting a pissed sigh, Bay followed the agent downstairs and to where the other groomsmen were gathered.

The church was beautiful with cathedral ceilings, marble and gold floors. Golden light streamed in through the stained glass windows and the skylight above.

Carlos, the groom, was standing in the middle of the group of groomsmen looking like he was about to have a heart attack.

Bay trod over to him with a grin. "Bro, you still have time, it's not a done deal yet. You want me to get the car and meet you around back? No one will see you leave."

The other guys chuckled.

Carlos, his olive skinned face red and sweating, palmed his black curly hair back and smiled weakly with a loud swallow. Soft organ music played in the background.

"Sure, you trying to get me killed at my young and tender age?" Nervously, Carlos tugged at the bottom of his tux, then the sleeves.

He fussed with his tie until Jules swatted his hands away saying, "Leave it alone, you'll fuck it up and she'll kill you for that too."

Laughing, Bay said, "A murderous bride, you sure you want to go through with this?"

Blinking nervously, Carlos nodded. "Yeah. I love Maggie, I can't imagine my life without her. I don't know what I did to deserve her, but," he glanced at the stairs as if to catch a glimpse of her, "I thank God for giving her to me."

"Then why are you so nervous?" Chuck asked.

"Bro, I'm terrified *she'll* get cold feet and bolt before I can get her 'I do' out of her!"

The men laughed out loud.

The reverend gave the sign, and Carlos fist-bumped each of his friends then went to the altar to wait for his bride. His groomsmen ushered the female relatives of both Carlos and Maggie to their seats.

The music changed, their cue for the men to get ready to stand with the bridesmaid they were walking with down the aisle.

As he walked slowly with a tall, full figured blonde on his arm, Bay didn't notice that with every step she was rubbing her massive breasts on his bicep, he was busy checking out the congregation in case Livy had slipped in.

But no, there was no sign of her. He couldn't believe how disappointed he was.

His jaw contracted as his teeth clenched. Well, she'd see he was a man of his word. As soon as the ceremony shit was done, he was going looking for her. And she was going to be one sorry little girl.

He pictured tossing her over his lap, yanking down those loose pants and panties, and wailing on that hot little ass for standing him up. Okay, he subtly shifted his pants, not a good time for a hard-on.

As everyone took their places at the altar, the men lined up beside Carlos and the bridesmaids next to where Maggie would stand, the music changed yet again, this time to the Wedding March.

All eyes were on Maggie paused in the threshold of the double doors thrown wide open. She looked nervous but was grinning ear-to-ear, and she only had eyes for the groom waiting at the end of the aisle for her.

Up on the altar, legs shaking like palm trees in a storm, Carlos only had eyes for her.

Smiling broadly, the bride's father brought her down the aisle to the organ's lilting music.

Watching their slow procession, Bay stood with his hands clasped behind his back, a movement at the back of the church caught his eye.

He forced his face to remain impassive, but inside he grinned.

Livy was slipping into a pew in the back of the church.

He'd nodded slightly to her when she looked in his direction, but then he forced himself to not look at her again.

43

The ceremony slid past him in a haze. He tried to pay attention to the couple repeating their vows, the minister's words of love and encouragement and faith, but, all he could think about was wrapping himself around that shy enigma of a petite woman sitting reverently in the pew.

At the end of the service, his back ramrod straight, head high, bridesmaid's huge breasts practically beating his bicep, Bay trod back down the aisle holding his breath until they reached the end.

When he passed the pew Livy had been sitting in, he allowed a quick glance, and his stomach fell.

It was empty.

After photos, the boisterous wedding party arrived at the reception. They immediately grabbed drinks and blended in with family and friends.

One hand in a pocket, the tux jacket tucked behind his wrist, and a scotch in his other hand, Jules found Bay standing off to the side staring glumly down at the drink in his hand.

"Hey, bro, what's going on? You've been pissy and morose all day."

"Bite me, J, I have not." Scowling at his bourbon, Bay tossed most of it down his throat. He hadn't wanted the teasing so he hadn't told anyone, even Jules, about asking Livy to be his date at the wedding. His sisterly date.

Most of the guys used weddings as pick-ups. Bay had never taken a date to one before.

His friends would have been relentless on him if they knew he'd asked Livy to attend with him. And worse, that she hadn't shown up. Here he was, a well-known non-dater, and he finally asks a woman out for something more than sex, and she actually blew him off. Shit.

"Seriously, Bay, you are normally one taciturn asshole, but today, you're downright cantankerous. What bug flew up your ass?"

Unbuttoning the jacket of his tux, then shifting the cummerbund to be a little more comfortable, Bay grumped, "Nothing, just fuck off-" he caught a hint of dusky rose, the color he saw Livy wearing at the church.

His stomach leaped into flip-flops, she was here.

"Bay, what-" but Jules was talking to air.

Bay was threading through the packed room, deaf to people trying to talk to him, his eyes on Livy who hovered by the door.

Before he could get to her, she found a seat at a table that was half empty, on purpose no doubt so she wouldn't have to talk to anyone.

His mind on Livy, Bay hurried to the table, and a big, voluptuous roadblock stepped in front of him- he almost ran right into her.

"Bay, honey," Marianna pouted, brushing the front of her body-clinging red dress against his body. "You haven't even looked in my direction all week. To make up for your lack of attention to me, why don't we go, I mean," she rubbed harder on him.

Plucking at his bowtie, her voice lusty, she purred, "This is a hotel after all. I'm sure we can find an empty room, and have us some fun."

"Uh huh," Bay muttered. Putting his hands on her shoulders, he moved her aside and kept walking.

Damn, Livy saw him, and the frown on her face showed she wasn't pleased seeing Marianna hanging all over him. He walked faster.

It happened again. A woman in a bridesmaid dress, huge breasts falling out of the ruffled strapless teal, her blonde hair curled and frozen unmoving on her shoulders, stepped in his path.

Batting layers of thick false lashes, she set a palm on his chest and mewed, "Commander, you ran off so quickly we didn't get a chance to talk..." She smiled coyly. "Or anything."

Plucking at a black button on his white shirt, she raised her chin up, lowered her lashes, and pouted her thick lips as if begging to be kissed.

He looked blankly down at her obviously not recognizing her.

With a sulky scowl, the woman snapped, "It's Gwen Waltimar. We walked down the aisle together for Pete's sake. We attended the rehearsal and the dinner together, what the hell is the matter with you? Are you blind?" Annoyance wrinkling her pretty face, she stroked his chest.

Bay tried to focus on her. With total lack of interest, he said with indifference, "Oh, yeah, sorry. Weren't you with a guy at the dinner?" All week his mind had been on Livy, he hadn't noticed any other females.

"He was nothing. Hon, come, you need to sit next to me at the main table, we're partners in this frilly circus." She grabbed his hand and tried to pull him with her. People were starting to sit down.

Bay looked away from the woman and saw Livy going out the door.

Cursing, "Shit," he jerked his hand from Gwen's grasp and jogged through the room.

Out in the wide, tiled hall lined with paintings, he jumped in front of Livy. "Leaving so soon?"

"Oh!" Livy squawked, stepping back so quickly she lost her balance.

Bay caught her arm and steadied her, but didn't let go, even when she tugged at it.

A bite of anger in her tone, she said, "You're doing it again, Commander, holding me against my will."

He responded mildly, "That's because you keep trying to run away from me."

"Humph," she snorted. "You had your hands full, real full," her voice chilled with sarcasm. "I remembered I had someplace else to be."

"Come on, Frosty, those women came at me. I have no interest in either of them. Now," he let go of her arm to drape his arm over her slender shoulders.

Turning her back towards the ballroom, he said, "I'm hungry and you need a drink to smooth away that sour look on your face."

"What!" Mouth bunched in insult, she pushed at him, but he held her with the strength of an iron bar. She berated him, "You are rude and- and a womanizer, and we are not on a date anyway, let go of me!"

His head fell back. He groaned at the ceiling then looked down at her. "Who have you been listening to, my little Frosty?"

She twisted her body to get free but he only strengthened his arm around her. "What does it matter, they say it's true."

Annoyance in his step, Bay moved Livy back to the reception.

When they reached the doorway, he stroked his hand down her back. His big hand wrapped halfway around her tiny waist. The feminine curve of her under his hand made his palm heat and his trousers grow uncomfortable.

"Livy, I wouldn't think you were the kind of woman to listen to malicious gossip," he admonished as he maneuvered her to a table near the head table and pulled out a chair.

She stood still, refusing to sit down. "The women all talk about you, they say you are a player."

Ignoring the other guests at the table trying to greet the couple, Bay said, "First of all," he placed his hands on her shoulders and gently pressed her down onto the seat. "I have not slept with any woman on this base. I don't fu- uh, sleep with women where I'm work-" he stopped.

He was about to say he didn't sleep with women he was stationed with. He sure as hell didn't want her to think he wouldn't have sex with her because she was stationed there, that would keep her mind cemented in the 'friend' category.

And the last thing he needed was to talk about his prior sexual exploits with the girl that he not only wanted to have naked under him, but wanted something more.

Throwing his previous partners in another woman's face like say Jessica or Marianna's would only incite them to want him more, they'd love the competition, but it would likely make this little honey close her legs and run for the hills.

"Anyway," he plopped down beside her. Shifting his chair to face her, he gripped the seat of her chair and turned her towards him. "I don't usually explain myself," he took a breath, said through gritted teeth, "to anyone."

Her lips tightened and her shoulders stiff, Livy pressed her back against the chair as if trying to put space between them.

Bay realized he was in her face and likely grimacing. Clearing his throat, he sat back, eased the hardness from his expression and said, "When I was staying on base a while back, I kept going to my bunk that was in a cluster of rooms

I shared with some of my fellow agents, and," he jabbed his fingers through his caramel locks to calm himself.

"This woman kept sneaking into my bed, nude, waiting for me. I turned her down, again and again, until I ordered her, in writing, to stay away from me and my bunk."

As if they were armor, Livy crossed her arms over her chest and just stared at him.

"Ahem," he cleared his throat again. "So, anyway, you've heard the old 'woman scorned' thing, she was pretty mad. She started a bunch of rumors." There was one that he'd raped her but this wasn't the time to share that.

Fortunately, he'd had an airtight alibi. He had been transporting a famous mobster to a different state to stand trial at the time she claimed he accosted her. The cops laughed her out of the precinct.

"She said I'd fu- uh, had sex with her and tossed her aside after I'd made promises that we would get engaged. I mean," he chuckled irritably, "everyone knows I don't- ah," he raked his fingers through his hair mussing the honeyed locks.

He didn't want to tell her he doesn't have long-term relationships with women. He'd already ascertained that she was the kind of woman that didn't do one and dones. Hell, this is why he didn't converse with females, he had to watch everything he was saying. With men, no one cared how rude or crude he was.

Livy sat back and smiled up at the server who set a plate of salad in front of her and another poured water for the table.

Several more people joined them at the large round table. Everyone introduced themselves. Bay knew most of them.

Taking a sip of ice water, keeping her voice low so the others present couldn't hear her, Livy said coolly, "It doesn't matter anyway, Commander. Since we are to be friends, I should not be judgmental of you, that is certainly not how friends behave. I apologize."

"Liv-" Bay bit his tongue, how was he going to transition smoothly from friend to lover without her thinking he tricked her? Hell, he'd boxed himself in.

Keeping the scowl off his face, he looked down at the dress she wore. "I, ah," he stuck a finger in his tight collar and tugged at it, the teal bow tie shifted crooked, a shade of color reddened the tips of his ears. "You look absolutely...stunning, Livy."

The dusky rose dress fit her perfectly. It had an embroidered strip that crossed the front of her neck and thin straps, the center was a diamond shape of bare skin.

He'd been chasing her down so hard he hadn't noticed what she was wearing. Bay swallowed tightly, freaking deliciously lush breasts mounded out of the diamond.

The sparkly bodice fit snuggly down to her tiny waist before it poured out into a flouncy skirt that swirled above her knees exposing the sexiest legs Bay could ever remember seeing. They were quite slender, showing how young she was. She wore very high-heels that made her legs look longer.

Livy looked down and put a hand over her breasts. "You think it's okay?" She didn't look happy. "I never wear stuff like this, so...revealing, but Maggie brought it insisting I look nice for her wedding."

"Livy," Bay leaned back as a salad was set in front of him, "trust me, it's perfect. You look perfect except for," before she knew what he was doing, he reached up and plucked the pins out of her hair.

"No!" Livy yelped, uselessly trying to keep the locks from tumbling down. Rich, fat cinnamon curls waved around her shoulders and down her back.

Slipping the pins into his pocket, he smiled and lifted a few curls. "Such a vibrant unusual color, extraordinary, gorgeous. Why would you want to hide such amazing hair?"

Shit, he knew she had been hiding treasures, and he was right. Fucking tits that made his hands itch and his mouth water like a horn-dogged teenager, and the hair of a goddess he wanted to feel on his bare skin.

"Now this," he reached out quickly again and snatched off the hairband she perpetually wore and tucked that in his pocket. "There, much better. Doesn't it feel good to have that shit off your head?"

Appalled, her hands on her hair, Livy cried, "Commander, what are you doing? Oh my gosh, you have no right!" With anxious fingers she combed through the waves. "Give me back my things," she demanded in an outraged whisper.

"Later," he had turned and started munching on his salad. He needed a moment away from looking at her in that dress.

Damn, she was breathtaking dynamite, and he wanted to peel that dress off and detonate her. He was already halfway there himself. Plucking a couple of rolls out of a warming basket, he set one on her bread and butter plate and one on his.

Calmly cutting his roll open, he slathered it with butter.

Beside him, Livy sat in shock. He figured in a few minutes she'd get over it. "Come on, eat your salad, it's good for you," he waved to a server to bring them a cocktail.

When the server came to take his order, he asked Livy what she would like to drink.

51

She turned stiffly, her lips still parted in shock, but she said nothing.

His gaze running down her, he said, "I think she'd like a nice glass of maybe chardonnay. No, bring her a rosé to match that amazing dress." It was all he could do not to gawk down her dress at those perfect round breasts.

Bay ate half his salad and set the plate aside and buttered another roll.

The man on his other side tried to start a conversation with him, but Bay knew he didn't have much time to work on Livy so he kept the conversation short.

They ate surf and turf with garlic smashed potatoes. At a slight sound coming from Livy, Bay turned away from the man who was persistent in engaging him in conversation, and saw a look of bliss melt over Livy's face.

Bay bent and whispered in her ear, "Good?"

"Mmm, heavenly." Licking her lips, she rolled her eyes and took a piece of lobster tail, dunked it in melted butter and brought it dripping to her mouth.

Bay watched every move wishing he was that lobster. The picture of the two of them, naked, sitting in a luxurious hotel room, drinking champagne and feeding each other chocolate covered strawberries, floated through his mind.

"You act like you don't eat much, Frosty," Bay commented while he patted extra butter on his potatoes. A server brought their drinks.

A pointed glance at his plate overflowing with more buns, and added butter on everything, Livy said smugly, "Huh, no kettle black there, I think. Uh, I mean you have no problem packing it away."

At his chuckle she sighed. "I haven't had an appetite in a long…uh, I mean, I'm not a great cook so this is like manna to me. The mess hall is good, but not like *real* food, you know?"

"Seriously?" He said as if it was the worst thing on earth. "A woman who can't cook," shaking his head, Bay took a swig of his bourbon, "that is so sad."

She giggled at his drama and took a sip of wine.

That made him smile. Between bites, he asked, "Didn't your mom teach you?"

Livy stared down at her plate, the giggles gone. A wistful note in her voice, she answered, "No. I attended an all girl's boarding school my entire life. We did studies, not homemaking. I mean, we were taught basics and stuff."

"That sounds kind of miserable," he replied, studying her expression. Sadness, loneliness, and something else he couldn't tell wandered across her face. Her eyes were too hard to see. "Where were you born?"

Livy pushed her food around now, like the joyous appetite she'd had was gone. "Oh, you know, a tiny place you've never heard of."

"Did you go to college or come straight into the company?"

Turning her head fully to him for the first time since they sat down, with a fake smile on her face, she said over-cheerfully, "Evgeny is a great place don't you think? How long have you been with them?"

Clearly she was avoiding his questions. But he answered her, "I was a Marine then came to Evgeny where there was less…bureaucracy."

Livy, as well as all the other occupants of the compound didn't know much about the secretive, specialized squad he headed. His team was only on the base for a specified training and planning a pending mission.

"Hmm, there are rumors that you are commander of an elite ops force."

Chewing on a piece of juicy steak, he nodded. "Something like that. So you were telling me how you came to be at Evgeny?"

"Oh, um, you know how things happen. Oh look, Maggie and Carlos are kissing, they make the cutest couple don't you think?"

Again she didn't answer his question and tried to distract him with the bridal couple.

Livy stabbed an asparagus and had it halfway to her mouth when Bay tried again, "Do you have any siblings? Are they still at home in…"

She set her fork down without eating the asparagus.

Bay could see her eyes darting back and forth as she thought about what to say. Hell, usually when he was conversing with women he could never get a word in edgewise. With this girl he needed a freakin' pick-ax to pry answers out of her.

"Um," her lips pulled in, her attention flittered anxiously all around then landed on the dance floor. People were dancing to the DJ's music.

"I…" her gaze flashed to the bride and groom who were heading to the dance floor. "Isn't Maggie beautiful? They look so happy, I hope they-"

"Come." Bay set his cutlery down, stood up, grasped her hand, and pulled her chair out and her to her feet all seemingly in one movement. "Let's dance."

Without letting her have a say, he led her through the crowd to the dance floor.

"No, wait, Commander, I don't want to dance." Livy took a step back to the dining area, but Bay held her hand.

"Yes, little Frosty, you must dance with me or I'll be forced to dance with Maggie's great aunt Elspeth. Geesh," he whined, "have you seen her? Has more hair on her chin than Chuck Houston does!"

Livy couldn't stop the giggle that slipped out at his description of poor Elspeth.

"Now," Bay took her hand and set it on his shoulder, clasped her other hand as he set his palm on her waist. She was suddenly rigid and anxious in his arms.

"Please, Commander," she said to his shoulder. "I really would like to return to the table."

"Livy, can you call me Bay?" Holding her closer, his grip loose, but firm so she couldn't tug free, he slowly, effortlessly moved her across the floor.

"Humph," she grunted, "you were quick to state your title that night, pulling your rank on me."

Bay drew her closer so her front just barely brushed his and stroked his hand up her back, and down. "Yes, well, you were hysterical and I couldn't let you drive in that condition. But that was then, and this is now."

He bent his head back to look at her, then plucked her glasses off her nose and tucked them in his pocket with the pins and hairband.

"Hey! Stop doing that! You can't just remove things from a person's body without their permission!" She put her hands against his chest pushing at him. Bay only pulled her closer, forcing her forearms to press on his chest. He dropped his hands to circle the small of her back.

Bay gazed at her, his pupils dilated at her beauty. More hidden treasure. "Livy, your eyes, why do you hide such incredible eyes?"

He searched his brain for a word to describe them. "Icelandic blue, you know, pristine crystal, blue ice, glacial, like the way you're glaring at me right now."

"Commander DaRocco, you are taking too many liberties for being a friend, an older brother of sorts. Please stop taking things off me."

A heavy sigh fell out, he said, "Okay." Then mumbled, "For now," and snuggled her closer. Anything else he peeled off her they'd have to be alone for.

Moving his hand from her back, he pressed her head gently to lie against his shoulder. She was a tiny thing, but the spiked heels helped so he didn't have to bend over too much.

Note by note she relaxed more and more, softening against him. They danced as if in a fuzzy warm cocoon. When the song ended and another started, they kept going.

Several times Bay felt a tap on his shoulder, which he ignored and hugged her closer. He wasn't giving up this moment.

God, she was soft and warm and curvy in his arms, breasts pressed against his chest, the scent of her in his every inhale. Yeah, he had a raging hard-on but he would dance the rest of the night with her if he could.

The song ended again, and the music paused.

Bay and Livy separated slightly, their dazed eyes connected for a breath before she lowered hers. The music started up and Bay was pulling her back into his arms when a body shoved between them.

"Baysie," Gwen the bridesmaid bustled her huge tits in pushing the couple apart, and quickly nestled against Bay's chest.

She griped, poking at his cummerbund, "You promised me you would dance with me, all the other groomsmen and bridesmaids are dancing, we're supposed to be dancing also. This is the bridal party song, and they want pictures." She turned her back to Livy and strung her arms around his neck.

Over her shoulder, Bay saw what she said was true, the bridal party was all dancing, but- ah hell, Livy was already across the floor and winding her way back to their table.

It would be the height of un-chivalrous rudeness to leave Gwen stranded on the dance floor.

Biting back an irritated sigh, he gripped her hand and waist, pushing her back from rubbing all over him. She felt thick and heavy in his hands after the slender, graceful Livy.

As soon as the dance was over, he raced back to their table.

A few of the guests were still seated there eating cake, but Livy's chair was empty.

His stomach dropped. She could be in the ladies room, but, his shoulders slumped, he doubted it. He went outside to look for her car and saw that his inkling was correct.

The crappy VW on its last legs was gone.

Chapter Five

Even though he was on the other side of the planet, Bay called Livy's number and left her several messages telling her he wanted to take her on a date. A real date.

She finally texted him back. It was brief, and cold, like her.

'Friends don't date, and right now, Commander, I don't have time for friends. Please don't call me again.'

Damn, he cussed a blue streak under his breath, she was shutting him out.

There was something she was hiding from, something that frightened her. It was in the way when her eyes weren't lowered which was most of the time, they darted around constantly as if she saw danger everywhere, in everyone.

The alarm showed in the way she drew in on herself as if in self-protection, and in the tremble of those gorgeous lips.

He needed to find out what it was so he could combat it. Just get his foot in the door then he could-

"Bullet! Heads up!" someone yelled.

Even with earplugs in, Bay heard him and ducked in time as a knife hurtled past his head. He quickly spotted the guerrilla one of his team had warned him of.

The man ran around a corner of a shot-out building, little left of it but crumbling mortar and bricks. Bay took chase. All around him in the dusty turmoil men shouted, screamed in agony, cried and cursed.

Bay's team had been sent overseas to an indigent country in an almost invisible town that wasn't even on any maps, to clean out a gang of marauding, murdering insurgents their intelligence told them was hiding out there.

The gang took glee in torturing, raping and killing innocent civilians. After looting them, they set fires to their homes until nothing was left but charred smoking wood and bones drying under the hot sun.

So far, the cutthroat rebels had managed to remain secreted in the bushy land and the sparse law officials had been unable to find and dispatch them to end their killing sprees.

With their expert skills, Bay's squad found the rebels almost immediately. Instead of running and scattering to hide somewhere else, the rebels open-fired on them.

When the DAK team had driven in, a barrage of bullets banged off the jeeps, pinging into the earth spraying up clouds of stones and dirt around them.

The squad kept their heads down as Roddy, driving wildly to avoid being a stagnant target, tossed them all about like jumping beans in the jeep as he hurtled behind some decrepit buildings to use as cover. The second jeep of DAK men followed them.

As soon as Roddy slammed on the breaks the men had jumped out swarming out in every direction.

Fitzgerald ran up some steps to climb to the roof to get a better visual while everyone else darted behind collapsed walls for cover while continuing to fan out.

Keeping his head low and his eyes on the man that threw the knife, Bay sprinted after him staying close to the shielding buildings.

The guy ran around a tree, Bay dashed straight across the knee-high grass and tackled him.

Before the insurgent could throw a punch, one powerful sharp twist of his head and the man was dead. Taking the deceased's weapons, Bay ran back to the core of the fighting.

The noisy chaos of shouts and rapid staccato gunfire, sporadic bursts of pulse-beating screams ricocheted all over the gutted ghost town.

Bay thought he saw something move way up in a big tree a few dozen yards away. Throwing his body against a wall under a cloth awning that was faded and filled with rips and holes, he scanned the area.

Hurrying to another tree, Bay quickly climbed up to a heavy solid branch and crept out on it on his belly.

Inching to the end of the branch, he pulled his Kalashnikov, the Russian AK-47 attached to a strap across his back around to the front, and braced his elbows staggered on the tree, then peered through the scope.

Dressed in brown and olive green camo, the insurgent blended in very well with the broad leafy tree he'd sheltered in, but once he got him in his sights, Bay slowly, steadily, squeezed the trigger.

The plugs in his ears muffling the sound, Bay's smile was tight seeing the man topple out of the tree, hitting a few branches before crashing to the ground.

Peering around, he saw another insurgent leaning over an overhang on a roof, his gun aimed at the top of Roddy's red head. Roddy had his own weapon trained on a man that was running across another roof.

Both DAK agents fired at the same time. Roddy's target on the roof lurched a few feet then rolled off, falling straight from the roof to slam on the dirt ground.

Bay's target just crumpled on the tar roof, his shotgun clattering on the asphalt.

Roddy swung around in surprise.

Bay jumped from the tree with a grin.

Roddy gave him a grateful thumb's up. This was not a surrender or capture day, orders were to leave none of the vicious murderers alive. It wasn't long before every one of the insurgents lay dead.

Climbing back into the jeep, Jules scolded Bay. "You had your head in the clouds, bro, and you almost bought it. Either grab her and fuck her or forget her."

Bay snapped at Jules who was climbing in the seat behind him, "I wasn't-" Jules' smirk shut his mouth.

Sitting shotgun, Bay turned around and said, "Let's hit it, Roddy. Maybe you can make the trip out of here a little less bumpy than the one on the way in, huh?"

Roddy slipped his dark sunglasses over his pale green eyes and threw Bay a quick grin. "Aye, aye, Commander."

The other jeep followed them out of the crumbling dusty, ghost town, now filled with more ghosts, and back down the dirt road that led to outlying roads that were more plain sand than gravel.

They headed back to the small elite, custom-made jet. They'd flown in landing on a long stretch of open, flat hard ground, and now the jet was hidden behind heavy scrub.

Driving the jeeps into the jet, they flew the hell out of there as swiftly and stealthy as they'd flown in.

Chapter Six

The landline phone rang as Livy walked past it.

She hesitated but didn't answer it.

Hovering by the phone, she waited for the answering machine to pick up. She assumed it was the girls wondering why she wasn't at Prontos yet.

How she let them talk her again into going to that stupid pickup joint she had no idea.

All they wanted to do was get trashed, make-out in dark corners with strangers, and then go home with them or with a different one.

The base was one big, promiscuous fuck-fest. Last thing Livy would ever want in her life was…her stomach revolted at the thought of sex.

Her voicemail's robotic voice stated for the caller to leave a message. No one spoke, but Livy could hear someone breathing, loud enough like they wanted it to be heard.

"Great, now I'm getting kids playing pranks, cold calling people." She erased the message. Then the phone rang again, same thing.

Getting angry, the third time it rang, Livy snatched it up and yelled, "Okay you guys grow up, you aren't funny!" and slammed the phone down hard hoping she hurt someone's eardrums.

Then it rang again, the same breathing came on. Aggravated, wondering where those kids' parents were, she unplugged the phone and went out the door and climbed into her car.

Driving as slow as molasses to the bar, she thought *yeah, maybe a drink would perk me up.*

Parking the VW, she glanced around the parking lot hoping she wouldn't see the commander's truck. He drove one of those big things, a black and gold Ram 2500.

Her chest tightened when she saw it parked in the lot. He had called her and left more messages since her text telling him she didn't want to go on a date with him, or anyone for that matter.

Thankfully, he had her glasses and hair things delivered to her home.

Yet, he asked her to call him so they could talk.

Honestly, what did they have to talk about? If she wanted friends there were plenty of females on the base, she didn't need the trouble a male friend would bring.

Besides, he didn't talk, he bossed her, and negotiated with her to get her to do what he wanted. Even that didn't make any sense, why was he bothering with her at all?

Huh, sighing, she got out and locked the car manually. It was too old to have a remote.

The commander must still be bugged that she had refused to file assault charges on Duke Rashad. It dug in his craw as a military commander that she wouldn't want the man that attacked her be incarcerated and answer for his crime.

Thinking about the commander brought to mind the wedding reception. The way they had danced, the way he had held her so snug, so intimately against his powerful body.

A warm fluid heat rolled up her legs as if she could feel right now the way she'd felt in his strong embrace, pressed against all those huge hard muscles.

Inhaling his very masculine scent, she had felt his hands, big and strong yet holding her gently, his nose in her hair, like a predacious animal he intentionally sniffed her-

Livy shook her head. The girls had told her he was a player, and he was obviously just flirting, it probably was as natural as breathing to him.

She pictured the commanding man. Even his face was hard, not ugly, just tough, kind of scary. He had jagged cheekbones, his mouth was strongly shaped but full, manly jaw covered with dark shadow considering how light the hair on his head was.

He acted innocuously cheerful, obviously a façade to hide his true violent nature that came out when he'd beaten Duke so viciously.

She thought about Commander DaRocco's eyes, Irish green she would call them, they were like chips of arrogant green rocks. They were hard too, formidable, ruthless aggression sparked icy in their confident depths. Huh, and they called her cold!

Her step slowed, then she chastised herself. What was she worried about? A man like him would never be interested in a mouse like her. He was probably wrapped all around some leggy, bosomy blonde and wouldn't even notice her arrival.

Livy entered the bar as unobtrusively as possible, last thing she wanted was anyone's attention on her. Her hair was pinned up in a severe bun as always.

She caught the reproving look on Ella's face as she took in Livy's regular outfit of loose blouse over baggy slacks.

Sucking in a deep breath, Livy joined the women at their table.

"Hi everyone," she said, docile eyes slanted down as she shuffled into a seat. Taking a quick peek around the bar, her stomach pitched.

Commander DaRocco was standing at the bar with his usual circle of friends, tough looking agents like him. The rumor was that they were some sort of secret assassin squad. The way they were built, the sharp hardness in their eyes, Livy believed it.

DaRocco wore a dark blue button down shirt with black jeans and boots. As she figured, with a slight disappointment tugging at the back of her head, Marianna was with him. Actually, she was all over him.

With a sneer of disgust, Livy turned away before the commander could see her ogling him. Huh. As if she would *ever* ogle a man. Especially a man-whore like him.

The women, Ella, Jessica, Farah, Wanda, and another girl Livy barely knew, Keisha, gave her varying degrees of friendly greetings.

Livy ordered a drink from the barmaid, her face red when she had to produce ID, yet it didn't really matter, as it was fake anyway.

She sat back, letting the women's conversations waft around her. She didn't join in unless she was asked a direct question, and thankfully, that didn't happen very often.

On her second drink, Livy was daydreaming, drifting away from the shrill voices at the table. She noticed Commander DaRocco never looked in her direction.

Still, she recalled his deep voice, it had the same hard edge as his face, his body, yet when he spoke to her it had sifted like a husky warm breath down her entire body- *oh*- a full-body shiver raced through her.

She reached for her glass hoping no one had noticed.

At the bar, Jules tipped a beer to his mouth, sucked a few gulps, swallowed, then he teased Bay. "Bro, your honey's over there, aren't you gonna go say hi?"

"Hey Bay!" "Bullet!" Keisha and Farah yelled at the same time, competing for his attention. He nodded at them but kept his gaze clear of Livy. He didn't respond to Jules' taunt.

Jules kept on, "Whatsup? A few weeks ago you were panting hot and heavy for her."

Bay replied with a slight shrug, "Yeah, well, she avoids me like I'm a fucking diamondback or something."

To himself, Bay had admitted that his attraction for her was too fierce. It distracted him from his job, his training. He'd almost gotten a knife in the head on that last mission because he had been thinking about her lips and her in his bed under him- fuck.

No good could come out of them being together anyway. He would only have worked out his lust for her until it finally left him, then he'd leave her, and she was the soft-hearted fragile kind, yeah, she would get hurt.

It was better they didn't get together. Her refusing to return his calls had nothing to do with his new determination.

"No," Bay sipped at his bourbon rocks. "I'm done chasing her tail. I'll stick with the easy stuff." His gaze canted to the blowsy Marianna.

She had finally stopped rubbing all over him like a hog rolling in mud, and flopped down on the stool next to him.

Now, the man beside her had his tongue in her ear, and his hand under her skirt. The way she squirmed and made gasping gushing sounds, Bay could figure what he was doing with that hand. However, her heavy-lidded eyes were on Bay.

Her tongue was out and circling her big lips. Super thick and hideously long lashes lowered over the clear invitation she was sending him. *What a slut*, Bay thought.

Her legs spread wider stretching the skirt. While the guy had his hand on her pussy and was working it, she was greedily soliciting Bay's attention even as the man pronged his fingers up inside her.

The blatant vulgar, public display made the bourbon crimp in Bay's stomach.

The man moved his other hand to cup the underside of one of her massive breasts. His thumb not even discreetly rubbed over her hard nipple.

As Bay turned away, the disgust rising up his throat, Marianna and the man locked lips, his hand was now up under her blouse. He squeezed her melon so hard Bay heard her wanton giggle. *Geez, get a room, or a brothel.*

He fought it, but his eyes twitched across the room to Livy. She was staring unblinking at one of the televisions up on the wall.

Across the room, Livy's heart started pounding, her pulse raced, her mind buzzed, she couldn't think for the fear that was elevating. Her gaze was turned up and glued to the TV, wide-eyed, her lips parted in morbid dismay.

It was a news report. She couldn't hear it but it was closed-captioned. The anchorwoman in a blue suit was speaking, there was a picture of a man behind her.

Terror radiated from Livy's eyes as she read the words streaming under the picture.

The newswoman looked like she was speaking quite cheerfully as the close-caption read, 'Hello, this is Kay Dorne from CHPS Channel 7 News. We are bringing you an updated report on an all-points-bulletin that is still out on Jered Michael Kenaz."

Pausing to heighten the shocking effect, she continued with fear-provoking awe in her practiced voice, "Convicted serial rapist and killer, Mr. Kenaz was in Blake Correctional Institute, sentenced to life in prison, until he escaped several weeks ago. He is still on the run and considered armed and dangerous."

The camera angled in close to the newswoman's face. Dark brown hair slicked behind her ears, matching brows like swans rose excitedly over taupe colored eyes.

Her expression theatrical, holding the microphone over ruby lips, Kay Dorne announced, "The DA's office had indicated at the time that only one victim had ever managed to escape the madman's clutches, Miss Elisabella Blossemia.

"Miss Blossemia was seventeen when captured by the maniac. Viciously beaten and assumed violently raped like all the others, she was chained in a basement for weeks waiting her turn while other girls were tortured and murdered." The anchorwoman broke off for dramatic effect before continuing.

"The brave young woman, Elisabella, was somehow able to escape. She spent months convalescing, stowed away in an unknown hospital back in her tiny country of," the woman glanced at her notes, tried to pronounce the foreign word and mangled it. "Um, ah, Joracocia."

Tilting her head at the camera, "Uh, anyway," she said with a laugh, "the parents of one of the girls who had allegedly lain dead right at Elisabella's feet, Jenna McQueen, attempted to have Miss Blossemia arrested.

"The McQueens charged that since she was the only one to ever escape his homicidal clutches, Elisabella was somehow in cahoots with Jered Kenaz and helped him abduct innocent young women for his perverse, sadistic, deadly games."

Livy's wide eyes were glued to the screen. Every word a puncturing icepick to her already damaged soul.

The anchorwoman appeared pleased with her story because she smiled wider as pictures of Livy, and Kenaz, and each of the deceased victims flashed behind her head.

Jered Kenaz was 6'3", 220 lbs., in his mid-thirties with thick black hair waving across his head of ridged square angles and thick bones.

His cruel smirk matched the sadism glowing smugly from thin dark eyes. Such inhumane evil emanated from those savage eyes, even the strongest of men couldn't suppress a shiver at such pervading malevolence.

Dorne droned on, "However, Miss Blossemia was cleared of any wrongdoing." The way she said that, it sounded like she didn't quite believe in the girl's innocence.

"So odd that such a good-looking man would need to...um, well, anyway, apparently Miss Blossemia went into hiding after her daring escape." She smiled broadly at her audience.

Shaking her head, she said stoically, "This station has tried to reach her for comment but to no avail. Is she waiting for Mr. Kenaz, perhaps as her secret lover to meet up with him somewhere?"

The woman's voice lowering with an evocative slyness, suggested, "Or, is she hiding in terror waiting for the killer to come and finish the job? Well, that's all-"

It all flooded back to Livy like a gigantic, blindsiding punching wave. The nightmare horror of the kidnapping, the rapes, the doomed girls. Poor Jenna butchered and dying, then lying there at Livy's feet, grotesquely decomposing for a week.

Livy's desperate escape, almost drowning in a rabid river. The weeks in recovery before being released from the hospital, then a longer mental recovery, if you could call having to live with the abomination of what had happened being recovered.

Followed by the sensationalized trial of Kenaz where Livy had been forced to relive every heart pounding, heart breaking second of her harrowing ordeal in front of a lurid audience that hung on every sordid word, and eagerly viewed excruciating leaked pictures of the slaughtered girls.

She had to tell a courtroom stuffed to the gills with reporters and ghoulish voyeurs in detail the atrocities visited upon the victims, as well as the violations Livy herself had suffered.

In the middle of describing when Kenaz was ripping off her clothes, Livy's parents had slapped their hands over their mouths covering not horrified, but mortified gasps as they jumped up and fled the courtroom, leaving Livy sitting completely alone with zero support.

When she thought it was finally all done, all behind her, she'd had to endure a civil trial.

Jenna's parents had claimed she'd somehow been involved, dredging up every ghastly component of the atrocious experience all over again.

She had even considered suicide at a few of her lowest points. Skulking outside her home and the courthouse, the media hounded her every waking, and sleeping moment.

To be judged and persecuted even as she tried to move on from her own horrific ordeal as a victim was a never ending torment.

Surviving was almost as bad as living through the horror. The nightmares alone made her want to dive off a cliff to erase them from her poor tortured brain.

Then it came to Livy, the phone calls with only deliberate heavy breathing, her skin prickled as goose bumps ran up her arms.

The authorities were supposed to warn her, call her if he ever got out. *Oh my gosh, he's been out for weeks- how on earth did he find me?*

Without a word, she grabbed up her purse and hastened towards the door. She had to hurry, get home, lock the doors, *oh God-* she stumbled blindly out the door and into the crisp dark night.

Her car, her mind so jumbled with stark terror she couldn't remember where she'd parked the car.

"Focus, Liv, focus, calm down," talking to herself, she remembered, she'd parked down the street.

Her legs as heavy as iron, wouldn't respond to her urges to move quickly.

As she made her way to her car, she glanced over one shoulder then the other, her rapid shallow breaths rasping in her ears, all the way down the street.

She had parked blocks down in front of a closed store.

The street was dark except for street lamps and a few closed shops that were lit inside with faint security lights. Heavy clouds loomed in front of the cool silver moon blocking even its spare illumination.

As she moved past the shops she caught a glimpse of her face in a darkened window. She couldn't see her eyes through her tinted glasses, but she knew they were round and blinking with rising anxiety, her skin as pale as ivory.

Most of her hair had escaped the bun, she hadn't made it as tight as usual being in a hurry, and she'd forgotten the hairband for the first time.

She pulled the pins out and stuffed them in her pocket, like the commander had done while they danced. The wind shuffled the curls around her head, across her back.

Her head cocked, were those footsteps? Did she hear someone behind her? Anxiously, Livy swung her head around but saw no one else on the street, only parked cars and empty, darkened stores.

Finally, she spotted her car. Even as relief started swirling, she saw that the streetlights around it were out.

The tension returning to her tight shoulders, Livy couldn't remember if they had been out when she'd parked. Great.

She approached the VW warily; Kenaz could be hiding right now behind any of the other cars parked along the murky street, ready to spring at her the second she was near.

Wishing she'd brought a jacket, the night had grown chilly, she gripped her blouse, holding it tight in her fist in front of her, half from the shivering cold, half from the mindless fear that was invading her frantic brain. The chilly wind swept up under her skirt freezing her bare legs.

A noise pricked her ears, *what was that*? Livy paused, blinked into the shadowed street. Had she seen someone, something move down there?

She listened, nothing. A slight sound of the wind rustling leaves and trash down the gutters, and the faint boom-boom of music from another bar a block away, but that was all.

"Okay, buck-up Livy," she remonstrated herself muttering, "you let him terrify you when he isn't even here and he owns you. Don't let him inside, keep him out of your head, girl." Sure, brave talk. He had owned her nightmares since she had escaped.

Through the blood pounding in her ears, she could hear her own footsteps now as she trod on some gravel on the walk. Tugging her blouse tighter, holding her breath, she reached her car. Fumbling the keys out of her purse, she looked down.

"Oh no," the wail gushed from her tight throat. Her front right tire was flat as a pancake.

Muttering, "Darn," her head down, she reached in her purse for her cell to call for a tow-

"*Oof-*" a grunt was knocked out of her as something plowed right into her. Livy slammed to the ground, her glasses and purse went flying, but she managed to roll as the dark figure stumbled trying to grab her.

Scrambling on the cement walk, Livy screamed at the top of her lungs.

"Motherfucking bitch," a nasty voice snaked from the male. Dressed in all black, a hood covering his face, he lunged for her.

Livy fell back on her butt kicking at him. She grabbed a handful of gravel and threw it at his eyes.

"Bitch!" he screeched, his hands clamoring at his eyes.

LOUISE FURLEY

Livy jumped to her feet and ran in a blind panic back up the street screaming.

"Get back here you bitch!" the man roared-

Livy could hear his footsteps pounding behind her. She ran as fast as her legs could go, head down, gasping for air, she couldn't breathe, her throat was too paralyzed with fear to take a breath to scream-

Blam!

She slammed into what felt like a brick wall. She hit him so hard she bounced backwards. He reached out and grabbed her, and snatched her back hard against his chest.

"No! Let me go! Help me! Help me!" Livy pounded her fists on his chest as panicked screams roiled up her lungs.

"Livy, Livy, baby, it's me, Bay, Commander DaRocco, you're all right!"

She fought him so frantically he had to wrap his arms around her to hold her flailing arms down. "Livy, calm down, you're going to hurt yourself."

He lowered his head, his nose in her hair, he breathed in her fresh scent, it went straight to his dick. That was something that has never happened to him before.

Stroking her hair, he said gently, "Okay, I've got you, breathe deeply, slow, baby."

His deep voice reached her, she stopped fighting him.

"Oh my God," Livy cried. Shuddering in his strong embrace, frenzied wheezes scraped from her heaving chest.

Twisting in his arms to look back, she shouted, "Look out- he was right behind me, we have to run-" Panicking again that the man was still after her she fought to break loose from Bay's hold.

Wrapping his arms tighter around her to hold her still, Bay looked over her head. All he saw was a dark street lined

74

with cars in front of closed shops. There was not a soul on the walk but them.

"Livy, honey, calm down, there's no one there, shh," he rubbed her back with light circles. "I won't let anyone hurt you, it's okay, I promise." He could feel her small body shuddering against his chest.

Swinging her head around, Livy checked out the street herself. Chest heaving, huge blue eyes round with fright scanned up and down both sides of the street.

When she saw what he said was true, she stopped struggling, still her rough panting shook through her, rattling her bones.

Bay held her against him, her breasts wedged hard on his chest, her fragrance wasn't the only thing making his balls sting and his erection rise.

He cradled her jaw with one hand to hold her focus. "Baby, what happened? Who was there? Did someone hurt you? Let me-" he ran his hands down her bare arms, then he held her damaged palms up. "You're hurt," then he crouched to examine her legs.

"Your knees are scraped too, Livy. I need to take you to the hospital."

"No- no," she panted, sobs strangling in her throat. "I'm all right. I'm all right," she repeated like a chant trying to convince them both.

He stood up. "Livy," his long fingers wound around her thin arms. "Tell me what happened." It was an effort to keep his eyes on her face, not on her nipples that poked through her blouse from the chilly air, and her breasts heaving with fright.

"I- I," she gulped down the sobs, took several deep breaths to gather her composure. "The report, the news, did you s-see it?" Her voice broke tiny, bleak.

Bay's gaze roamed her face, her glasses were gone, he could see how haunted her huge eyes were. He stroked the soft skin of her cheek. "Yeah. Honey, I," he drew a heavy breath. "I already knew about your...ordeal. I, uh, well, honestly, a couple days ago I ran a background check on you."

"You," she put her palms on his chest and pushed back.

He let her, but he didn't release her arms.

"You looked into my history? How could you? They changed my name, my being here at the base is part of a victim relocation plan to keep me...safe, anonymous." Her lids lowered hiding her pain.

"Yeah, well, I have a pretty high security clearance. It's your business, Livy, I haven't said a word to anyone."

He didn't tell her how horrified he'd been when he read what she had endured.

Now he understood why she'd shut herself off from the world. He had hoped they would grow close and eventually she would open up to him and he could help her. Regrettably, she had shut him down.

"I saw the stricken look on your face when you got up and fled from the bar. Then I saw the news report." He shrugged. "I followed you to see if you were all right."

She was shaking. He slipped his arms around her and drew her to his strong, masculine warmth, and gently stroked her hair, her back.

"I heard your screams, I ran to you. Tell me what just happened, Livy, I'll call the MP's."

Unceasingly scanning the street, through chattering teeth she told him, "I uh, I went to my car. The streetlamps were out. I don't remember them being out when I parked there. Then, my tire was flat, now I realize it was to stall me, distract me so he could-" her breath caught, small hand fluttered at her flexing throat.

"Okay, honey, steady, tell me what happened next. Are you sure it was a male?"

"Huh," she choked a sob, then wiped at her eyes. With a short nod, she said, "Yeah. He was big, like- like Kenaz."

A shiver roiled through her body. Bay felt it, he drew his arms more tightly around her.

"He had broad shoulders, and he was strong." Her eyes crunched closed tight and she shook her head back and forth as another violent shiver rolled over her.

"So strong. And, uh, he spoke, cursed at me, it was definitely a man. I couldn't see his face, and he spoke in short, cut off words, but I'm sure it was him."

As she talked, Bay petted her, rubbed her back softly, trying to calm her, give her his support. He uttered in a hushed, soothing tone, "Okay, baby, then what happened?"

Her eyes snapped open and she continued her frantic perusal of the area. "Uh, I was reaching in my purse to get my cell to call a tow truck or something, when he- he jumped me, knocked me down. I rolled and kicked at him, threw stones in his eyes. That stopped him long enough for me to get on my feet and get away. I heard him coming after me," her voice trembled.

Sniffing, she sucked in a long, rippling breath to calm herself. "I guess when he saw you he ditched."

Relief in his voice, Bay said, "Thank God I came after you, Livy." His heart quailed at the thought of what would have happened to her if he hadn't.

He shoved his hand in his pocket for his phone saying, "I'll call the MP's-"

Her head bounced up, she shouted, "No!" Embarrassed, and worried about drawing attention to herself, she spoke more quietly. "Please, Commander, you have no idea the media circus I went through the last time. I-" she wiped under an eye, lowered her head.

"I can't go through that again. No police. You call them and I will not speak to them. I- I'll find a taxi or something and run away. Please," she looked beseechingly up at him.

His sigh somewhat annoyed, he couldn't resist her pleas. She was so scared, how could he deny her and add to the torture she'd already had to endure in her young life? She was now shivering nonstop, he rubbed her arms to warm her,

"Okay, come on, let me get you out of here." Taking ahold of her arm, he started to walk with her back towards the bar.

Sniffing down another deep breath, Livy pushed her long curls off her shoulders letting them coil down her back and shook her head.

Wearily, she dragged a trembling hand across her forehead and attempted to force strength into her shaky voice. "No, I need my purse, my keys," she pulled away from him to go back to her car.

He held her taut, curved her back around to face him, bringing her close. Holding onto her upper arms, Bay lowered his head to connect their eyes.

"No, Livy, you go back in the bar, I'll get them. I'll change the flat and drive your car to the front of the bar to collect you."

"No, please, Commander, I- I can't. I mean, you can go back to Prontos," she tugged to get loose but he held her still. "I need to get my stuff, besides, I don't have a spare."

His brows arched in disbelief. "You don't have a spare, Livy? You should ha-"

"Commander," she sighed her nerves out. "Have you seen my car? I'm lucky it came with a key."

His mouth pulled wryly to the side. "Gotcha. Okay, I'll walk you inside, my friend Jules will watch over you, and I will go get your belongings." His long fingers still coiled around her upper arms, he unconsciously squeezed them, his thumbs stroked her skin.

Shaking her head, she objected, "Please, Commander, I want to go get them. I- don't want him to think he won, that he's scared me." Her fingers splayed on his chest.

He glanced down at them, so small, dainty on his huge hard chest. Picturing them moving down his body, his groin flamed. Damn he wanted her, but right now she needed him to help her.

"I don't want you going there, Livy. Hell, he could be waiting with a knife to ambush you again, or he could have a gun."

Glancing with worry down the dark street, she shook her head.

Damn she was so stubborn. He swiped his sleeve across his brow, his brain shuddered again at the thought of what could have happened to her if he hadn't followed her out.

Livy mumbled, "You, um, I mean, I'll be fine. He's probably gone by now. It might not have even been…him. Maybe he was just a- a- robber and I was in the wrong place at the wrong time. I'll get my phone and wait for a tow truck, you can go back to your friends."

He paused and studied her.

Her skin muddled ashen, eyes still wide with terror, her limbs shaking. Such a tiny thing, and yet she was fighting him on this.

"Uh, sure, yeah, okay," he said drily. "I'll just trot myself back to the bar, plop down, order another beer and chit-chat with my friends while you walk back alone in the dark to your car while some murderous maniac waits in the bushes for you. Uh, huh, come on, let's go."

He crouched, pretending to tie a lace but surreptitiously pulled out the gun at his ankle and tucked it in the back of his waistband. Then he gingerly took her arm and was surprised when she didn't pull away from him.

They walked back to her car to retrieve her things.

As they moved on down the street, the closer to where she'd parked the car, he tucked her in tight to his body under his arm in case the fucker was still lurking around.

Bay was trained in this sort of thing, ambushes and the like, he could scan the area without looking like he was. His body and brain were on high alert, but he held her gently. He didn't need for her to feel his tenseness, she was already scared out of her mind.

When they neared the car, they could see her purse on the ground, keys beside it. Bay bent, grabbed her keys and purse and handed them to her.

She peered inside the purse. "Everything's here." Her glasses were a few feet away. Livy knelt to pick up the specs.

Holding them in her hand, she said in dismay, "He came back here and- stepped on them on purpose. They are totally smashed, that wouldn't have happened if they'd only fallen off or if they got stepped on once."

Since her purse was still there and nothing was taken, it seemed pretty likely that it hadn't been a robber that assaulted her. A shudder rippled from her head down to her toes.

Bay took the glasses from her and tucked them in a pocket, this time she wasn't getting them back. He'd studied them when he'd taken them off her at the wedding. They were plain tinted glass she used to hide behind. "Come on, let me take you somewhere safe."

Staring bleakly at her car, she said in a small voice, "I want to go home. I have to call a tow-"

"Livy, don't make me pull rank again, I'm taking you somewhere safe." He guided her towards where he'd parked his truck.

Opening the door for her, he said, "Here, it's high, put your hand on my shoulder to balance." He took her hand and set it on his shoulder then put his hands around her waist and pretty much lifted her inside.

When she settled, he closed the door and jogged around to hop in the driver's side. Turning on the ignition, he pulled out of the lot. Heading down the street, he said, "I think a hotel-"

"No. I want to go home. I'm not letting him run me out of my home. I'll feel safer there. You take me anywhere else and I will leave and go home anyway." Her hand went to clutch the door handle.

"Hey, you gonna jump, Livy?" Bay pushed the button on his armrest ensuring the doors were locked.

"I will if I have to." She yanked on the handle, but it didn't budge.

"All right honey, take it easy, I'll take you home. Just chill." Cranking the wheel, he turned the truck around to head for the house she was renting.

He'd have to figure out what to do next to protect her once they got to her home.

Chapter Seven

She only lived a few miles from the base, but it was in the poorest, most crime-ridden section of town.

Bay pulled up and parked in front of the small, dilapidated house she rented.

Peeling ancient white paint with olive shutters, one that hung from only one hinge, a few uneven cement steps led up to the olive painted door.

Bay put the truck in park.

Livy turned her wry expression to him. The side of his face lit from a streetlight, the rest of the world was dark. She noted blandly, "You didn't need to ask me my address."

"Hmm," his reply noncommittal, he shut off the engine.

Her hand on the door handle, Livy's voice heavy with weariness, she told him, "You don't need to turn it off. Thank you for bringing me home. I guess I'll see you around at the base." She jerked at the handle but it didn't budge.

She plucked at the lock but it didn't unlatch. Brows down, lips pursed she said, "Commander, unlock my door, please."

He opened the driver's door and slid out then leaned in and said, "You stay here. Give me your keys, I'm checking it out first."

Eyes rolling, her irritation clear she said, "No. This is my home, you can't tell me what to do. Now, unlock this door immediately." She jerked hard on the handle showing her exasperation.

"Ah, obstinate woman." Sighing, he leaned in further and snatched her purse like he had that night when Duke Rashad attacked her.

"Dammit, Commander, you can't just-"

He rifled in the small bag, pulled out her keys and tossed her purse on the seat.

"You," he pointed a broad finger at her, "will stay here until I come and say it's all clear. He knows your car, he knows you were in the bar, he could have followed you home before and know where you live."

He stood, closed his door and clicked a button on his remote. She glared at him through the window. He shook his head at her misplaced and ill-advised bravery.

She wanted to be courageous and not back down from the freak that was stalking her, but this was not the time or place. When he was either dead or safely behind bars then she could run about freely and exert her independence.

Furious, Livy scrambled across the seat behind the wheel to unlock the door. But, for all she tried, she couldn't get it unlocked.

Dropping the remote in his pocket, Bay smiled grimly at her powerless anger, then turned and strode to her house.

He slowed when he reached the steps, the door was ajar a fraction of an inch. He glanced back at Livy, watching him crossly through the window. He figured she lived with her nightmare of terror day and night, there was no way she would accidentally leave her door open.

He turned sideways as he pulled his gun out of the back of his pants so she wouldn't see it, then crept silently up the steps.

Standing to the side of the door, he peered through the open curtain. There were no lights on, nothing moved inside. Suddenly, he jumped down the steps and jogged around the house disappearing into the dark.

Seeing him do that, eyes wide with nervous curiosity, Livy sat up straighter. Putting her fingers on the dashboard, she leaned forward to look out the window trying to see through the gloom of dark night.

Livy sat on tenterhooks. What on earth was he doing? Why didn't he just go through the front door?

Then, the front door opened and he hopped down the few steps stalking quickly back to the truck.

Unlocking the driver's door with the remote, he opened the door to a livid Livy.

She charged out of the truck not realizing how high up she really was, "Commander! How dare you-" with a short scream she tumbled out having misjudged the high step.

Bay caught her with his big hands, pulled her in and held her against him. When he didn't set her down right away, she wriggled against his warm body.

Even without a jacket and his shirtsleeves rolled up his rocky forearms, he radiated heat, warming her. Breathlessly, she said, "Commander, you can let me down…now."

He held her so their eyes were level, mouths close, so close their breaths misted tickling each other's lips.

Livy gripped his thick shoulders, her voice a bit husky she said, "Uh, Commander, please put me down."

Still he hesitated. Then, the edge of his lip nicked up. "Yeah, okay, as soon as you call me Bay."

"Huh," she grunted. "Sure, and in a second you'll pull rank on me and be the bossy commander again. No thanks. Now," her voice stern, she gave a little kick, "put me down."

"Ah, so stubborn." He sighed, and set her gently on her feet. She started immediately for the house, he grasped her arm stopping her.

"What? You can leave now, Commander, I-"

"No. Livy, wait."

Annoyed at being manhandled and controlled, she jerked at her arm demanding, demanding, "Let go of me."

Still holding onto her, Bay said quietly, "Listen, Livy, someone has been in your house." He waited for his words to hit her.

Her head swung sharply. "What? What are you talking about?" She gave a tug on her arm.

He took a deep breath; let it out and explained, "Your door was open. If someone was inside they would have seen the truck lights in the driveway, that's why I went around to the back to catch them if they were escaping out the back. Someone-" She wrenched from his grasp and ran towards the house.

"Goddammit Livy," he cursed and jogged after her.

He caught her at the door. "Hey honey, take it slow."

He'd left the door wide open, she paused with her hand on it. "Could- could someone still be inside?"

Bay shook his head. "No, I cleared it, and the back yard. But, you need to be prepared for-" he set a hand on her lower back to slow her, but she moved through the doorway, gasped, and stopped dead.

"Oh my gosh, what happened?"

The place had been trashed. She didn't have much, the furniture came with the house. Someone had knifed the cushions and pulled out stuffing, knocked over tables, threw magazines around.

She ran into the bedroom and cried out.

Every drawer had been pulled and dumped, her pillows slashed. Bay came in quietly behind her.

"I- I don't understand, why would someone do this? A burglar broke in? What was he looking for? I have nothing worth stealing."

"Livy, it's more likely it was the same person that tried to grab you earlier."

"But why? Was he looking for something? You see I don't have anything of value, why don't you think it was a robber?"

He glanced around. "The way your stuff has been tossed around, but most things like in the kitchen were barely touched. If someone was looking for something there wouldn't be anything not searched.

"The fridge would have been dumped, glasses and plates out of the cupboards so he could look inside. No," he shook his head again, "whoever did this, did it deliberately to scare you."

"But, who-" she broke off, her lips pulled in at the cramp in her stomach. "Jered Kenaz, it has to be him."

"Yeah, well, grab a suitcase and get some stuff, you're obviously not staying here."

"What? No." Frowning, she shook her head looking around in desperation. "I have nowhere else to go. I have no family here and I haven't been here long enough to make any real friends."

Looking at the damage, she said hopefully, "It's really not that bad, I can clean it up, it won't take that much." She started picking clothes up off the bed and folding them.

Bay slammed his hands on his lean hips and barked, "Are you fucking kidding me, Livy? This asshole broke in, babe. The lock had been jimmied, the entire place is all windows for fuck's sake, you aren't safe here. We will call the cops-"

Shrieking, "No!" Her voice sharp, she stated, "No police. I told you, I can't live with the media spectacle that would create all over again. No. I'll just put everything back where it was, everything will be fine like it never happened." She stared blankly at the blouse in her hands.

"Ah, shit, Livy." Bay crossed his arms over his bulky chest. "You can't stick your head in the sand and pretend this didn't happen. Fine, no police, but you are not staying here, so pack some shit and let's go."

She plunked her hands on her hips and glared up at him. "I just told you I have nowhere to go. I can't afford a hotel room. Now, I appreciate you driving me home, but I'll be fine. I keep a baseball bat under my bed, ever since..." she trailed off, her eyes lowered.

"So, uh, please go now and let me get this cleaned up." She put her hands to his crossed arms and tried to give him a little push. It was like trying to shove a cement wall, he didn't even twitch.

Feeling tingling from her hands on him, Bay pictured her in some skimpy lingerie, tits and ass hanging out everywhere, waking up in a daze to a killer in her room and trying to fight him off with a bat. The fucker would be laughing his ass off as he took it from her.

His stomach heaved at the thought. "You gonna fight a gun if he has one?"

At her rounding eyes, his voice cold, hard, he said, "You have five minutes to get the shit you need and then you're coming with me. You're staying at my place; there will be no arguing about it. You don't pack, I will, and I will haul your pretty ass over my shoulder and take you out of here."

Eyes wider, mouth open appalled, she gasped, "Are you kidding me?" Her voice grew shrill, she said, "You would force me to go with you?"

At his determined clenched jaw and pressed lips, her brows lowering, Livy shook her head in disbelief. "I don't believe it. You're pushing this responsibility thing as a commander a little too far. Thanks for the ride home, now get out and let me be in peace."

Lips pulled in, her face reddened in vexed anger. She didn't look around at the jumbled mess of her belongings strewn everywhere, it was like she needed to keep her eyes on him or she'd fall apart. The trembling of her small pointed chin belied her angry bravado.

He glared at her for three seconds, then pushed past her, stalked into her closet, found a suitcase in the tiny closet, pulled it out and slammed it on the bed. Opening the lid, he grabbed up clothes off the bed and started tossing them into it.

He held up a lacy yellow bra and stared at it. Her cheeks pink, she snatched it out of his hands.

"Commander, what are you doing-"

He grabbed the bra back from her and tossed it in the suitcase. Gathering more clothes to throw in, he scolded her, "It's bullshit you live here in the first place. For fuck's sake, it's dangerous as hell and you have zero security." Seeing a few pairs of shoes near the closet he grabbed those up and tossed them in the bag.

"You're insane! Stop it! Stop right now, Commander!" Livy yelled at him.

Ignoring her, he went into her bathroom and grabbed her meager toiletries. Stomping back into the room, he threw everything into the case, slammed the lid closed and snapped the locks. He stood it on its side with the handle up, then faced her. "Well? You coming?"

"You- you- you-" she sputtered, backing away from him. "I am not leaving, this is ridiculous! I can take care of my- no! Get away from me!" she shrieked, throwing her hands up defensively as he stomped over to her.

He bent, grabbed her under her thighs and lifted her over his shoulder. Stomping back to the bed, he grabbed up the suitcase and strode out passing through the living room and out the door, kicking the door closed behind them.

"Stop! You let me down this instant!" She kicked at him, pounding her small fists on his broad back.

He suddenly smacked her butt hard then clamped his hand over it. Stunned, she stopped moving.

"You keep fighting me, Livy, and I will paddle that ass into tomorrow."

"You- you- you-" she stammered against his back as he carried her out.

At the truck, he opened the back door and tossed her suitcase in. Then he opened the passenger side and shuffled her in, then closed the door in her face, clicking his unique remote that locked her door, making her unable to unlock it from the inside.

When he climbed in and turned the engine over, she started in.

"How dare you! This is kidnapping! I'm going to your superior and tell him-"

"Uh huh. Here," he held his cell out to her as he put the truck in reverse. "Lieutenant Colonel Garrett Miles, speed-dial #3. He knows your situation, and he knows me. When I tell him about your car and now your house, trust me, he will support my actions 150%."

Livy crossed her arms and glared at the phone but didn't take it.

"Put your seatbelt on," he told her.

"Humph," she huffed, facing out the front window.

"Ah, okay, Livy, you know by now I mean what I say, so," his gazed flicked down her body then up to her angry face. He half turned with his arm curved on the backseat looking out the back window to backup down the driveway.

"Either you buckle up, or I'll paddle your ass then do it myself." His mouth quirked, he almost hoped she'd resist, he'd take any excuse to touch her.

Apparently that wasn't okay with her because she snatched the belt pieces and jammed them together, then sat fuming, glaring out the window.

They drove in silence to his place. He stopped at a gate and knuckled in a code then the gate opened, he drove through and parked in the garage below the building. He got out, retrieved her bag, then helped her down.

Stepping a few feet from him, looking around, she asked, "What is this place?" The structure was two stories, windows jutted out like crooked building blocks set on top of each other.

He lightly grasped her arm as he sensed she was going to run, and led her to an elevator. As soon as the door pinged open, he hustled her inside then stood between her and the exit.

As they rode up, he said, "I share living space with my...team. This is kind of like a group of villas bunched

90

together, we have our own space, our own privacy. The place is secure as hell, you will be safe as shit here."

"But-"

The elevator door slid open with a double ping and he took her arm pulling her out to a hallway.

Setting her suitcase down, he turned to her. Holding both arms, he forced her to stand in front of him then gave her a little shake so she'd look up at him.

"Don't fight me on this, Livy. You're staying with me. I have two bedrooms, you'll have your own private space, and the building, the garage is secure. I'll have someone repair your door right away to deter thieves, and get the flat tire fixed and your car brought around here. I'd prefer you just stay put until we get this bastard caught."

He forked a hand through his hair making it stand up in spikes, then wrapped it around her arm again. "But, I already know what a stubborn female you are. I assume you will insist on going to work, to training?"

Brows drawn down in obstinate anger and tightened lips answered his question.

The side of his mouth ticked up, his fingers prodded into her arms. "Yeah, as I thought. At least you'll be safe on the base." He started to pull her from the elevator to the hall.

"Commander, please stop dragging me around." Livy jerked her arm from his grasp.

Ignoring her annoyance, he picked her case up and said calmly, "You can't get out of the parking garage without the code." He trod to a door, unlocked it and strolled in.

She stared after him. Then realizing there wasn't anything she could do…at the moment, she followed him.

A wide, white-tiled foyer opened to a large, masculine living room. Most of the furniture was dark blue leather on a lighter blue carpet.

Vertical white blinds at the floor to ceiling windows were closed tightly against the peering night. A faux, ivory brick wall separated the room from the kitchen.

Bay strode through the living room and down a hall. Reluctantly, Livy followed him keeping a distance between them. He turned into a room.

Livy stood in the doorway and watched him set her case on a chair.

The room was champagne walls with pastel yellow plaid curtains. A gleaming hardwood floor was covered with scattered yellow rugs. The room had a dresser and a desk with a chair, and a small divan in yellow print was at the single bow window.

When he turned quickly to her, Livy gasped and took a step back.

He frowned at her fear of him. "There is a bathroom through there," he nodded to another doorway. "It should have everything in it. My mother and sisters were here last Easter," he said it like it was an affectionate burden.

"They always make sure it's well supplied." He started towards her and frowned again when her face paled and she backed up into the hallway, shrinking against the wall as he neared.

Forehead wrinkling in consternation, he growled, "Hell, Livy, if I was going to attack you, hurt you, I've had plenty of opportunities already. You don't need to be afraid of me."

Huge blues wide and wary at him, Livy stayed cowed against the wall.

Bay swallowed his sigh of pique that she would think he would hurt her. However, considering what she'd gone through when she'd been abducted, and then tonight, it was reasonable that she would be frightened of everyone. Especially him as a big man with a fierce reputation.

He said quietly, "Come on, I'll show you the kitchen." He moved past her making sure there was a wide space so she wouldn't jump out of her skin.

She waited until he was several feet ahead before following him. He led her to a huge kitchen in blue and white with a round table and chairs, and an alabaster island. It all looked pristine.

"I have a woman that cleans and keeps the fridge stocked. Please feel free to help yourself to anything, okay?"

He watched her, but she said nothing.

In his most amiable voice, he asked, "Are you hungry? Would you like something now? I'm not a great cook but I can make a mean ham and cheese sandwich."

His crooked grin should have taken her nerves down a notch, but she just stared at him with a shake of her head.

All of her bravado and anger had dissipated now that she was alone with him, and basically imprisoned in a strange place.

"Livy, listen," he took a step to her and frowned when she blanched and crossed her arms over her chest in a protective stance.

Changing course, he went to the cupboard and took out two glasses and filled them with ice from the front of the fridge, then opened it and took out two sodas.

Moving slowly, he trod past her out of the kitchen. "Come on, Livy," he said quietly.

She hesitated then followed him. He went into the living room and set the glasses and sodas on the coffee table. He popped the tab on one of the cans and poured it into a glass.

She stood in obvious discomfort, set the tip of a finger on the arm of the couch to brace, and looked like she was on the verge of running.

"Sit down, Livy, there is nowhere for you to go. You're making me feel like a mass-murdering rapist and I'm really not liking it." Seeing her pupils dilate, he realized that was a poor choice of words.

Bay knew he looked like a big bruiser, it came with the job. And he knew she'd been through living hell, but as he said, if he wanted to hurt her he would have already.

He waited while she contemplated his sincerity.

When he didn't pounce on her, she gingerly perched on the edge of an arm of couch.

Silently, he let out his held breath and handed her the soda. He poured himself one and was going to sit next to her but realized that would not relax her, so he plunked down on a chair placed to the corner of the sofa.

Apparently comforted by his distance, she slid down carefully to sit on a cushion, still eyeing him warily.

Drawing in a breath, he said, "Ah, listen," he watched her take a tiny sip of her soda. "Livy," he leaned slightly forward towards her. "I can't pretend to know what you've gone through," he paused as the color sank back out of her already pale complexion.

"I uh, maybe I was a bit highhanded in the way I brought you here," he smiled at her one arched brow, good, her moxie was returning.

"But, shit woman, you were attacked in the street, your house was broken into and deliberately ransacked, and," he took a deep breath, "the man that…held you prisoner is on the loose.

"Hey, I know you've got to be terrified, and I don't want to add a whit to your fears, seriously. But, baby, I could not leave you there in that unlocked shit rattrap you call home in that fucked up neighborhood."

"Commander," she said, "there was no space for me at the base, which apparently you knew. I am more in training than actually working, so I am certainly not on your pay-grade status," her tone lightly sarcastic as she pointedly looked around his obviously expensive home.

He sat back, his legs wide apart like men sit. Scratching his honey-colored hair, Bay said, "Yeah, I get it. It's just, shit, Liv, don't you have family that can help you out? I mean, you're so young, and after that whole horrible ordeal, hell, if you were my sister, wife, daughter, whatever, I'd make sure-"

"Yes, well, maybe you would," she cut him off. "But my family..." The pupils widened in her blue eyes again, this time with pain. "I..." she drank some of her soda then looked towards the shuttered window as if she could see outside.

"Livy," he leaned forward again setting brawny forearms on his knees and clasped his hands together. "Can you tell me, I mean I have the general idea, and, really, I don't want to dig into your private shit, but, help me to understand...what you're feeling."

His deep green eyes darkened as more pain flashed over her face taking the last bit of color with it. "I..." how does he say this without sounding nosy? "I want to help, if I can."

They were both quiet for a few minutes.

Uneasily settling back against the couch cushion, Livy took a shuddering breath. Her head down, she peered up at him through a veil of rich curls, and sighed. "O...kay."

When she saw he wasn't making any alarming moves towards her, his jaw was gentled, eyes warm and nonjudgmental yet interested, she sighed again.

"Uh, well, you've read the reports, saw the news. A man, Jered Kenaz," his name on her lips came out twisted, ashamed, tormented, and filled with guilt.

"Um, he grabbed me, took me right off the street just like…earlier," a shiver ran through her slender body, the hands holding the glass clenched it.

"Except, that time I didn't get away."

Chapter eight

*H*earing the anguish in her tight voice, Bay said quietly, quickly, "Liv, hey, you don't have to tell me. I want to understand, but I don't want to upset you more than you already are. Let's just forget about it for tonight, let's-"

"No," her eyes flashed angrily, and with a hint of shame, "you asked, you can just sit and listen. I've never told anyone, except, the shrinks." She said the word shrinks as if it was soiled. Her pupils shrank as the memories flooded.

He settled back, so she continued, "I, uh, like I said, he abducted me right off the street. I never even saw him coming. He punched me, knocked me out. I came to in a van.

"I knew it was a van because I was lying down, and the floor was hard but I could feel the vehicle moving. My hands were tied behind me, my ankles bound, I was blindfolded and gagged." Her hand swept over her eyes in remembrance of the blind fear.

"Such…senses deprivation, it's hard to describe the free-floating terror, you can't see, talk, move. You can't see the very real danger around you, yet you know it's there."

Bay nodded, recalling his own violent past. "Yeah, I've experienced it."

Her gaze jerked to his and she saw he had suffered at the hands of others too. Bay understood the helplessness, the fear of dying, or worse.

"Uh huh," her voice relaxed some seeing he wasn't fooling with her, or being nosy, he'd been there and felt what she had.

Bay had watched people die, many tortured until they'd begged for death. He himself had been tortured, except, he had knowingly put himself in harm's way doing his job, and, he wasn't a helpless young girl in the hands of a sadistic rapist killer.

Her voice quiet, Livy said, "He kept us in cells. We could see each other. We could see when he took a girl, dragged her out, heard her screams. Once he removed one he never brought them...back. Then he started...bringing us out to watch..." Tears sprang, filling her beautiful blues.

"Liv, don't-"

"Raped," she gasped through her throat tight with the pain of remembrance. "He raped them with his...penis, and with horrendous objects. Their screams were..." In her brain forever, she could hear them every minute of every day.

"He...got off on torture. Tied them up, and hooked electric wires to their, uh, nipples, and, lady parts, even their tongues, lips, ears." Her body scrunched in a cringe of vivid recollection.

She kept her gaze from Bay, just stared blankly at the wall. "And," the deep breath she took shook, "he used knives and, uh, other...things." She stopped talking, staring off into space.

Bay waited, then said quietly, "But you did get away, Livy, you survived." He patiently waited again, watching the emotions flicker over her face. His groin twitched recalling the feel of her draped over his shoulder, his hand on her ass.

She was stunningly beautiful. Without the big tinted glasses to hide her face and eyes, he could see soft, rounded cheeks, a small slightly upturned nose in a heart-shaped face.

Large, Icelandic blue eyes that changed as her emotions fed through her. They darkened to almost cobalt when she was relaying her tribulations.

He'd seen them briefly turn silvery light when she had been lightly sarcastic with him, almost playful, when she'd let her guard down.

"You escaped," he prompted.

"Hmm?" It was almost as if she was back there and he had intruded into the horrific memory.

Swallowing hard and blinking rapidly, she turned back to him and said, "Yes. He...had taken Jenna out. She had been there the longest, she had heard and seen every monstrous thing he'd done, every girl he'd killed. That was torture in itself. Letting her see what he did to the others, so she could dwell on what would happen when it was her turn.

"He decided he liked having an audience, so, he would bring us all out and bind us to chairs so we could...watch him. Like he was a show, an actor on a stage in a play we'd paid to enjoy. Jenna, was," her eyes flicked to him then away.

Livy swallowed hard. "Out of her mind with terror. She was almost not even sane anymore. I talked nonstop and told her stories to keep her from thinking of...when it would be her turn. Or mine..." she petered off again.

Bay waited for her to drag back from being right inside the memory.

When he saw she was stuck, suffering with the images as if she was still there, he said sharply, "Livy!" Bay hated to watch her relive the agonizing experience, but, he hoped it would be somewhat cathartic for her.

She hadn't sounded too impressed when she mentioned she'd spoken with shrinks, and she appeared more at ease when she understood that he could relate to what she'd experienced, to a degree. Torture, death and horror.

Blinking at him, her lids lowered, she licked her dry lips, and reached for her soda.

After a few sips, her breath expelled harshly. "Yes, then it was our turn. We were the last, three of us, he brought us all out. Tied us to chairs. He hammered the chair legs to the floor so we couldn't move them and try to untie each other while he was distracted with his...fun. We had tried it once," she drew a hard breath.

"He instantly stabbed one of the girls to death in his rage. And, then, again later, he abruptly killed one of us remaining three."

Livy's eyes closed, her shoulders slumped. She lifted her lids to display tears blurring the blue. "For some reason he got angry with this girl, Christine. Christy was one of us last three." She clutched the soda in both hands.

"I don't know what she said, suddenly he...just hauled off and slammed the hammer into her head, again and again until there was...nothing left of her face, her head."

The picture she drew was grisly, harrowing, stomach roiling. Blinking away the picture, her mouth hitched with wry sadness.

"Was probably for the best, at least she didn't have to suffer the rest of the torture he'd planned for her before dying. Losing his temper had saved her from worse agonizing pain..." Livy closed her eyes.

"Shit, Livy," Bay's voice strained with what she had seen. He craved to go sit with her, pull her into his safe embrace and comfort her.

But, he sighed, he knew she would shut right down and fight to get away from him. He forced himself to stay in his chair.

"Yeah." Agreeing with him, Livy went on, her voice weak and faltering at times. "Jenna was screaming, she knew she was next. The veins on her neck, so taut, red and swollen; her eyes blind with terror, she just nonstop screamed. He started by untying her." Livy's stare went blank again as the old images rolled in her mind.

"He held her by her hair, so tight she couldn't fight him, and he brought her to this...table. It was slanted almost vertical. He pushed her face first onto it so she couldn't fight him while he put her wrists and ankles into cuffs that held her spread uh, eagle, on her stomach. Then he cut her clothes off her.

"The entire time he was taunting me, telling me I was next so I should watch to see how much Jenna loved what he did to her. I tried to stop myself but I couldn't, I cried and screamed with her. I cried for my daddy to come and get me. I begged, pleaded, screamed, but...he never came and Kenaz never stopped."

Livy lifted the soda to her lips but didn't drink any. Cupping the glass with both hands again she set it in her lap. "He, you know, uh, sodomized her, then he uh brutally forced other things in her."

She took a heavy breath, exhaled hard. "Then he un-cuffed her, turned her over to lay her on her back, bound her hands above her head, legs spread again and cuffed.

"Blood was pouring down her thighs, she was only whimpering now, her throat too raw from screaming hysterically and crying in agony. Her chest...just hitched and heaved with her sobs.

"He...did her again, raped her, the same, things. He laughed while he was talking to me, and she was bleeding and crying, he laughed like a savage fool."

Livy's eyes closed, her voice trembling whisper, "He did his torture stuff, electric shocks and cutting. Especially he liked cutting, slicing her sexual parts. Uh, he did this for," she dragged in a deep trembling breath.

"Hours and hours and..." her breath tumbled out wearily. "She had lost so much blood she no longer fought, or cried, or made any sounds. So, he tired of her and slit her throat. He untied her and let her crumple at my feet, beside Christy. Then he left the room. The cabin, it was. He left the cabin."

"Livy," Bay urgently wanted to go to her, comfort her, but he knew his touch would not comfort her. "Please, stop, let-"

Her lips moved, but no sound came out. Eyes wide and blank, unseeing, Livy said, "He was gone for a few days. I was faint with hunger, thirst. The girls decomposing right by my feet, it was, the smell, Bay."

She peered up at him, he nodded in understanding. He'd been around enough dead bodies to be well acquainted of the ungodly smell.

Seeing his nonjudgmental empathy, the comforting nodding of his head, reassuring warm green eyes filled with grief at her pain, she went on, "Then, he returned for me. Told me I was the last in that area. He would be moving on to stay ahead of the law, he told me he had another place. Bragged about it, and described it."

She waved one arm as if indicating the area. "He told me in detail about the land, the city, everything. He taunted me that it was my fault I'd been taken, my looks. He liked my...angelic, uh, he described my looks as angelic. Said we were all beautiful in different ways, but he'd saved me for last because I looked like such an angel.

"He said he was dying to cut every pretty piece off my face, and body," sobs gurgled up Livy's throat but she gulped them down.

"But you got away," Bay repeated, trying to pull her back from the black crevasse he saw her mentally sliding into. He could now understand why she went to such efforts to hide her beauty.

"Huh," she snorted. "Yeah. I got to sit and watch him rape, and mutilate, torture and kill other young women knowing my turn would come, and now it had. I had watched him though, carefully, looking for a weakness, a mistake, something to help me get away.

"He untied me, stuck his hand in my hair and grabbed as tightly as he could. So tight my head bent back, I thought my neck would snap. I was helpless to even hit at him."

Livy's head tilted back as if pulled, her eyes wide with the frightful memory, how beyond hysterically terrified she'd been.

"He jerked me from my chair and dragged me backwards across the cement floor to his inclined table. As he dragged me, he clawed at my clothes, tearing them off as if he couldn't wait. Seeing my bare skin scraping on the jagged floor, bleeding, amused him.

"Lifting me by my hair, he pushed my face into the metal table. I was…totally naked at that point. He uh, you know, molested me, but uh, didn't completely penetrate me.

"Then, he suddenly flipped me around, said he wanted to watch my face as he raped me, wanted to see me cry and beg as he took my…youth. My virginity. Said he was going to f-fuck me front on first, then he would, turn me onto my belly and, continue."

Lowering her head, Livy put a hand to her throat feeling the spinning pulse throbbing there. She took a quick sip of her soda then leaned over and set the glass on the coffee table.

"But," her mouth thinned into a queasy smile. "I had watched him when he hammered our chairs to the wood floor, the time he...hit Christine with the hammer. When he let me go to reach for the cuffs, I- lunged for the hammer he'd left on the side table where he kept his tools."

Bay leaned forward in anticipation, hoping she'd put a nasty hurting on the evil creature who'd abducted and tortured her.

"The other stuff, the things he used for torture, knives and scalpels, screwdrivers and things were too far away to get to. But, he'd left the hammer close, he'd just negligently dropped it after he killed Christine. It was still gummy with her blood. *And tissue, bones, brain matter-*

"I grabbed the hammer and swung- I'm a small woman and he was huge, I only got him in the kneecap, but it was enough for him to collapse with a dreadful scream. He reached out and snared my leg. As he tried to wrench me off my feet, I swung the hammer again and hit his arm."

Her lashes flapped up and down rapidly as her tale finally had some retribution. Still, she wasn't a violent teenager and it revolted her.

"Oh, Commander, the crack sound it made, sickening," her face twisted at the gruesome memory. She shook her head. "He screamed again and fell forward, and I ran straight out of the cabin. Thank God he hadn't locked the door. I don't know if he came right after me because I wasn't running for long."

They were quiet again while she gathered her thoughts. Her long toffee-tinted lashes fluttered on her soft cheeks.

The desperate haze in her eyes cleared as she moved mentally from the cabin of atrocities and to the outside.

She continued, "I was in a forest. I just ran blind as fast as I could, so blindly I didn't see the edge. I hurtled right off an overhang and dropped like a rock into the river. It was good, and bad. Bad, because it was freezing and I couldn't swim."

His voice rasped rusty from his pity for her plight, Bay asked huskily, "And the good, Livy?"

"Hmm, yes." Her eyes shifted back and forth as she continued recalling the unspeakable nightmare. "The current was so swift it kept me on the surface. They told me I had been swept near this man standing way down river fly-fishing, and he managed to grab me. The next thing I knew I woke up in the hospital."

"But you were able to tell the police where the cabin was. They caught him."

"Not at the cabin. I had no idea where that was. It was deep in the forest and I had gone over a cliff and hurtled downstream away. By the time they located it, he was way gone. But," her blue eyes gleamed with vengeance and a slight smile curled the side of her lush mouth.

"I told them where he was going next because he'd gloated about leaving so the police couldn't track his pattern and catch him." The half-smile grew in satisfaction.

"He had taunted me about where he would be living, knowing I would be dead and not able to tell the police." She glanced at Bay then quickly away.

Her sad little chuckle held no humor. "He forgot he told me. Plus, apparently he had seen me go over the cliff into the river, he assumed I was dead. So they set up surveillance in the small village where he had told me he planned to move to next."

Her delicate shoulders rose with a deep breath. "After I escaped, they had me sit with a police artist to draw his image. He had mentioned the name of the town he was going to so the police monitored the only main highway going into the rural area. They watched the grocery stores and hotels. He was nabbed buying supplies in a small store."

Bay nodded with approval. Admiring her for her heroism, he said proudly, "Yeah, good girl, you saved yourself and were instrumental in the capture of a monster."

Livy's gaze rose to his, she blushed and sat back against the sofa cushion.

After some silence, Bay said softly, "You had to go through the trial? That must have been tough."

Her big eyes turned up to him, he saw the profound pain in them, it told the story.

"The worse, Commander, was after he was sentenced and I thought it was all finally over, Jenna's family accused me of being complicit with that fiend. Because I was the only one to get away.

"They said I wasn't beautiful like their Jenna, that I was too plain, too homely to attract him; therefore he must have been using me to capture other beautiful girls. They claimed that Kenaz liked my looks because he was a freak and liked other freaky things."

Her eyes flashed briefly to him then away. "That's why I know you were messing with me when you were pretending to ask me out." Her eyes lowered, she whispered, "I'm just an ugly little mouse."

Damn, Bay thought, how fucking conflicted she must feel about her own looks. She hasn't been hiding her beauty, she hides behind clothes and glasses because she no longer knows who she is, what she looks like.

Her reality is distorted by what other people have said to her. The rapist told her she was angelic and beautiful, Jenna's family told her she was homely, the women on the base disparage her, yet men like Duke Rashad insanely desire her enough to attack her. She must be confused out of her mind.

He bent forward, his fists clenched, he opened his mouth in anger but she kept talking.

"There was no evidence of course, so, when they couldn't get me charged with anything criminal they went after me civilly. They won."

"What?" Bay barked. Taken aback, he blinked then slammed his fist on his knee and yelled flabbergasted, "What? That's ludicrous! How the hell could they? That's fucking ridiculous, outrageous-"

"Uh huh. They won. Somehow they convinced a jury that I was like a- a- Lolita or black widow or something. That's why no matter how much I earn, my pay is garnished to pay them the restitution they won. Don't ask me how much the lien is, I...I don't want to talk anymore, please," her voice small and pitiful tugged at his heart.

"Shit, Livy, I'm so sorry, I didn't mean to dredge it all up. I just wanted you to tell me how you felt so I could, I don't know, understand, be empathetic. I guess I shouldn't have said anything." He rubbed the back of his neck in perplexity.

"You seemed so down on the psychiatrists, I thought maybe someone else that had lived life and death situations, been imprisoned and tortured could, er, ah, anyway..."

She grunted, said with derision, "Yes, the shrinks." Sitting back, she toyed with a long ringlet.

"My parents sent me to a few. I didn't talk for the longest time, then I thought maybe they could help take the nightmares, the every second, the every breath of every day horror away, so I started telling them."

Her mouth crimped in shamed anger. She spewed her resentment, "They got off on it. I didn't see it at first, I was so naïve and all. They asked so many questions, but only about the torture and the sexual stuff. Not about how I felt, or anything.

"Or how I could learn to defeat my demons. How to fight the terror that it would, could, happen again, or- or- the damned survivor's guilt, or, even, how to live with the shame." She pushed the heels of her palms against her eyes to staunch the tears.

"No, they kept asking for more and more specific, graphic details of when the others were raped. They wanted step-by-step descriptions of how they were tortured. Describe exactly what he shoved into their bodies, what made them scream the loudest. They were titillated by our torment!"

She slapped her palms on the cushion in rage. "And me. How was I splayed naked on the table and where did he touch me? Did he grope inside me, if so, where, front or back? Both? Did he beat me? Whip me? Rape me-" she broke off with an infuriated, mortified choke.

Swiping at sliding tears she huffed then said, "Anyway, I finally realized they were getting off on what I was telling them. So I stopped talking completely. To them, to everyone.

"My parents were frustrated. They thought I was just being difficult and why couldn't I cooperate after putting them through that humiliating trial and all. They meant *their* humiliation of family and friends and co-workers knowing what had happened to me.

"My face was plastered all over the newspapers, the net, discussing every grisly, lurid, detail. My parents wouldn't even sit in the courtroom when I testified. Said it was too disgusting to listen to.

"Plus, they felt guilty that they weren't able to rescue me, that if Daddy hadn't ignored my calls that day they may have saved me and maybe some of the others, but," she shrugged, "they also blamed me."

"Blamed you?" His voice rose, he'd moved to the edge of his seat.

"Yeah. Said I must have been trying too hard to not be so- so- plain. That I dressed too provocatively, or walked too sexy, or…whatever. They didn't mean to, they just couldn't help themselves. It was partly my fault too, I blamed them too, my dad, for not coming for me."

"I can understand that, Liv, a little girl, a seventeen-year-old girl crying for her father to come and save her, anyone would feel that way." He leaned over and pushed his soda in a circle on the coffee table but didn't drink any of it.

"Yes, but, he could have. He could have found me. My cell was in my sock. I had no purse that day because I was just walking over to a friend's house. Kenaz didn't find it at first.

"My hands were still tied behind my back, but I managed to get it out of my sock and called my father, but he didn't pick up. I tried again, three times, it went to voice mail." Her humiliated gaze rose to his then shifted away as her cheeks pinked in gall.

"Uh, so, anyway, Kenaz liked to get to know his new captures for a few minutes their first night. You know, play with them, see what they felt like, and, stuff." Her cheeks darkened in mortification, telling him about the bastard molesting her.

"I couldn't fight him with my wrists bound," she sounded like she felt guilty that she should have been able to fight off his groping hands.

Livy sighed in recalled despair. "He found the phone. To say he was angry would be an understatement. I got many good strikes and, other punishing things, and that was that. He took my hope and left me locked in the dark cell."

The tears let loose spreading from the corners of her eyes and rolling down her face, over her cheeks. "The other girls kept quiet, they were too afraid of his enraged attention turning from me to them."

"Hell, Livy," he couldn't take it anymore, Bay moved to the couch and pulled her into his arms. He cradled her face against his chest, stroked her hair, mumbled nonsense words of comfort as she cried.

He held her for a while, he was surprised she let him. His shirt was soaked, but her sobs lessened into hiccups. Eventually she felt loose in his arms, weakened, drained.

"Hey, baby, it's okay, it's over, you're safe here with me," he huddled her into the corner of his arm and cupped her face.

Her eyes were like twinkling wet stars, blurry blue stars, her plush lips trembled as she struggled to gather her control.

"Here," he pulled a pillow off the couch, yanked the case off and handed it to her.

She stared at it not comprehending.

"Wipe your eyes, honey, blow your nose."

"But, it's a pillowcase. A decorative pillowcase."

"Yeah? So? I don't care. The washing machine won't know the difference between it and a handkerchief."

Livy started giggling.

Bay eyed her with suspicion, was she turning hysterical on him?

"It's just," she giggled and wiped at her eyes. "I'm picturing a washing machine with this pissed-off expression, like, 'You're putting *that* in me? Like, 'You trying to pass that plaid doily off like it's a plain white hanky? Puh-leeze, like I can't tell the difference,' and he sniffs indignantly."

Seeing the amused expression on Bay's face made her laugh harder. The tension in the room like a thundercloud of doom from her telling her devastating story evaporated.

Which was fine with him.

The terror was gone from her beautiful face, the tenseness in her shoulders lessened, and she had the cutest girlish laugh.

Bay slipped his hands under her hair and lifted her locks off to slide behind her back. Stroking his hands over her shoulders and down, he wound his long fingers around her arms, he wanted to kiss her so badly, and knew he couldn't.

If he put the moves on her after what she just told him, she would run screaming from the house. He rubbed his thumbs on her arms. She yawned slight and weepy.

He said with a tender smile, "Okay, you're exhausted, honey. How about a sandwich before you hit the sack?"

She stiffened, moved from his hold and set the pillowcase on the arm of the couch. "I, uh, no, my stomach," awkwardness pushed the pink back into her cheeks.

Putting more space between them, she made moves to get up. Her eyes darted frantically to the door, she said with a bit of panic, "I…need to leave. Just-"

"Okay, relax Livy, we've already beat that horse to death. You are staying here. Come on, you go to bed, in your own bedroom, lock the door. Do whatever you need to, to feel safe. Go on now, you know where your room is." Bay nodded towards the hall.

She sat and just blinked at him for a minute. Long lashes sweeping up and down over blue beacons of fear and weariness.

His tone calm, he said quietly, "I'm not going to walk you there, Livy, because I know it will only frighten you. So, you just go ahead. Okay? You get hungry or thirsty at any point, rummage for anything you want in the fridge or cupboards."

Again, she guardedly watched him.

Bay sat back and benignly dropped an ankle over a knee, laid his arm casually across the back of the couch indicating he wasn't moving.

He was right. Big and built of solid muscles, he was a terrifying tower of male strength that frightened her to death. But, he sat impassively, nonaggressive, nonthreatening.

She said in a small voice, "Um, okay, you sure?"

He smiled. "Yeah, I'm sure, go on now."

The wariness made her shoulders rigid as she stood up cautiously. "Okay, then, if you're sure." She kept looking back at him until she reached the hall.

He could hear her run down the hall and the bedroom door slam, and lock, and it broke his heart.

Chapter Nine

The next morning, when Bay got up and entered the living room rubbing a bleary eye, he saw Livy was standing by the door, dressed.

A bright fake smile on her face, she said, "Time to get to the base."

Frowning, he muttered, "And good morning to you too." Smothering a yawn, he grumbled, "Cripes, woman, we need to eat." Another big yawn, he rifled his fingers through his hair, skewing the uncombed locks worse than they already were.

His voice deep and rough with sleep, he mumbled, "And coffee, I gotta have coffee." A white t-shirt stretched across his thick chest. He scratched at his chest and looked with drowsy eyes towards the kitchen. He wore pajama bottoms that hung low on his hips.

Her eyes sifted across his chest, down the tight abs and lower. At her attention, Bay felt his dick rising to it. "Yeah," he coughed and turned, grunted like a caveman, "coffee. Food."

A blush rolled up her neck to her face. Looking away from him, Livy moved closer to the door and said stiffly, "Okay, you eat, I'll catch a cab."

Adjusting himself when she looked away, he said, "Your car has probably been brought to the garage downstairs by now."

"Good, I'll take that," she reached for the door handle.

His drowsy calm turned to irritation. Combing his fingers through his hair in agitation, he told her, "The tire isn't fixed yet, it was towed. Just fucking chill for a second. Let me eat and shower."

He glowered at her. She didn't see the glower because she was looking everywhere but at him.

"I already spoke to the lieutenant colonel. He knows what happened, says you don't even need to come in today. Actually, he said take the week off. Stay here, Livy, you'll be safe while I look for the motherfu-"

"No," she stamped her foot. "I refuse to let Kenaz control my life. I am going to training. I'll call a-"

He moved in front of her and grasped her arms, giving her an irritated shake. "Shit, Livy, slow the fuck down. I said I would take you, give me a break. It'll go faster if you can make something for breakfast while I shower. There's cereal, or eggs, toast, I'll eat whatever if you can do that?"

She had cleaned up, he could smell her fresh fragrance, the long curly hair was damp and shining. She wore slacks and a neat white blouse with short sleeves and a wavy collar.

Even though the clothes were way too big for her, she still looked good enough to eat. Her soft flesh under his palms sent tingles down his body to his already hardening dick. It wanted more than a slight touch.

Livy glared at him for a moment, then sighed giving in. Shrugging off his grasp, she snapped, "Fine. Go take your shower." She set her purse on a table and went into the kitchen.

Bay snatched her purse and took it with him. No money, no phone, she wasn't going anywhere without him.

Fifteen minutes late when he came out, he was combing his hair. Still wet from his shower it had turned a dark caramel color. He wore a black, long-sleeved shirt and black slacks, dress boots. "Wow, hey, something smells good," he said entering the kitchen.

On the table was a plate of buttered toast, jam, crispy bacon, a plate of sliced tomatoes, two glasses of orange juice and Livy was setting two plates containing omelets down.

"I made a pot of coffee, you want milk? Sugar?"

"Yeah," Bay stood still. Damn, the scene looked so domestic. "Ah, I mean no, I like mine black."

Livy had found an apron from God knows where, probably his mother's, and tied it around her tiny waist. Her hickory toned hair was up in a ponytail, cheeks flushed from cooking at the stove.

Fluffy yellow eggs with some green and white things sticking out, and toast looking tasty. The smell of sizzling bacon and rich coffee permeated the air, he took a deep breath.

What was wrong with his fleeing instinct? Normally seeing a female still around the next day gave him the heebie jeebies and he'd be inching, quickly, for the door.

But, Livy, shit. He felt nothing but warmth in his stomach, his heart. She looked so perfect there in his kitchen and he didn't want her to leave. Ever. Damn, he is so screwed.

"Well, sit down then, Commander, you know we have to get going," she ordered while pouring two mugs of coffee. She set one down next to a plate she nodded at for him.

"I hope you like mushrooms, onions and green peppers. They were in the refrigerator, I put them and some ham in the omelets. Oh- I forgot the milk and sugar," she bustled to the fridge and stuck her head inside.

"Ah," Bay settled onto a chair and snagged a piece, and then another piece of toast letting the hot bread drop from his fingers onto his plate.

As he reached for the grape jam, Livy came over and set the milk and sugar down then went to her own chair. She didn't notice Bay staring at her.

She picked up her glass of OJ and took a sip then caught him gawking at her. "What's the matter? You don't like eggs? I thought you said they would be okay. All right, wait a sec," she put her hands on the table to get up. "I think there was oatmeal in the cup-"

He shot his hand out and set it over hers. "No, wait Livy, I love eggs. This all looks," he waved his hand over the table, "great. I, uh, I'm not used to this, a woman in my home, and cooking for me." *Other than my mother.* "This is great," he repeated and stabbed his fork in the omelet.

He stuck a huge piece in his mouth, chewed, and moaned. "Girl, you can cook, you said you couldn't cook but this is unbelievable. Shit," he took another bite then bit off a chunk of bacon washing them down with a swig of steaming black coffee. "I'd love to hire you to be my cook."

"Uh huh, good luck with that," she chuckled and dug into her own breakfast. After chewing a bite of omelet, she reached over and took the unused cream pitcher and poured a drop into her coffee.

"Hmm," he gobbled a piece of toast, part of it bulged in his cheek as he talked. "Can you cook real stuff too? Like dinner, you know meatloaf, spaghetti, things like that?"

She gave him an impish grin. "Well, eggs and bacon are considered real stuff, but yes, I can cook pretty much anything."

Nonchalantly he sipped his coffee, said, "You told me in the mess that day that you couldn't cook." He stared levelly over his cup at her and watched the pink creep into her cheeks.

Clearing her throat, she said, "Uh, yes. Well, you were deliberately flustering me, I couldn't think. I said I could cook, but that I wasn't great. And, uh, groceries, I just can't affo-" she bit the words off.

"Honey," he slathered butter on his toast and took a bite. "I would call this great cooking. More than great, superb. Did your mom teach you after all?"

"Um, thank you. Actually, my grandma taught me when I was home on breaks." Her face lost the perky smile.

"She's gone, huh?" he murmured, attacking the rest of his food. He heard her unfinished sentence about not being able to afford good food, the embarrassment was clear in the reddening of her cheeks and her averted eye contact.

Nodding sadly, she said, "Yes, a couple of years ago. Thank goodness it was before I was taken, I don't think she could have survived my-" Livy broke off, lowered her eyes.

He said quickly, "Yeah, I understand, my gramps and I were close. He taught me how to fish and repair cars, washers, stuff like that. I guess we're lucky we had the time we did with them."

Bay finished his orange juice and watched Livy thoughtfully, and was rewarded with a soft smile.

"You're right, Commander. What a perfect thing to say."

"Sure. Listen, Livy, can you please call me-"

But she was already jumping up and gathering up the empty plates. "Okay, you've had your shower and your breakfast, we need to go, unless you want me to call a…well it would have to be a bus, I don't think I have the money for a cab."

Her head swiveled back and forth with a frown. "I could have sworn I set my purse on that table."

"Yeah, here, let's get these dishes up and we can hit the road." He hurried to distract her. He forgot he took her purse to prevent her from leaving without him.

They got everything cleaned up, Livy *found* her purse in the living room, and they hustled down the elevator to his vehicle. Her VW was parked next to it, the tire still flat.

Once they climbed in his truck, she said, "Oh, I thank you so much, Commander for getting it here. What do I owe you?"

He grunted backing out of the parking spot and heading towards the exit. A twinge of guilt slithered in his belly. He had told the guy that brought her car not to fix the tire. He wanted her to at least have a day of his protection until he could work on her for more.

Glancing back towards her car, Livy said, "I know a tow has to be quite a lot of money, so," she rummaged in her purse and pulled out her checkbook.

"I don't have the cash right now, so just tell me how much and I'll write you a check. Just, uh," her cheeks turned bubblegum pink, "if you could wait until after next week to cash it." Her head bowed over the checkbook as she pressed the pen waiting for him to tell her the amount.

"Hell, Liv," he growled passing a hand over his hair. "I don't know, forget about it."

She turned to him. He was staring hard out the windshield, vein pulsing at his temple. "Please, Commander, you brought me home, then put me up at your place and fed me, I must pay my obligations."

Sure, that's what he wanted to be to her, an obligation. "Really, Livy, it's no big deal, forget about it. Which class do you have first this morning?" He already knew but he asked to change the subject.

"Commander, really I won't be beholden to you or anyone," she said tersely. "Just tell me how much I owe you."

His mouth tipped up, he glanced at her. "You repaid me by cooking me breakfast."

Rolling her eyes, she replied, "That's hardly comparable to towing my car here. I have to pay you-"

His head swiveled in her direction again, gaze stroked down her form. He cut her off, "How about you let me take you to dinner, that will be payment for me."

"Oh, come on, that's ridiculous, you don't owe me! Now-"

"Okay, then," he glanced at her again; she looked so earnest he wanted to fucking grab her and kiss the shit out of her. He wanted to pull over the side of the road, strip her, arch her naked over his engine and fuck her until she screamed his name, and not Commander.

He took a deep breath instead. "I am not going to accept any money for the tow. How about you cook me dinner and we'll call it even?"

Livy stewed for a minute. The thing was, her check was likely to bounce regardless of when he cashed it because her paycheck barely made her rent and electric. She had only the basics on her phone, and no data or internet, she couldn't afford any extra frills.

"Are you sure?" Her brow furrowed as she looked at him, she didn't sound too sure about it herself.

119

A wide grin split his face, and it felt funny because he didn't often genuinely grin. His job was tough, he wasn't kidding when he'd told her he had life and death experiences so he could relate to her situation.

"Yeah, that would be great, Livy. A home cooked meal would be worth way more than a tow. Okay then, when?" he asked, happy about the way things were going. "How about tonight?"

She sat flustered. She had no excuse not to, she had nowhere to go, no plans. Wait, her home was destroyed.

"How about in a couple of days, I need to get my house straightened up. I'm going to need the locks changed, I think."

Ya think? He said, "I've already got a crew on it, Livy. They're working on all your locks including your windows and putting in an alarm system and motion lights, should be done in a few days." His shoulders drew up preparing for her outrage. And it came.

"You what!" she shouted. Twisting her body to turn completely to face him, her mouth dropped, eyes blazing incredulous.

"Come on, Liv, you can't live in that shithole like that. The guy got in because the doors and windows are child's play to break into. You live in a crap-assed neighborhood with no protection. If the alarms I'm having put in go off, the cops will be there in minutes."

He was considering setting her up in weapons training, to get her a gun for defense instead of, for God's sake, a baseball bat. The training would be free on the base, but that didn't matter, his plan was to train her himself.

A small smile lit Bay's face, she's mad now; she would really be pissed if he gave her a gun, as a gift. Hmm, his stomach twitched with a smile, that could be worth a lot of dinners.

"You- you- you-" she huffed and puffed, face indignant red. "How dare you!" she blurted aghast. "You can't do that, Commander. I can't afford that. I can't afford a television for heaven's sake. You must call them all this instant and cancel everything!"

He didn't look at her, disregarded her infuriation, it wasn't changing a thing. "No can do, Liv, it's already in the works."

"But- but, I can't pay them, aren't you listening to me?" Anger and frustration curdled her words. Her face scrunched, she clenched her fists.

"Shit, calm the fuck down, it's taken care of." Trying for levity, he grinned at her before turning back to the road. "I guess I'll be getting a lot of home-cooked meals, huh?"

"Oh my, God," she despaired. "You can't do this, you can't take over my life without my permission. What are you going to say to your girlfriends when they come over, introduce me as your cook? No," she shook her head vehemently, "you call them all off right now."

"Fuck, Livy," he snapped, angered, what'd she think he was, a goddamned whoring cad? That he'd have her there and fuck some other broad while she was in the kitchen making his dinner?

"I have no girlfriends, I am not seeing anyone, and for the record, you are the only woman I've ever had in that home other than my family. Now, we're here, quit fussing. You go do your thing and I'll meet you out front of the mess at five to take you back to my place."

He parked his truck and was already getting out and coming around to her side.

"Wait, what?" she blathered as he opened her door. She started sputtering more but he reached in, grabbed her around the waist and swung her out and to her feet.

Stumbling back from him she continued dissenting, "My car, I need to find a tire, I can charge it on my-"

He growled, "It's in the works. Go on, now, I'll see you at five," he turned her around and gave her a little push.

She resisted. "Wait, Commander, I just told you I'm not coming to your place to cook until later in the week, I'm going home after work today."

He tossed over his shoulder, "You need a ride, your car is in my garage, honey, meet you at five," and he strode away, his long legs eating up the grass of the quad.

Livy stood with her mouth hanging open at his dominating behavior, like one of those alpha males she kept hearing about. She didn't know what to think. Why was he doing this? Did he think she was some sad charity case?

Her brows drew down, complexion darkened. "I am no one's charity case," she groused to the empty space he'd left.

"How dare he. I am not some stray cat he can take in for the night, order around, feed, and dump off at the pound or something." She trudged angrily across the lawn to her first group of classes.

Her buildings were on the east side of the compound. Her current classes and training revolved around strategy and air-intelligence.

Everyone except the instructor turned to her when she entered the room. Bay had told her he'd called ahead. The LC had sent the instructor word she would be late with his permission.

She slid into a chair beside Ella Carmichael. The fluorescent lights above bouncing off her platinum hair, Ella grinned at her.

After her third class, Livy went into the mess for lunch with Ella. They joined Wanda, Keisha and Marianna already halfway done with their food.

Wanda's hard toned body was attired in a uniform of a black T and camouflage cargo pants and boots that tied up the front. Her black hair was pulled back in a ponytail.

She raised a brow over an almond-shaped, kohl-lined brown eye to Livy. "Girl, the word is you were seen driving in this morning with Bullet DaRocco."

Marianna narrowed more finely-lined eyes with a sneered, "Really?"

Livy felt the heat rise up her face. "Yeah. It was nothing. My car had a flat and he offered me a lift, no biggie."

"Hmm," Marianna's narrowed eyes slicked up and down Livy before dismissing her with a sniff. She fluffed a few blonde curls on her shoulder and looked down then adjusted the already low décolletage of her blouse lower. Her breasts were as big and round as white bowling balls and she reveled in showing them off.

In her camo-type uniform, Wanda was the only agent amongst them. The rest of the women wore civilian blouses and slacks, or skirts.

"You jealous?" Wanda goaded the blowsy woman.

Marianna sneered again at Livy. "Of her?" Her lids flapped in distain. "Seriously, this is the conversation we have lowered ourselves to? A scrawny child's crush on hot Bayou DaRocco?" Her full upper lip curled.

"She hasn't a snowball's chance in hell of getting that soldier's attention. She's so frumpy dumpy, and too skinny, right? Obviously he would prefer a *real* woman, one that can take his rough ways." She sniffed scornfully then turned her back to Livy.

Her dark eyes matching her smooth skin, "Hey," Keisha said, "let's talk a better convo, anyone see the Housewives of LA last night?" That was apparently a more interesting topic than Livy; everyone started gushing at once about the reality drama.

Livy sat quietly not wanting any more attention drawn to her. Apparently no one caught the news, or didn't recognize her, she sighed with relief. Last thing she needed was these catty girls to snag onto her experience with a rapist murderer.

She couldn't live with the gossip, the stares, the whispering and pointing fingers and shaking heads, the curiosity, the pity, the accusing looks, the vapid interest in the graphic details like the shrinks had.

Men wanted her because they thought she'd be an easy lay, and maybe could teach them a thing or two after experiencing such sadistic sex, being sexually assaulted and all by a freak.

Which thank goodness she had not been raped, but people chose not to believe that she'd managed to escape before Kenaz could complete the full act. He'd committed other atrocities on her but she had been saved the ultimate violation.

Then there were the other men who thought she was tainted or damaged so they didn't want to get near her.

The girls talked around her, their voices buzzing nonsense while Livy's mind wandered as she suffered through the grotesque memories of Kenaz, and now he was on the loose and might be after her.

Then, there was the puzzlement of why Commander DaRocco was doing those things for her. He must want something. What could she possibly have that he would want?

Perhaps he relished being attached to the salacious attention of the media, wanted to glow in her mongering orbit. Or, maybe he wanted to show off to his superiors how he was helping some poor loser trainee with a huge baggage of *issues*.

That made her mad. She was not going to be some guy's altruistic Medal of Honor for aiding her. She was no charity or pity case. Ella jabbed her elbow in Livy's side startling her from her musings. "Huh, what?"

Wanda said, "We're going for happy hour after classes, you want to come or you going to hang around with those big eyes hoping Bullet notices you?" The girls snickered.

Marianna snorted, "Like that'll happen."

Livy opened her mouth to decline as she usually did, last night was bad enough with her face plastered all over the news, the attack, the flat tire...the commander. She needed to dodge him. The pub would be a good avoidance.

"Yes, yes, I'll go," she said with a firm nod.

"Okay then." Ella stood up. "I'll call Farah and Jessica, tell them to meet us. All right, back to boring classes. I have AI this afternoon. I'll see you, Keisha, there."

The girls all got up and went in their separate directions.

After her last class, Livy accepted a ride with Wanda to the bar. Her stomach roiled, she was supposed to meet the commander at five to get a ride to her car. She texted him that she would see him tomorrow.

While she was in Wanda's car, Bay texted her back.

"WTF? Where are you going?"

She hesitated, then typed, "Out." Really, it was none of his business. Her phone pinged immediately.

He texted, "Wait, Livy, who are you with? Tell me where you're going and I will come there."

Rolling her eyes, he was back to being her dominating big brother. She texted, "Big Brother, I will see you tomorrow and maybe I can catch a bus to your garage." Wanda said she'd give her a ride home later tonight.

Her phone pinged a half a dozen times, then it rang. She shut it off and dropped it in her purse. She was not going to be someone's philanthropic good deed for the day. She was not some needy victim.

"Wow," Wanda said, glancing at Livy's cell as she put it away. "Someone is into you. You got a honey stashed somewhere we don't know about?" she teased.

Shaking her head, Livy fixed a few loose pins on her bun. "No, just someone trying to get kudos from his boss."

Wanda said to her, "Listen, I need to swing by my mother's house and take something to my sister. D'you mind if I do that before we hit the bar?"

"No, I don't mind, I'm in no hurry to be anywhere." Livy shifted more comfortably in her seat.

Chapter Ten

Bay was beyond pissed. Livy was not where he told her to meet him, and she'd stopped responding to his texts and wouldn't answer his calls.

"Damned woman," he groused. Doesn't she realize the danger she's in? Petite and delicate, thin really, she would be no match against that madman if he chose to come after her again. The thought ran shivers through his body.

He hopped in his truck and drove to her place. The lights were off. Still, he parked and crept up to peek in the windows.

The alarm and sensors would be installed tomorrow. He'd lied telling her it would be a few days hoping he could get her to stay at least couple of another nights with him.

He knew she was determined to stay in her own home even though it was not safe because she was embarrassed to accept help. Bay also figured she was also doing some magical thinking that as long as she didn't answer the door she would be okay.

He wandered around the house until he was satisfied she wasn't there. That just made him worry all the more, where could she be? He'd checked the base, the gym before he'd left.

Maybe she was going to the bar with the girls, he pushed the thought that maybe she had a date right out of his head.

He jumped back in the truck and drove to the tavern.

Parking in front of Prontos, he got out, pocketed his keys and strolled inside.

Scanning the interior, he nodded here and there to people who waved or smiled at him. He saw the girls Livy had been with before at a table. He headed straight for it ignoring his own friends that were gesturing for him to join them.

"Hey, ladies," Bay greeted them with a roguish smile. "How's everyone doing this evening?" He couldn't jump right in and ask where Livy was, they would leap on his interest and Livy would be mad that he'd brought unwanted attention on her.

"Bullet, honey," Marianna nudged her chair over and with a pout, patted the empty seat beside her. "It's been so long since you visited with me, us, have a seat, sugar."

"Yeah," Keisha said with a broad, toothy smile, "sit with us, have a drink."

He hovered, looked around, there was no sign of Livy.

His friends sitting up at the bar were grinning at him like dogs. He pulled out the chair and sat down but shifted it away from Marianna. If Livy came in, the last thing he wanted was for her to see Marianna humping his leg.

He ordered a beer from the barmaid who came right over, and ordered a round for the table. "So," he said, "you ladies just doing happy hour or this going to be an all-nighter? It is Friday night after all."

"Bullet," Marianna hitched her chair closer to his and set her huge tit on his arm. "I'll pull an all-nighter with you.

Hell, I'd pull anything you wanted pulled." She batted her lashes lewdly at him. The other women laughed.

"Thanks," Bay said, accepting his drink from the barmaid. He subtly moved from Marianna by tossing some dollars on the barmaid's tray.

Avoiding responding to Marianna, he took a hefty guzzle before setting the bottle on the table with his hand wrapped around it. "Aren't there a few of you missing?" He said casually, "Usually there are more of you girls hanging together, right?"

Marianna leaned against him. She stroked a hand over his shoulder and into his hair where she twirled a lock around her finger. "Aren't we enough female flesh for you, big man?" she cooed in his ear.

Bay sat back in his chair away from Marianna.

Her blouse was unbuttoned to her navel, her tight skirt was all up around the tops of her thighs. She had a strong, musky perfume that made his nose wriggle, and he didn't want it clinging on him.

"Yeah," he muttered non-committal. "I don't see Wanda, she staying home tonight?"

Ella sipped at her lemon martini. Her lashes wriggled the bottom fringe of her straight platinum bangs. "No, she's coming. Supposed to have been here by now. She's bringing Livy."

"Gawd," Marianna groaned, "why do you guys insist on including that ragamuffin?"

Bay sat up straight. "What do you mean that they should have been here by now?"

Ella shrugged, her blonde hair whisked across her shoulders. "They left when we did."

Bay dragged a hand down his face, scrubbed his chin. "Do you think they went somewhere else?"

The girls were quiet, they didn't really care too much. People showed or they didn't.

Farah replied, "I heard Wanda say something about needing to go to her mother's house maybe."

Bay stood up.

"Where you going?" Marianna almost shouted at him.

"I gotta get another drink and I need a word with Jules. I'll catch you all later." Bay threaded through the crowd to his friends.

When he reached them, he said to Jules, "Hey I'll be back in a few," and split before they could ask him any questions.

As he left the building heading for his truck, he pulled out his cell and typed into it. He had told Livy he had high clearance, it was nothing to obtain all of Wanda's family's addresses, and he drove straight to her mother's.

When he paused in front of Wanda's mother's house and saw Wanda's orange Porsche wasn't there, her family had big bucks. He took off for Wanda's apartment, and she wasn't there either.

"Damn that girl," he muttered curses under his breath.

He drove past Livy's house again like a fucking stalker, saw she still wasn't there, and with nowhere else to check, he headed back to the bar steaming with frustration, and increasing worry.

Back at the tavern, he pulled in and parked next to Wanda's Porsche feeling a tad relieved. Hopefully, Livy would be inside.

He pushed the door open, loud music and clamoring voices hit him in the face as soon as he entered. The place was knee-deep teeming with people, almost every table in the white oak and cedar trimmed bar was taken.

130

Along the varnished curving bar counter, every stool was taken.

Bay discreetly checked out the space under hooded lids until he saw her sitting with the other girls. His abs sucked in clenching, then relaxed with a heavy relieved exhale.

The fucking little bitch, making him worry and run all over town looking for her. Of course he'd never tell her he did that, she'd think he was a creepy stalker. And she already had one of those.

Bay contemplated going straight over and giving her a hard time, but then that would put focus on her and the other broads would give her shit. He'd have to wait and catch her alone, or, maybe she'd come to him. Yeah, sure.

The corner of his mouth nicked up. Blowing him off was her way of letting him know she didn't like being told what to do, being controlled. *Sneaky minx*, he thought with a shred of admiration, she had balls.

Actually, ovaries. He guessed the female counterpart would be. Whatever, she had pluck, but that wouldn't keep her safe. Brass balls wouldn't stop a bullet or a murderer out to get her. When he reached his friends, he waved at the bartender.

"What the hell, Bay," Jules said, tipping his bottle of beer to his lips. "What was that all about? You came in for like five minutes then blasted right out. What's going on?"

Bay downed his own drink the bartender brought and shook his head. "Later, no big. I'll fill you in later, I don't want anyone else to know."

"Whatever," Jules shrugged.

The group of men all had their eyes tuned up at the TV monitors watching the game.

Bay watched too, trying to enjoy the beers and the game with his friends, but his gaze kept sliding to Livy. He didn't

131

once see her look in his direction. She was drinking, and laughing sometimes.

The girls were taking turns buying shots for the table and at first it appeared Livy was reluctant to accept anything.

Of course he knew she had very little spare money to spend, but he saw Ella whisper to her and then Livy accepted the drinks placed in front of her, albeit reluctantly.

But now, a couple hours later, he could see her cheeks and ears were bright pink and she was laughing a lot more, yeah, she was getting tanked. And, she looked different.

She no longer wore the tinted glasses because the asshole smashed them, and her hair was slipping out of the bun, she finally just yanked the pins out and let it fall.

A grin tugged up the side of his mouth at the other girls watching Livy unconsciously sift her fingers through the lush curls. The unique color looked as if someone had taken a glossy wand to it.

So damned pretty, Bay wanted to drag his fingers through the rich cinnamon locks seeing the gold flecks flickering under the low lights, like gold coins in a wavering fountain.

Then he would grab a handful and wind it around his fist, drag her head back to raise her mouth to his, watch those silvery blues widen at his roughness, then soften sultry while he kissed the living fuck out of her. He felt his dick swell.

Guys were hitting on her all night, and he couldn't believe that the unfathomable feeling that was digging into his craw was jealousy. What would he do if she actually got up and went out the door with one of them-

"Oof-" an elbow jabbing in his side broke his ruminations.

"Eyes back in head, bro," Jules chuckled next to him.

Bay scowled at him rubbing his ribs.

Hunched over the bar, Jules laughed. "It's a good thing you're no longer into her, because if your tongue got any longer you could paint the side of a barn with it."

"Fuck you," Bay muttered under his breath and tilted his head up to watch the television.

A few minutes later he saw Livy stand up on what looked like very unsteady legs. She stumbled and grabbed the edge of the table to steady herself. The other girls thought that was just hilarious. Livy giggled a little then picked up her purse.

She was going to the ladies room or- wait, hell, she was headed for the front entrance. The women at her table waved goodbye and yelled things out to her as she meandered crookedly through the crowds.

Bay saw guys following her with their eyes, then a few got up and started after her.

He stood right up and moved away from the bar with Jules' words hitting his back with a sarcastic chuckle, "Yeah, nice seeing you too, bro, catch ya later."

Bay strode quickly around the perimeter of the room, hoping no one would notice he was going after her, and he could reach the door before the other men did.

He managed to get outside right after Livy did. He grabbed the door handle and held it from moving, thwarting the other men's exits. He waited until Livy was a few feet from him, then he released the door, shot his arm around her waist, and hustled her quickly to the side of the building out of sight, so when the men broke through they wouldn't see them.

He was still trying to avoid having people see them together, for her sake. He of course didn't give a shit if someone saw him with the gorgeous woman.

The edge of the building cut off Livy's tiny squeal at his grabbing her and pulling her beside the wall. When he let her go, she swayed and had to put her hand on the wall to keep from toppling over.

Brows down over blurred eyes, she frowned up at him. "Commander? What are you doing?" Then she giggled.

"Great, Livy," he couldn't censor the anger in his voice, "you're so drunk you weren't even scared some strange fucker just grabbed you and dragged you out of sight?"

Her brows furrowed lower, then settled in a straight line as she blinked up at him. "But it wasn't a stranger, it was you. I know you, you're Commander Bayou DaRocco who takes in stray cat charity cases."

"Huh?" What the hell was she saying? Ah, she's trashed.

Suddenly Livy turned and started walking away from him, her heels teetering over the loose gravel.

"Hey," he called out going after her. "What are you doing?"

She tipped her head up at him like he was a dimwit. "I'ma goin' home. See you." Her head fell back loosely then she shook it, and giggled. "Not tomorrow, it'sss Saaturday, no shcool," she slurred and kept walking.

Bay strode casually beside her. "Yeah? And how are you getting home?"

She looked down at her feet then back up to him again like he was dull. "Hmm, I thought maybe I would spread my wings and fly home." Flapping her arms like a bird she broke into giggles, and kept walking, heading for the main street.

"Funny, you're a real comedian. You know how far away your house is from here, Livy?"

Her slender shoulders rose in a delinquent shrug. "I'sss no matter, tol' Wanda I can use the fresh air. Bye now," and she trod away from him.

Eyes rolling, Bay went after her, caught her arm. "Come on, Livy, your car and clothes are at my house. I'll take you there." Not that he'd let her drive anyway when they got there.

She slid her arm from out of his grasp. "No, I'ma fine, goodnight, Commander," and took two steps before stumbling.

Bay grabbed her again keeping her upright. His tone friendly, light, he said, "I don't think so, come on, I'll drive you."

"No, don't wanna, yer too bossy. I'ma not a charity cat, lemme go, I'm walking." She tried to pull from his grasp, but his fingers were wound tight around her slim wrist. She dug her heels in the gravelly asphalt and started fighting him harder.

Great, any second now they would have an audience, that shit he didn't need. Big bruiser soldier knocking tiny woman around, that's what it would look like.

"Goddammit, Livy." Glancing around quickly making sure no one saw them, he bent and put her over his shoulder like he had when she wouldn't leave her house.

"Hey," she mumbled incoherently against his back.

He strode quickly to his truck, he could tell she was barely conscious now, her head was flopping limply on his back.

Unlocking the door, he slid her inside and buckled her belt, closed the door and went around to climb in the driver's side.

By the time he hit the main drag her head was against the window and she was out. Good, she couldn't fight or argue with him if she was asleep.

When he reached his home, he plugged the code into the gate, it opened and he parked in the garage.

Bay got out and came around her side, opened the passenger door. "Hey, Liv," he said quietly, unbuckling her belt. "We're here."

"Hmm," she mumbled without moving or opening her eyes.

Still good, no arguing. Bay slid his hands under her and lifted her out of the truck into his arms. He kneed the door closed and carried her to the elevator.

As he stepped inside, she stirred.

Her heavy lids lifted, she peered blurry blues up at him. "Co- Commander?"

He smiled down at her. She looked so soft and sexy sleepy, vibrant curls half covering her eyes and trailing over his arm. "Yeah, Bay, remember?"

She looked around, confusion wrinkled her brow, "Um, you- uh, you're carrying me, why are we in a metal box?"

"Ha," he barked a laugh, damn she was so fucking adorable. "We're in an elevator, Livy."

She woozily pondered that as the elevator rose. "Why?"

"Why are we in an elevator?" he asked. She nodded.

He told her, "Because we're at my house, you remember, you have to take an elevator to get from the garage to the residential part."

She still looked confused, but not angry or worried. She snuggled down in his arms, put an arm around his neck, a palm on his chest, and laid her head on his shoulder with a cozy sigh.

Ahh, she felt amazing in his arms, he could carry her forever. Soft and sweet, her hair smelled like wildflowers, he lowered his nose into the burnished locks.

The elevator door slid open and he trod down the hall then set her down to open his door.

She swayed back against his chest, Bay rolled an arm around her and walked her inside. He flipped the lights on, she moaned and covered her eyes.

"Okay, Liv, I'll get you to your room, come with me." His hand on her back, he started to usher her through the living room, but she stalled.

"Commander, why are we here? I need to go home." She twined her fingers together and turned that pretty face up to him, blue eyes wobbling trying to focus.

"Livy, your house isn't safe right now, don't you remember you said you would be fine staying here in my spare room for a few days, a week or so maybe." Sure, a lie, but he didn't know what he would do if she insisted on going to her house.

The safety measures weren't in place yet, the damned place was as easy as a crackerjack box to break into. He would have to force her to stay here if she persisted in leaving.

Her forehead wrinkled as she thought hard. "I did?"

"Yeah, sure, come on, don't tell me you're so drunk you don't remember," he said it with fake exasperation.

She stared up at his wide innocent eyes, then her blurry gaze flicked around the room. "Um, yes, sure, I, uh, remember." Her hand went to her stomach, she rubbed it.

"You hungry, Livy?" She'd been drinking on an empty stomach, not a great idea. Damn she was such a fucking innocent, the girl needs a keeper. And fortunately he knew a guy that fit that job.

She nodded.

"Okay, you sit on the couch and I'll get you a sandwich," and strong coffee, "okay?" He watched her digest his words, then she stumbled over and plopped on his couch.

Hopefully, he could fill her belly and that would make her sleepy and she'd go right to bed without pondering being in his place.

Fill her belly, not the best thing to be thinking about while she sat on his couch pushing her heavy locks off her shoulders to let them coil down her back.

The way she lifted her graceful arms, sensuous as hell, the fullness of her breasts pushed against the cotton blouse outlining them. Yeah, he wanted to fill her all right, shit, he needed to go get busy. Bay turned on his heel and hurried to the kitchen.

When he came out, Livy was on her knees, on the couch.

He carried a plate with two ham and cheese sandwiches on it, the coffee was percolating. "What, uh, are you doing, Livy?" He came to her and set the plate on the table.

She struggled to her feet, her legs wobbly on the cushions. "C'mere, Commander," she coyly crooked a finger to him.

Bay took a couple of hesitant steps to her. "What are you doing?" he asked again. Livy leaned over and set her arms on his shoulders.

"Uh, Livy…"

"Shh," she combed her fingers through his hair. "Wow, Commander, your hair is really soft. I thought a tough guy like you would have, you know, like rough hair, but yours," she stroked her fingers through the locks. "It's pretty, like honey-wheat."

Hell, he knew he should stop her, but, her face was so close to his, he could smell her scent, see the silver tinsel amongst the icy blue, the black pupils enlarging with heat.

Those plush lips almost on his, and her fingers, shit, raking through his hair, he could feel the tingle in his balls.

"Uh, this is not a good idea, honey," he went to clasp her wrists, but she grabbed ahold of his hair and jerked his head forward and pressed their mouths together. *Oh shit-*

Chapter Eleven

Bay's brain instantly spun into a mindless whirl.

He could feel inexperience in her kiss, but that only turned him on more, if that was even possible.

He splayed a hand across her back feeling the lightness of her shoulders, her spine, felt the warmth through her shirt on his palm.

His other hand cradled her head, her soft hair spilling through his long fingers. He pushed those plush lips apart, bit the full top one then thrust his tongue inside, and almost shot his seed at her throaty moan.

Dizzy lust thickly clouded his brain. Bay pulled her in, held her tight against his chest groaning at the soft feminine breasts wedged against the muscled slabs of his chest.

He chased her tongue, during his pursuit he licked her teeth, shoved his tongue almost down her throat before he caught hers and sucked the shit out of it.

His dick strained at his pants yelling at him to yank her drawers down and drop her on her back on the couch. He could take her in- *hell*.

He gripped her shoulders, gasping, he pushed her away.

Groaning, "Ah, Livy," at those blues misted like a dusky sky he almost jerked her back against him to shove his tongue back down inside her youthful softness while he took possession of her entire body, outside and in-

Murmuring softly, "Listen, honey," he gently pushed her until she was on her knees on the couch cushion.

Her head cocked to the side, "You don't like me, Commander?" Her full lips pushed out in a sexy pout. "They said you do any girl you meet."

Dammit, he scowled at her. "Cripes, Livy, that's not fucking true."

"I've seen you, Commander, girls hang all over you." She slanted her head with a sensuous smile, lids half-mast, her fingers went to the buttons on her blouse and she started pulling them apart. "You want them, but not me?"

Bay froze. He needed to stop her, she was drunk, she didn't know what she was doing. But he couldn't move, speak, just watched her undo the blouse to expose lush fucking breasts spilling out of a lacey black bra.

His eyes bee-lined to them, he was powerless to look away. "I, uh…"

One shoulder raised coquettishly, her head tilted sideways, the glorious hair waved partially over one eye, the other peered up at him so sexy, inviting, a fucking siren.

Bay gulped hard over the lump in his throat.

Her delicate fingers went to her jeans. She unfastened the button and lowered the zipper, he could see the matching black lace, red flushed up his neck.

He rushed to grab her arms to stop her. "No, ah, no, Livy, we can't, you're drunk."

Even as he denied her, his eyes were glued to those voluptuous creamy breasts. His hands itched to clutch them,

find and rub her nipples with his thumbs and fingertips, tweak the shit out of them.

She tugged her arms from his grasp. His hands fell to her waist, her tiny, curved waist. His fingers dug into the supple flesh, his gaze dropped to the lacey panties peeking out from her open jeans.

His dick swelled so painfully he thought he was going to explode. Unconsciously, his hips were rolling, mimicking the sex act.

She lifted her hands to the buttons on his shirt and started undoing them, and he was incapable of stopping her. She had three or four undone and she sifted her hands inside to splay her fingers over the darker hair that covered his chest.

Okay, he needed to stop her now before it was too late, and it already almost was. He stepped back from her so fast she almost fell off the couch. He shot a hand up to her shoulder to steady her then released her as if she was on fire.

Hell, he was the one on fire, his balls were blistering, cramping in his pants.

"No, Livy," he said as sternly authoritative as he could. "It's time for bed, I mean to go to sleep, you're going to your room now."

Those full puffy lips pushed out in that cute pout drawing his heated gaze from her breasts to them. "I'm not sleepy, don't you wanna play with me?" She sounded so child-like, but the playing with her that he wanted to do was anything but childish.

Bay cleared his throat. Keeping his eyes on her face, he said firmly, "It's time for bed, Livy, come on." He grabbed her arms and lifted her off the couch to her feet then led her though the living room and down the hall.

Peripherally he could see her blouse drifting back and her tits bouncing as she walked, her jeans were still undone.

God, he wanted her so badly it hurt, his groin stung. But she was drunk, he couldn't take advantage of that, and if he did, she would hate him tomorrow. If she remembered. That would be even worse, her not remembering their sexual uniting. Fuck.

He practically dragged her down the hall and thrust her into her room.

His words rushed out before he changed his mind, "There ya go, hon. See you in the morning," and pulled the door closed almost in her face.

Bay leaned his back against the door, one, to catch his breath and strengthen his shaking legs, and two, to prevent her from coming back out. He only had so much control and most of it was expended.

He waited a few minutes, then sure she wasn't coming out, he adjusted the hard-on straining at his jeans and trod down the hall to the kitchen. He needed to pound back some alcohol.

An hour of bourbons, and slightly light-headed, Bay turned out the lights and headed for his own bedroom. He looked at Livy's, the door was still closed.

Filled with half regret and half relief, he padded down the hall to his room.

After a quick, icy shower, he pulled on pajama bottoms and feeling a bit drunk now himself, slid in under the covers preparing to dream about the beauty sleeping just down the hall from him.

Sometime later, a noise woke him.

Slightly foggy from the bourbon, he sat up, shoved the hair out of his eyes, and swung his legs around off the side of the bed.

Hearing something off, he stood up. He wasn't worried about intruders, the security he and his other agents had installed themselves was virtually impregnable.

But, he had a houseguest and maybe she was wandering around needing something. Huh, he snorted, he needed something himself, and she had what he needed.

Shaking his head, Bay didn't turn on any lights; he had left his door open in case Livy called to him. Now, that she was probably more sober, it was unlikely. He chuckled dismissively, however, she might have required his assistance with something, or was hungry.

He traipsed barefoot on the carpet down the hall, turned the corner and almost ran right into her.

She gave out a little squeal and jumped back, her hands went to her throat. She blinked rapidly as if trying to recognize him.

"Hey, Livy, what's going on?" He kept his voice low, calm, set his hands loosely in a nonthreatening stance on his hips.

Her rounded eyes dropped to his bare chest and widened. Not normally self-conscious, but this girl brought out a lot of firsts in him, Bay splayed an awkward hand over a pec.

"Oh, Commander," she averted her eyes, stammered, "I woke and was…disoriented. I didn't know where I was. I," her gaze drifted back up to his chest before quickly dropping to stare at the floor.

"I got scared, I thought I was back with, him…" Confusion mapped over her face. "I mean, I knew I wasn't in the…the…cell, but still, I couldn't…" she trailed off,

144

embarrassed and confounded. She wrapped her arms around her body, hugging it with a shiver of fear.

Bay's heart broke at her fright and disoriented confusion. "I brought you home from the bar last night. This is my place, remember?"

He went to reach a hand out to her, but lowered it. "You remember my bringing you here?"

Her eyes scrunched, she rubbed them, then opened them. A bit sheepish, she said, "A little, not really. I guess I drank too much."

He studied her, wondering how much she did recall. A pink blush was filling out her cheeks, yeah, she remembered being on the couch with him.

Changing the subject to settle her, he asked, "You want something to eat or drink? I put those sandwiches in the fridge."

The curls waved, separating around her breasts, she was wearing shorts and a big t-shirt. She must have changed before crashing earlier.

Bay's eyes strained keeping them on her face. Clearly she wasn't wearing a bra, her tits were almost visible in the thin, white cotton. Good thing the air conditioning wasn't on.

He dug his fingers into his hips to keep them to himself, he could feel himself hardening already.

"No, um, Commander. I'm sorry I woke you."

"Livy, really, I don't mind. Listen, I'd like you to call me Bay."

Ignoring his statement, she looked around the room and asked, "Could, I mean, I don't want to go back to my, that is the, room alone. Can I sleep on the couch?"

His gaze traveled her face. Her brow was creased, lips pressed together. He asked gently, "You scared, Livy?"

145

She didn't answer him, her eyes lowered in self-conscious shame.

"Uh, sure, if that would make you feel better." Bay felt guilty, maybe if he hadn't pushed her to talk about her horrific experience she wouldn't be suffering right now. He wanted to offer her to sleep with him or him with her, but that would surely freak her out.

"I'll get you a pillow and some blankets." They walked together to the living room and she waited while he retrieved the linens and pillow.

Laying a sheet on the couch, he said, "Okay, here you go, lie down." He stood while she settled down on the cushions then he drew the blanket over her.

His heart clenched at the two blue torches that blinked in torment up at him. The blanket went over her chin, her head rested on the pillow, the long curls rolled over the side of the couch.

"You gonna be okay here, Liv?"

Her voice tiny, "Yes, I'm fine."

"Ah, okay. I'll leave the lamp on." He crouched beside the sofa and couldn't help petting her head, her hair. "You need anything at all, Livy, I mean it, you call out for me, or come and get me, okay?"

"Yes," she nodded.

"Okay, then, goodnight." He leaned over and kissed the top of her head. Standing up, he went off to his own room. Damn, she looked so vulnerable lying there, so scared, and so fucking desirable.

It wasn't long after when he heard noise again. He couldn't sleep anyway knowing the dainty young woman was sleeping on his hard couch when she belonged in comfort.

146

Bay got back up, went into the living room and to the couch.

Livy's head was thrashing back and forth. Wretched moans gagged from her lips, her hands flailed at something as if she was trying to fight it off.

He sat on the edge of a cushion and caught her wrists stilling them. He spoke quietly, "Livy, wake up baby," he kept talking softly until she became aware of his presence.

She stiffened and moved to sit up. Leaning back against the cushions, haunted eyes, huge and anxious shimmered in her pale face.

Grumbling, "Aw, shit, baby," his heart felt like a vise was squeezing it. "Come on." He scooped her up in his arms and carried her out of the room and down the hall to his room. He set her gently on his bed.

She didn't say a word, just slid with graceful moves under the covers and laid her head on a pillow.

He liked a lot of pillows, there were at least five in the bed. The blinds were only partially closed, Bay preferred to be able to look out at the night sky.

The moon was huge and amber, it generated slight illumination through the window gilding the side of Livy's face and neck.

Bay hesitated, but she just stared up at him without a word. Sighing, he let his restraints slip off and climbed in with her. Only in pajama bottoms, he should have put a shirt on.

Murmuring, "Livy," he slipped his burly arms around her and pulled her into his embrace. He waited for her to protest, but she allowed him to hold her without pushing him away.

Surprisingly, she stroked her hands up his bare chest ruffling over the hair and brushed her fingers around his neck.

"*God*," he moaned and covered her mouth with his. He thought he'd died and gone to heaven when her soft as pudding lips opened and accepted his foraging tongue.

His greedy tongue lathed the outside of her lips, sucked and nibbled roughly at them before moving inside, sliding over her teeth, tasting every part of her he could before he besieged her tongue.

She was tentative at first, as if she'd never kissed before or not very much, which Bay couldn't comprehend. He'd wanted to devour the sweet plums since the second he'd laid eyes on them.

There had to be a hundred men lined up vying for the chance to plunder them. And the rest of her ripe little body that was now snuggling so soft up against his hard frame.

Bay could feel her plump breasts squashing against his chest, her nipples brushing the mat of hair over his stone-hard pectorals.

Wrapping an arm around her, holding her to him, he spread his big palm on her slim back then stroked it down her spine, along the inner curve of her lower back, and down to clutch her exquisite bottom.

Every time he'd seen that fine ass swaying as she walked away from him, his hands had itched to grab ahold of both cheeks and squeeze the hell out of them. His groan wafted her hair over her ear and the side of her face. Still, he paused, giving her time to object or push him away, but she didn't.

Her name a question, "Livy?" he pulled back slightly from her.

Her eyes were half-mast yet shining, parted lips already red and swollen and he'd only just begun. Her lashes rose then lowered, sweeping over the pink round cheeks, she sighed, "Hmm?"

Damn he was gone on this girl, and he knew it. "I want you, Livy." He webbed his long fingers cupping the side of her face while he kissed her soft, then, a starving man on a deserted island he sucked the tender meat of her mouth.

Moving to suckle the fat of her round cheek, he licked down her face to nip and suck hard on her neck, then back up to claim her mouth again.

The urgent raiding of her lips so ravishingly intense, hungry bear growls rumbled deep inside his chest revving to devour every inch of her.

Bay had to force himself to back off, slow down, get a grip before he ripped her shorts off and rammed himself inside of her.

When he let up enough for her to take a breath, Livy's rushing breathing matched his, shallow and fast, her lids heavy.

She licked her lips as if wondering where his had gone. Her girlish voice hushed and breathy, needy, "Commander?"

"Ah, please, Livy, call me Bay," he tried to keep the irritation out of his voice. He had the most beautiful girl he'd ever seen, or wanted, finally in his bed and she kept a wall up, using formality as mortar.

Softening his voice, he smiled at her while stroking his hand up her neck, up the side of her face then caressed her smooth skin with his calloused fingertips. "Say it, baby, say my name."

If she couldn't say his name he had to get her the hell out of his bed because there would be something really wrong with making love to a woman who called him by his rank.

He wanted her to make love to the man, not the title. He needed to ensure she wasn't feeling forced by his being in a position of command.

Her lips curved in a pretty bow, eyes twinkled up at him. Softly she whispered, "*Bay.*"

His heart crimped. "Yeah, baby." He shifted to partially cover her smaller body with his, keeping the bulk of his weight off her, but enough that he could feel her curvy suppleness under him, pressing so damned feminine and warm against the hard slabs of his body.

His mouth descended on hers and his hands skimmed up her body to cover her breasts. "Shit," he groaned as he felt them. Cupping their weight, squeezing them, they molded in his hard hands like fucking plump pillows.

Beneath him, Livy licked at his lips that were sucking at hers, their breaths mingling warm on their skin. Her body squirmed against his, pressing her breasts up to fill his big rough palms.

"Damn, Livy," his breath grated the words. He grasped the bottom of her shirt and pulled it up. "Lift, baby," he murmured. When she raised her back, he pulled the shirt off and dropped it off the side of the bed, his eyes riveted on her bare breasts.

Shyly she gazed back at him. With a little self-conscious murmur, she moved her hands to modestly cover her nudity.

"You're so fucking gorgeous I can't stand it, Liv. Shit baby, don't hide from me." A groan growled deep in his chest as he pushed her hands aside and gripped her just under her chest.

His long fingers wrapping around her slim torso, feeling her delicate ribs between his fingers, he had to stay cognizant of his powerful strength and restrain himself from squeezing her too hard or he'd bruise her.

Staring at her beauty, his own breathing rasping loud in his ears, Bay's heart pounded with every heavy breath. He webbed his thick fingers to cover her chubby breasts. Skin on skin, grasping huge handfuls, when he kneaded them hard, a deep moan wrung from Livy.

She slipped a leg over his. Twining the svelte limb over his muscular leg, she clutched it and wriggled closer under him as he gripped and kneaded the hell out of her full flesh. Groans rolled out of him like helpless drool.

Bay refused to allow his brain to think about what they were doing. She was probably still half drunk, he'd imbibed himself diminishing his own self-control.

And, she was obviously not very experienced, and so fucking fragile after her ordeal, he was clearly taking advantage of her fears of being alone, and the likelihood that she was still buzzed.

He stuffed those thoughts as his hands filled with her fine tits. Damn, he had wanted to clutch them every time he'd seen her, feel the sinuous flesh flush in the skin of his palms.

He moved his head to kiss down her face, along her jaw, down her neck where he latched his mouth on her satiny skin and sucked so sharply she cried out. He paused, but she only bent her neck so he could access more of her.

Knowing he was marking her, but he couldn't help himself, he wanted his mark on her. How caveman of him, he almost chuckled at his male need to mark his claim. Next he'd be pissing on her.

It didn't stop him from licking and sucking down her neck to her collarbone. Gripping her breast, he moved lower to the swell of it, and sucked his claim on that too.

Livy moaned, writhing on the mattress. Her fingers dug into his biceps, she couldn't get her small hands around them. Her back arched, offering her plump globes for him to devour, to crush in his hard hands.

His tongue flicked over her pink nipple before he possessed that too, sucking it in his mouth and practically chewing on it. With his other hand, he pinched her other nipple, tugging on it then pinching it again.

Both nipples, so small, little sweet-peas like her, peaked and hardened in his mouth and hands. Her cries grew louder, more ragged as her body squirmed, his strong grip on her woman's flesh held her in place.

Bay groped both breasts roughly then moved to his knees, and put his hands on her shorts. His eyes on her flushed face, heavy-lidded eyes and panting lips, he unbuttoned her shorts.

"Baby, you okay? I'll stop if you say, you have to let me know." *God, please don't say stop.*

Luscious hair like rich mink spread in curls around the pillow framing her pretty heart-shaped face. Blue beamed heated passion mixed with faint disorientation up at him, her hands fell beside her head as if in surrender.

"I…" her lids fluttered then opened glassy, her shoulders rolled in a shiver. "You, you're making me feel…"

"Feel what, Livy?" Bay sat back on his heels with his hands splayed on her hips watching her struggle to focus her blurry gaze even as her body undulated in need.

"I…" she whispered licking her lips. "You make me feel so good…Bay." Her shoulders rolled in, long lashes swept down then up with another delicious shiver.

"Ah, shit, Livy, you are fucking hot sin. I want to make you feel better than good, I want to blow the top of your head off. Will you let me?"

Her eyes tilted back in her head then back to him, the side of her plush mouth curved up. "Yes, Bay." Her hands still beside her head, palms up, trusting him.

He moved to lean over her, brushing her lips with his, then he knelt back and drew her shorts down her shapely legs and tossed them. He paused to drink her in.

She lay topless in her black lace panties, eyes thick with passion looking up at him with trust and heady desire. She moved a hand to set on his wrist, her other hand raised, and she slipped the tip of one of her small fingers in her mouth, and, hell, his groin twisted, she licked it.

He could tell she wasn't deliberately teasing him, it was more like she missed his mouth, his lips and tongue roiling with hers. She was trying to touch where his mouth had.

He set a big palm over her woman's mound and felt the warmth of it even as she gasped and shifted her hips.

Her arms bent as she moved them on the mattress lifting her back off the bed. "Commander, I..." She blinked eyes so filled with arresting desire, confusion, she licked her parted lips.

"Bay, baby, please." He put a hand to her shoulder and gently pushed her back on the mattress, still fighting the thoughts that what he was doing was wrong. He caught the top of her panties and slid them down her legs and off. Now she was totally nude he could not take his eyes off her beauty.

"An angel, sweetheart, angels pale beside you, Livy." He parted her thighs and cupped her sex, she bucked with a sudden gasp and a shimmy away from his hand.

"Shh, sweetheart," he murmured. "Let me pleasure you." He held one thigh keeping her legs spread, and stroked his fingers up her slit then over her plump folds, and smiled

153

at the gasping moan from the beautiful woman lying naked on his bed. The first, and last to be in this bed.

Her back rose and twisted, stretching with her breathy gasp to one side, then to the other before bending up presenting her bare breasts to him.

Of course he accepted the invite, bowing to suckle first one, then the other while he played with her slit, feeling her silk spilling into his hand.

His fingers silky wet, he rubbed circles on her lady's bud, his hair wafted over her skin as he moved from nipple to nipple. Sucking a bead into his mouth, he flicked his tongue hard over it, biting it, before doing the same to the other.

Her entire body rippled, her hips lunged up to his hand, her back arched thrusting her breast into his mouth. She cried, "Oh God, Bay, what are you doing to me?"

He chuckled. "I hope I'm driving you as insane as you do me." His mouth compressed, teeth grit to hold back his own craving need.

Livy's sweet voice raw with body-stinging needles prickling her all over, spooled out in scratchy whimpers with the sensations razing her body. Her face creased with the intensity of her body's reaction to his ministering fingers.

Seeing her hips writhing, and her breasts billowing with her frantic breaths was putting him over the crest.

A vein pulsing at his temple, mouth clenched, Bay strained to hold himself back from just ruthlessly shoving those creamy thighs wide and savagely impaling her.

"Do- do-" she stammered through chattering teeth, her head falling back, gasping. "Do what you- you need to, take me, Bay, please." Eyes closed, her head thrashed back and forth on the bed, hips bucking up to his hand.

Swallowing down his own racing desires, knowing she was relatively inexperienced, Bay held himself back from launching himself between her thighs. Last thing he wanted to do was hurt her.

What he did want was more of this, of her, he would do whatever it took to get it, keep it, keep her. Nudging her legs further apart, he moved to kneel between them, then squirmed down to his stomach.

Stroking her woman's flesh, shifting down the bed, he spread her nether lips and covered her sex with his mouth.

Chapter Twelve

"*U*h!" Livy squealed.

Bay's head was between her legs, his hair brushed her thighs, and he was licking her sex.

"Bay-" she started to sit up, her hand to his head.

"No, relax, sweetheart." He put his hand on her chest and pushed her again to lie back.

"Don't think, just feel, trust me. You are way fucking tight, really small, baby. I need to... make you ready to take me."

He was burning scorching hot, even inside the pajamas his cock seared her leg like a burning branding iron as he slid down her body, and so fucking hard he could jab holes into the universe.

Moving his mouth over her mound, he licked up her slit to lath her clit wickedly hard, so coarse and rough, her unruly whimpers burst out in jagged cries. Her hips bucked at his face. He held one thigh down to immobilize her, but she was no longer trying to get away from him.

At the rushing sound of her pitchy breaths and little moans Bay bit her hard bud and carefully moved a thick finger into her tiny opening. Her nether lips and his hand were slick with her silk, but, she balked at his intrusion with a whimper.

"Shh, Livy, just feel," he murmured and moved his finger deeper and licked her sex faster. Lathing and biting her clit, he struggled to work a second finger in her, stretching her. He paused.

At his hesitation, she came down from her thrilling fog. Livy wriggled, her voice hoarse, she cried, "What, what's wrong Bay? Did I do some-"

"No, no, beautiful, never. It's just," he kissed her clit while moving and curling his fingers inside her searching for her most sensitive spots. He smiled against her sex when he felt her squirm and gasp a moan.

"You are really, ah, tiny, and I'm..." He sucked her bud into his mouth grinning at her squeal and the gush of silk. He murmured absently, "I'm kinda big, but this should help."

Damn, he thought, *she hadn't many lovers, or they were small themselves*. He stroked her, alternating stabbing his fingers, then his tongue then his fingers into her until Livy was writhing and thrashing all over the bed with whimpering gasps and harsh cries.

Her chest hitched, flat belly sucked in as amazing sensuous sounds slid from her throat urged him on.

Livy's brain was heating along with her tingling body; she thought any second she was going to explode ballistic!

Other than the freak that had molested her while he held her prisoner, Bay was the only man who had ever touched her, kissed her, this intimately.

He was driving her insane with need, she didn't know what the need was, but her body was screaming for something.

Gasping, "Bay, I," her head rolled back, she cried out as he bit her bud, sucking it at the same time he plunged his fingers into her sheath.

She barely registered the throbbing hard length of him rubbing against her leg whenever he moved up to suck and kiss her belly before shifting back down to chew her stinging tenderness.

The broiling need balled in her sex and was reverberating out through her body like a sound wave until she felt she couldn't stand it anymore. It built and built and-

"Go baby," Bay urged, sucking hard on her while pronging his thick fingers in and out. "Let it go, I have you, relax your body and let it go, Livy."

That did it, his deep voice, dark and husky, she felt her body release. The flames struck, slashing at her like blasting burning whips until her body burst, convulsions rippled through her.

"Bay!" she screamed, her body folded up then fell back down as her body shook and shuddered, shattering into a million brilliant pieces. Through the uncontrolled lancing spasms, Livy faintly heard his richly masculine voice talking her through it.

"Good baby, good, I've got you, Livy, love." His voice faded in and out as it whirled around her spinning head.

When the spasms lessened, her belly hitching with cutting gasps slowed, Bay gently removed his fingers and rolled off the bed.

On her back, chest heaving with racking pants, Livy gasped, her pulse racing madly with her spinning head. Like a jellyfish she laid splayed, weak, sucking air in through her constricted throat. She felt his warmth, his hands leave her.

"Bay?" her voice small, faint.

"I'm right here, sweet." He shrugged his pajama bottoms down, and scrabbled quickly to his dresser to grab a condom and hurried back to her before she could gather her wits and come down from her orgasm.

Her body still shuddering, he slid the condom on and climbed back on the bed. Her legs were closed and tucked up.

He put his big hands on her thighs, pushed her legs down and apart, and moved between them. "Livy," he whispered.

"Hmm?" A luscious warm glow radiated all around her body, shivers continued rippling throughout. She felt her nipples harden as he moved his large strong body between her legs.

She could feel his muscular legs pressing against hers as he pushed them further apart.

"Tell me you're ready, Liv, tell me now." A hand on her thigh, Bay nestled down to set his forearm next to her shoulder.

His shaft hard as iron, ready, begging to drive into her, he gripped it in his fist, pressed it at her opening, then drew the head up and down her cleft getting himself slick with her silk, and stirring her sensitive clit.

He whispered against her mouth, "Tell me, Liv." His tone urgent and raspy with the need to be inside her, deep inside her. He leaned back slightly to look at her, see if she was all right with what they were about to do.

"Bay," her sigh shuddered out making her breasts jiggle drawing Bay's heated gaze. "I…I'm ready," she whispered. Her hands went to his biceps then moved to his chest. She spread her fingers over the matting of hair and smiled.

"So manly, Bay, you are one of the most masculine men I have ever…seen," and sighed as she stroked her hands over his thick chest.

A chuckle at her words turned serious as Bay pushed his thick, steel length into her. So tight, she was so small he could barely move in deeper.

She was too tight. Apprehensive, he started to ask her, "Livy…are you a-"

Her hips buckled under his, a wince puckered her face, she cried, "G- go, keep going, uh." She winced, her words scraping.

He paused. "Am I hurting you? You're so tiny, tight, are you-" he started to ask her again but her vagina rippled over the head of his cock squeezing it, nearly undoing him.

"Fuck Livy!" he barked and shoved into her so hard she shrieked at the sudden, harsh painful thrust that broke her virginity.

Bay stopped only partially inside, majorly nonplussed. If she was a virgin, he should have breached her hymen with his fingers, how-

Livy's chest billowed with her crying gasps, she tried to close her legs but it was impossible with his big body between them.

"Livy, fuck, tell me you are not a virgin," he demanded bracing up on both elbows. He didn't move further inside her.

Her voice tight with pain, "Not," she gasped, "anymore." Then keened, "It hurts Bay." Her channel squeezed his shaft so hard his cock swelled and jerked like a thick spastic bat against her inner walls.

Trying to control his dick that wanted to rampage into her, Bay forced himself to stay unmoving, propped on his elbows, his head hung, hair dusting her face. He must not have inserted his fingers deep enough in her before.

"God, Livy, why the hell didn't you tell me? I didn't know, I never would have done this." He raised his head, forehead wrinkled, mouth an iron line.

He'd taken her virginity and fucking hurt her, hell, he didn't know what to do now.

Tears oozed out of her closed eyes and rolled down her cheeks. Her woman's channel hugged his girth, involuntarily squeezing it, making him groan.

"Shit, Liv, don't cry, please don't cry, I'm sorry. I didn't know. Shit, I knew you were inexperienced but, fuck, I never would have done this." He needed to pull out of her, but...damn, he didn't want to.

He was right where he'd dreamed about being for months. He gently brushed at the tears that spilled.

"You- you don't want me, you don't want me now that you know I've never had sex before? Or- or is it because you got what you wanted and don't care anymore." The tears rolled, Livy turned her head away, chest hiccupping with her silent cries.

Bay cradled both sides of her face using his thumbs to wipe the tears. "God baby, no, not at all. I want you more than air to breathe, trust me. I've wanted you from the second I saw you in Prontos that first day.

"Hell girl, I've bugged you for dates, blew up your phone, stalked you, hunted you down when you were supposed to wait for me and brought you here. I was worried half to death when I couldn't find you."

She turned her head away, his hands still cradling her face he forced her to look at him, and his heart tripped. Her big blues swelled with dejected tears.

He sucked in a deep breath. "But, had I known you hadn't, I mean, that you were a virgin, shit, I would have...waited, until we knew each other better, so you were

161

more…comfortable with me. I sure as hell would have gone so much slower, made sure you were," he exhaled heavily, "really ready for me. And, damn, made sure that this was what you really wanted. Hell, I knew we had both been drinking, but shit, I figured you still…knew…I don't know…"

The thought flickered through his brain again, now singed with guilt, that he had taken advantage of her fear and slight intoxication.

Their faces close, eyes connected, he caressed her face.

"I hate like hell that I hurt you, Livy. Tell me, how do you feel, right now, you know, about this…sex. Do you want me to stop, to pull out, or…can we, keep going?"

Dots of perspiration at her temples dampened the tendrils over them, he gently brushed them back, his fingers so strong and large against her small, feminine face.

Grunting, "Bay," she wriggled under him, he croaked a groan as the movement squeezed his dick. Forehead wrinkled in uncertainty, she asked with awkward vulnerability, "What do you want?"

"Ah, Livy," he laughed lightly. "Are you fucking kidding?" He wrapped both arms around her, holding her close, his voice filled with heartfelt desire, he said sincerely, "I never want to leave this place, inside you. I'm right where I've always wanted to be."

His expression turned serious. "I just…don't want to hurt you any more, or take advantage of your…inexperience."

His mind tapped at the back of his brain reminding him he had been since he'd met her, and earlier when they were kissing, doing his damnedest to seduce her.

Murmuring, "Um," her long lashes lowered over demure eyes, then they rose as she peered with a decidedly sultry shine. With a delicious smile, she said shyly, "It, I mean you, actually," she squirmed under him, "feel kind of...good...now. The pain has subsided, mostly. Okay, then, let's-"

His cock throbbed inside her making her sheath suddenly constrict.

"Fuck, Livy!" He grunted with a wince as he forced himself to hold back from coming. "I'm like ready to fire, you can't move like that."

Finding out he took her virginity knocked him for a loop. Happily, he was still inside her, still hard as a rock, still wanted to feel his dick slide in and out until their combined friction made them both strike nirvana- he could feel her giggle rifling his shaft, it jumped and she gasped, then giggled again.

"Livy," he warned.

"It doesn't hurt that much anymore, Bay. Can we," her cheeks reddened, her eyes slanted away. "I like what you, uh, did, to me, and I feel...very, uh, filled, but still, it feels good, you inside me. I can feel you...throbbing and twitching against, my...insides," her voice trailed off in embarrassment.

Grinning wide, he said, "Yeah?" He cupped her face and kissed her softly. Rubbing her temples with the pads of his thumbs he shifted inside her.

Her groan about set him off again. He carefully drew out partway, then slowly pushed back inside, going slightly past where he had stopped before, and her rough moan told him to keep going.

"*Uhh*," the sound dragged from her as he pulled back drawing her natural lube, and then shoved in deeper, more and more, feeding his length into her until he sank to the very end of Livy.

"Bay, ungh," she groaned when he started to pull out again, her hands went to his shoulders then around his neck to pull him down to kiss.

Their mouths ground together as he picked up speed, rocking into her, the friction sharper with each rougher thrust.

Bay slid a hand under her bottom to lift her so he could plunge deeper into her. Which he did with such a hard thrust a grunt shoved from her and she was pushed away from him.

Laughing, he wrapped his arm around her to hold her from sliding up the bed. "You're so slight, Livy, I have to watch my strength."

"Mmm," she pulled his head down slipping her tongue in his mouth. She murmured against his lips, "I like it...harder."

The red in the apples of her cheeks deepened and she yelped when he drove savagely into her again and again at her words.

"More than happy to oblige, sweetheart," he growled in her ear. "If I hurt you, you tell me, okay?"

Nodding, her hair shuffled on the pillow, lids heavy, she smiled. "Yeah-" and before she got the word out Bay upped his game, his speed.

His thrusts rocketing hard to the very end of her, he rammed into her graceful body like a rough hammer. His big hand cradling her butt, he lifted her higher to meet his demands.

"Wrap your legs around my waist," he grunted, propelling into her.

Livy lifted her legs to cross around his waist and bucked her hips to meet his furious, ever increasing harder strokes. But now he started driving so fast, his shaft hard as iron pounding into her she couldn't keep up. She just clung to his shoulders grunting and crying out at his savage thrusts.

Every other plunge, he twisted to rake over her clit and rub over her most sensitive spots in her channel. Raspy mews gasped from her as he drove faster and faster.

Livy hummed in his ear, erratic with the grunts he pounded out of her.

When her hums scraped through her throat, and her breaths were rapid shallow huffs, keeping his driving rhythm Bay said, "Look at me, Livy."

When her eyes stayed tightly closed, he commanded, "Open your eyes Livy, say my name."

One hand cupping her bottom, the other rounding her shoulders to hold her close for his brute plunges, Bay's own breaths were gushing pants, growls, low thundering groans, as he felt her silken sheath clutching at him every time he dragged out of her and then slammed back in all the way to her womb.

Hearing her breaths erratic and rough, he let go of her butt and gripped her face lifting it and demanded, "Livy, open your eyes and say my fucking name."

Her neck arched, head fell back. He shook her, and she cracked her lids up. Limp disoriented blues crashed with his enflamed dark greens.

Bemused, she slurred, "You have such a potty mouth, *uh*," his hard thrust shoved a sharp gasp from her.

"Say it, Liv," his bark a harsh command, "say my name.

"Bay- Bay- Bay-" she chanted grunts with each thrust, so hard and deep he was going to split her wide open.

Bay watched the spiral of her climax start filming her dazed eyes. Her pupils spilled covering the blue. He reached between their writhing bodies and plucked at her clit to push her off the precipice.

The gasps started up her throat as the flush spread over her creamy chest, up to singe her face, her blues turned blind, unseeing.

When her eyes rolled back in her head as it arched back with her clenching screams, he slammed his mouth on hers capturing it while he took her body into climatic rapture, and then he let go-

The orgasm seized his balls like a crushing fist. Bay paused deep inside Livy, then the fist squeezed hard and his balls erupted, he drove wildly, insanely into her.

Losing all thought, his brain screeching with exultation as he skyrocketed, hurtling to the edge of Earth, and off, he soared with the flight of an eagle as his swollen seed burst from his manhood still pounding in a frenzy into Livy.

When the convulsions struck him, he moved his mouth to curse his ecstasy in her ear, grunting and roaring her name he sniffed her neck like a wild beast and sunk his teeth into her flesh.

His body shook and heaved over her, a masculine bulldozer striking her soft curves, bruising with his big hard body slamming in and on her, until, grinding against her sweet pelvis, the last of his seed spewed and he slowed, trying to catch his breath.

Body shuddering, he thrust a few more hard times, snapping his hips wildly. Bay was dizzy with gripping euphoria he'd never experienced before in his life, with any other woman. It was all he could do not to collapse on her. Yet he still dropped with a moan.

He partially lay on Livy, panting, swallowing hard, overcome with strange overwhelming bliss, he couldn't move. Nothing felt better in this lifetime than having Livy under him like this.

Wrapping his strong arms around her lissome, still quivering body, his lips mumbling near her ear, he huffed a mantra, "*God Livy, God Livy, God Livy...*"

"Bay," Livy stirred under him, his weight was too much for her. She put her palms on his huge biceps and pushed at him.

"Yeah," he groaned, and rolled on his back bringing her with him, keeping his arms wrapped around her as if he thought she was going to leave.

Livy sighed and snuggled against his sweating, still heaving body. Her hand on his chest, fingers splayed through the hair as her own body continued coming down from the orgasm that still rocked her.

In a few minutes, Bay shifted and slid his hand in her hair. Sifting the locks through his fingers he bent his head to kiss the top of hers. "Livy, baby, you okay?"

Her languorous slither against his body, her palm stroking up his chest answered him. He chuckled. "Yeah," he grinned, "me too."

They lay still, heart beating against heart, then, Bay reluctantly got up to take care of the condom and came back with a wet and a dry cloth.

"Here baby." He gently cleaned her while she giggled. "This will hold us until we can take a shower."

"Hmm, that sounds like you plan on us doing that together." Her voice warm and satiated, and slightly uncomfortable with the big tough man tenderly wiping and then drying her.

He dropped the cloths on the floor and pulled her back into his arms, right where he'd always wanted her.

"Oh yeah baby, it's a long holiday weekend. I don't plan on us leaving this bed the next couple of days except to shower and order take-out, maybe catch a movie in between while we regain our strength. That okay with you?"

Livy snuggled in his embrace, nodding, her hair swept over his bare chest making him shiver with the tickle of it.

"Yes, that sounds wonderful."

"Good," he cupped her face drawing it up so they could kiss.

Chapter Thirteen

$\mathcal{T}$he weekend went just as he planned.

They christened every room and pretty much every stick of furniture, kitchen table, counter, wall and living room carpet.

Periodically they would order something to eat, or Livy would prepare something. Bay had proved himself a danger in the kitchen other than making sandwiches.

Livy had laughed for an hour when she walked in on him throwing a lid on top of a pan that was on fire, then accused him of doing it on purpose so he wouldn't have to cook.

They watched some television and a few movies. Good thing she'd brought a suitcase that first day after her house was broken into. Not that he let her get dressed much.

Livy was puttering around the kitchen and wandered into the living room to find Bay.

As she passed the wall, an arm snaked out snatching her around the waist, then two huge arms, biceps bulging, lifted her up, her legs wrapped around Bay's lean hips.

She scolded him, "Bay, I just got dressed."

"Yeah, against my request." He smothered her words with his mouth, kissing her until she forgot what she was saying. He shifted an arm under her butt and pressed her up against the wall. "I like this skirt."

"You do?" She smiled. "I think the flowers are so pretty they-" He was shoving it up around her waist. She squawked, "Hey, what are you-"

"Uh huh. I prefer you not wearing anything at all, but if you must dress, I want you to always wear skirts. Nothing to get in my way, slow me down." He gripped her panties and just tore them off her and tossed them.

Pushing his fingers inside her, he growled, "But there'll be no panties at home. I'll buy you more to replace that one, and likely others that I know my shy little girl will insist on wearing out in public, but none at home."

Her body squirming on his fingers with a mewling groan, made his leering grin sexy and hot. Pulling his fingers out, he went for her blouse.

"Bay," chastising him with a pouty grin, her arms twined around his neck. Bracing her against the wall, his fingers started on the buttons on her blouse.

She giggled scolding him, "You are so bad."

"Hmm." He reached around to unclasp her bra. "And no bras either when we're home. I want to feel these babies all the damned time. But out in public, yeah, you wear a fucking iron corset, I don't want any other guy looking at my luscious tits."

He unsnapped the clasp and her breasts sprung free. "Oh yeah," he groaned, "mine, so perfect." Groping one of her plump globes he squeezed and kneaded it with a hard grip.

Livy chuckled. "Uh, I think you are confused, these are my breasts, Bay." She raised her head for his kiss.

170

Against her lips he murmured, "No baby, they are mine. Every round inch of you is mine." He tugged her blouse and bra off letting them fall to the floor.

She pulled back. "Wait, we spent a weekend together. I mean," a blush brightened her cheeks. "I'm already in shock that I slept with you without us having a relationship, we never even went on a date. In my book that makes me a…" she ducked her head shamefully, "a slut."

His grin straightened as his brows drew down. "Hell, Livy, don't start any shit. We did have a date, we went to the wedding together."

"It was the reception," she informed him. "And we didn't go together, I drove myself and we attended as friends."

"Seriously, Livy?" He frowned. "It was a date. I agreed to your 'let's be friends big brother' crap just so you would agree to go with me. I don't wet-dream about fucking my friends or little sister, sweetheart. And I chased the hell out of you, girl. So," he kissed her again, "you are not a slut, and I don't want to hear shit like that come out of your mouth ever again, you hear me?"

She sifted her fingers through the front of his honey hair. "You really are bossy, you know."

He shrugged. "Comes with the rank, it's a habit. I don't want any foolish shit coming between us, so I'm not letting it get a foothold in. We have plenty of time after this weekend to go on dates, or whatever you want to do. We'll do whatever makes you happy, Livy."

Her arms slid around his neck while he bent his head to suck a nipple. Livy said in a quiet voice, "So, the girls said you are only good for uh…one night and you never see the girl again, they, uh wanted to prepare me just in case."

She didn't want to let him know the girls had teased her about being interested him, and had quickly informed her that Bay was a one-night-stand kind of guy.

"What?" Hs green eyes darkened. Hazy with lust, he raised his head scowling. "What the hell are you talking about? Prepare you for what?"

She shrugged one slim shoulder, tossed her head flipping her hair back. "You know, that if we ever...um, got together that I shouldn't expect to see you again-"

"Aw fuck, Liv." He cupped her breast and pinched her nipple in irritation. "You are so different, it's a mountain of difference." His gaze aiming at her chest, he fondled her breast.

"First of all, you are the only woman I've ever actually pursued, or dated, or brought here to this home, or even slept with on the base. I have a rule, well, had."

He looked down at the bare globe clutched in his hand. "I purposely don't sleep with anyone on the base or whom I work with."

"But, I-"

He nodded, his heated gaze stroked over her face, eyes drifted to her lips. "Yes, you are at the base. But, like I said, you were different. The first moment I saw you I had to have you, rule be damned. I've never felt that way before, Liv. I've never felt the way I do about you for another woman."

She was quiet, her gaze scanning his hard face, forest green eyes, his honey-wheat hair tousled from her running her fingers through it.

He had shaved that morning, yet already a dark shadow covered his strong jaw. Her eyes dropped to his mouth, and she unconsciously licked her lips. His were full yet masculine, and the man could kiss. He could almost make her come with just his kisses.

He hadn't actually denied what she'd said about him doing only one night stands. Not sure how to respond to his declaration, Livy said, "Um, so, after tonight, tomorrow is Tuesday, I guess I should go home this evening and then we won't see each other again except I guess around the base."

His brows slanted down in anger. "What are you talking about? You don't want to see me again? Why?" His big hand clenched her breast so hard she winced. He loosened his grip but didn't release it, his thumb brushed roughly over her nipple.

Her blue eyes rounded at him. "You just said, I mean, what the girls said, you don't see a girl more than once so I figure-"

Barking, "Motherfucker, Livy, do you not listen to me?" He let go of her breast to wrap his fingers around the back of her head and hold her while he kissed her with insistent needy hunger.

When he moved his head back they were both panting, eyes glistening with the ravenous lust he kindled.

"Let me be clear, Livy," Bay said as he stroked her head, her neck. "I want you, I have not stopped thinking about you," breaking off, his green eyes glimmered, he swallowed, Adam's apple bobbing.

"I've not stopped desiring you from the start, and I mean desiring a relationship with you. If I had only wanted just sex I never would have hit on you because of us both being at the base. I just," he forked his fingers through his hair then slid them through hers letting the curls coil sensuously around his fingers.

"I want to be with you, Livy. For fuck's sake, I don't kidnap a person's car, or force every woman whose home has been broken into to stay in my house, or hunt all over town for them when they aren't where they were supposed to be." Worrying that his choice of wording might frighten her, he took a breath from his stalking rampage.

Bay stroked his fingers down her cheek and over her lips, hovering his fingers there until her lips parted and he slid one of them inside her mouth.

"God, Liv," he moaned when her tongue swept around his fingertip. His pupils dilated into black nickels. Then he realized she wasn't saying anything.

Reluctantly removing his finger from her lush mouth, he curled it under her chin lifting it so their eyes met. "Livy, talk to me. Understand you are different, you are what I want. You are not a- a one night stand for me. I want a relationship with you. Do you want one with me?"

His voice was confident, strong, but a shred of concern filtered in. He studied Livy's face, the black in his pupils melting with the heat he felt for her and the way she made his heart feel. Hell, even after a lust filled weekend it still skipped a beat every time he saw her.

His stomach started churning when she didn't answer his question. "Livy, talk to me, baby, tell me what you're feeling, thinking." He tenderly kissed her. "Please talk to me."

She responded to his kiss. Lids drooping over sultry eyes, she opened her mouth to his gentle kiss that quickly turned ferocious with his hunger.

Bay pulled back quickly, he didn't want them to get distracted. He wanted an answer to his question, the right answer, then they could distract each other all day long.

He said with gentle command, "Livy, answer me."

"Bay, I-"

They both jumped when someone knocked on the door.

"Ah, fuck, ignore it, Livy, you were saying," he prompted.

"Um, I was going to say-"

Bang- bang- bang, the pounding was louder.

"Shit, Bullet, you in there you fucker?" Roddy slurred from the other side of the door. "Come on, open up, I know you're there, your fucking truck is in the garage. Come, on, I got a bottle of Jack I wanna share, come on," he pounded harder.

"Motherfucker," Bay cursed under his breath and lowered Livy to her feet. "Honey, go in the other room while I get rid of this asshole."

He waited while she tugged her skirt down, grabbed up her blouse, tossed it on and hurried out of the room.

"Dammit," palming his hard-on, he sighed watching her go. Tomorrow was a workday and was coming at them fast, he wanted to savor their time together now.

He jerked the door open and Roddy almost fell inside.

Bay stood in the doorway with his hand on the frame preventing him from entering.

"Hey, bitch," his ruddy face reddened from the alcohol, the pale green eyes also red and fuzzy, Roddy held up a bottle. "Come on, drink this with me. You're the only fucker home. I left Jules a note to come over here when he gets off training. Let me in-" he tried to push Bay aside but Bay was like a steel wall.

"No, I'm busy. I'll see you guys tomorrow, tell Jules to take a hike, I'll call him later," and he went to close the door.

"What the fuck?" Roddy's intoxicated mumble slobbered out in a slur, "You ain't too fucking busy to drink with me, boy. We only got a week before we go on the mission and we can't drink much while there, so," he lifted the bottle and grinned, and tried to push past Bay again.

"No, man, I said I'm busy. Go away." Bay went to close the door.

Roddy's eyes narrowed at his friend and squad leader. He took in the tousled hair, unbuttoned shirt, the top button on his jeans was undone, and, Roddy grinned at Bay's obvious hard-on.

Then he saw Livy's bra and panties on the floor and snickered. "Oh fuck, son, I got it, you got a broad in there. Well, that's fucking new, who is it? Is it that-" He tried to peer around Bay but the commander moved to block his view of the room.

"None of your fucking business," Bay growled. "Get lost," and he closed the door in Roddy's face.

But the agent's snickering made it through the door.

Bay didn't give a fuck, but he didn't want Livy having to endure any raunchy jokes or whatever.

Locking the door, he tramped off down the hall peeling off his shirt on his way to find Livy.

Chapter Fourteen

$\mathcal{B}$ay's first mistake was that he wanted to fuck Livy so badly when he got to her that he forgot their conversation.

She waited for him in the hall just outside his bedroom.

Without a word, Bay scooped her up grinning at her surprised squeak and carried her into the room.

Setting her on her feet, his mouth was fastened on hers while he quickly peeled her clothes off then his, and pushed her to bend over forward on the bed.

Naked, in a strange position, Livy said breathlessly, "Bay, what are you doing? I can't-"

He grabbed up a condom off the nightstand and slipped it over his raging boner. "Yeah ya can, hold still, don't move."

He came up behind her and nudged her feet apart and set his hand on her back pushing her down when she went to stand up straight.

"Perfect, Livy," he stared at her ass, her shapely legs. "Goddam you are the most stunning female, your parents told you shit about your looks to keep you humble. You're fucking gorgeous, don't move," he gruffly ordered again.

"Bay," her voice wavering, she turned her head but couldn't see him. She was nude, bent over, legs spread and butt up in the air.

Bay very slowly stroked his palm down her back to her bottom, then suddenly clenched both round globes in his hands with a rasping moan, "So perfect, Livy."

He grinned when she squirmed but she moaned too. He slapped her bottom sharply three times and laughed at her shriek.

"Oh," she gushed, wriggling her butt at him. "What are you doing? You can't spank-"

Whack! He smacked her a few more times, and grinned when instead of balking, she shoved her gorgeous bottom up higher and wiggled it.

Bay whacked her again, then kneaded her cheeks. He slid his fingers into the crack until she protested and he moved them under to feel her sex. "Ah, sweetheart, so fucking wet for me, I can't stand it," and he suddenly thrust into her.

A gasp choked out of Livy at the sudden penetration, it roiled into a heavy groan as he started to move, sinking deeper into her before sliding out then rocking back deeper each time.

He reached up and grasped her breast almost crushing it in his soon to be out of control desire. "Ah, baby," he uttered, suddenly whipping in and out of her. Squeezing her breast, he moved his other hand to fondle her clit.

Livy's hips rushed back and forth at his with her rising shallow breaths and tiny squeals with his every thrust. Their bodies slapped against each other, the erotic sound urging them faster.

Within seconds Bay could feel her starting to come apart. Clutching her breast he moved his other hand to grip her hip to hold her still while he pummeled into her too fast for her to keep up.

Hearing etching screams ripping up her throat as she hurtled over the moon, he pinched her nipple hard and roared along with her as they both came in dazzling splendor, grunting, gasping together.

Until her strength failed and she fell on her stomach on the bed and he tumbled on top of her growling against her neck, and he kept pumping until he had nothing left.

They didn't move for a long panting while.

Finally, Bay crawled off Livy and dragged her up on the bed then flopped down beside her. Pulling the condom off, he tied it and dropped it in the little trash can near the nightstand. He'd moved the box of rubbers from the dresser drawer to the top of the nightstand for quicker access.

He pulled her to him to spoon her, and gasped in her ear, "God, Livy, you are so flaming amazing, tell me this will never end." He plucked up some of her hair stroking it off her damp face.

Her cheeks were red, chest slowing its quick shallow breathing, she didn't say anything.

"Livy?" he whispered, inhaling her scent. Then he realized with a smile that she had fallen asleep.

Sighing, he gathered her as close as he could and dropped his arm over her and followed her into dreamland.

Bay's phone kept buzzing. He threw a hand over it, lifted it to peer at it with a bleary scowl, then dropped it down and cuddled her closer.

At the sixth time it buzzed, he groaned and sat up.

Livy was barely awake, her eyes closed, lids fluttered every time the phone buzzed.

"Livy, baby, I have to go to Jules' place for a meeting with my team. I should be back in an hour or so. I'll get us some take-out, okay?"

"Hmm," her lips didn't open, nor did her eyes, she just burrowed down deeper in the bed.

Grinning, he chuckled, "Okay, I'll take that as a yes. I'm gonna grab a quick shower and go." He bent and kissed her lightly on her forehead then took off to shower.

Yawning, Livy stretched her arms up over her head. "Gosh," she sighed, twisting her neck back and forth. "There is not a single part of me that isn't sore."

A sated smile lifted her lips as she replayed the last two days with Bay.

"Make that pleasantly sore." They had made love so many times she actually lost count.

She turned her head to the empty spot beside her on the bed then looked up at the clock on the nightstand. He had only been gone less than thirty minutes and she already missed him like crazy.

She sat up and swung her legs over the side of the bed. "I wonder if I should go home. It's Monday evening and we both have to work tomorrow."

The thought of leaving him pushed her lips out in an unhappy pout. Darn, she didn't want to go.

Leaving the bed to take a shower, Livy thought about what he had said to her about wanting a relationship. At least, that's what it sounded like he was saying.

"Well," she smiled, "I guess I need to stick around to discuss it, to make sure."

Her shower was long and hot, and after all that sex she felt as relaxed as a boneless cat.

Pulling on jeans and a blouse, Livy glanced over at the sound of buzzing. Bay had left his phone on the nightstand by the bed.

Thinking maybe he was calling her since he knew she always kept her phone in her purse and seldom looked at it as no one called her very often, she trod over and bent to see if it was him. It was a text.

As she read it her insides froze, her heart raced, stomach plunged.

The text read: "Fucking A Bullet, you banged Frostine the Snow-girl! Proud of ya, you did what no other guy could!

You're my hero, your strategy worked! Yeah, you won the bet, Hope Livy didn't freeze your balls off! You gotta spill all the dirty deats, bro. I'm running late for our meeting, cya in a few."

The message was sent over an hour ago but just came through now.

It was from one of his agents, Roddy Curtis, they called him Punchy. Frostine?

"Oh my God," Livy's heart stopped beating and sank like a rock. Bay had called her Frosty before, alluding to her being so cold to everyone. She thought it was an affectionate pet name.

Her brain reeled. Stumbling, Livy grabbed the headboard of the bed to keep herself from falling over.

Roddy Curtis confirmed what she had always thought, that she was a big joke that Bay would be laughing that he nailed the homely girl and won a bet.

Her hand at her throat, she wondered how many men, and women, were sitting around laughing at her right now.

That must be where he was, not at a real meeting, no, a laugh-fest to ridicule Livy for Bay winning her over. With his planned strategy. Damn. She was such a fool.

Livy never cursed, but right now she felt her entire life has been a curse.

Sobs racing up her throat, she cried, "I have to get out of here before he comes back-"

In a panic, she ran around grabbing up her things and throwing them into her suitcase.

She raced to the elevator. On the way down to the garage she prayed that her car tire was fixed and she could get out of the garage. She knew the code to the gate, she'd seen Bay punch it in.

The elevator door opened with a ping and she hurtled out and ran to her car.

Thank God the tire was fixed and the keys were in the ignition. The door was unlocked. She jumped in, turned it on and headed for the exit that also was gated.

As she approached, the gate automatically swung opened. By the time she was at the perimeter gate, tears were streaming so hard she could barely see the numbers to punch in the code.

Her heart felt like lead, her stomach a broiling turmoil, her head was spinning with his betrayal. She had finally allowed herself to trust. The sobs ripped out of her chest as she pulled out to the main road. She would never, ever trust anyone ever again.

It was hard not to speed down the road, but she forced herself to stay within the speed limit, she couldn't bear for a cop to stop her and see her a hysterical mess. One more person to mock her.

When she reached her house, she wearily trod up the steps, drained, empty, a shell of nothing.

The door was locked. It was a new lock, she didn't have the key. Swallowing more tears of frustration, she wandered around the house and checked the other two doors, they were all changed.

He did as he said he would, why would he spend his time and money getting her house made safer?

"Huh," she snorted, he probably did it on his mission to show everyone what a great guy he is, meanwhile snickering that he locked her out of her own home.

"I'll show him." Livy looked around until she found a baseball-sized rock. She went to a side window and bashed the rock into the glass and almost broke her hand.

He'd had hurricane-resistant windows installed, *great*. Still, they can be broken so no one is ever trapped inside.

She stood back and threw the rock repeatedly at the same place until the glass cracked.

Even then, she had to pound on it to get the glass to break through.

Once she cleared the jagged remains, Livy climbed in the window.

When she was standing inside, she had to wipe away more useless tears as she thought about what to do. She couldn't lock the door because he had the keys, and she was damned if she was going to get them from him.

Glancing around, she saw that someone had also cleaned everything up and put things back, it was like the place had never been broken into.

A shiver raced through her. The whole weekend in bed with Bay had pushed Kenaz right out of her mind. He was out and he knew where she lived.

She couldn't leave and lock the doors, the window was broken. She didn't have the funds to replace the locks. Something on the wall caught her eye.

Humph, she snorted, he had an alarm system installed. "Geez, that man goes to a lot of trouble for recognition of being a great guy. If people only knew what a rat he really was."

"Well," she spoke out loud to herself, "I can't stay here." She went into the bedroom to pack up the rest of her meager belongings. While doing so, she started thinking about where she could go.

She remembered her cousin had a cottage near the lake. No one would know about it, and her cousin lived out of state, it was a summer get-away.

"Yes," she decided firmly with a sniff. "I can go there to lick my wounds and not have to see everyone laughing at me, or face Bay's smirking self-satisfied grin."

Choking back sobs, her heart breaking with every item she gathered, she hurried to pack and get out.

A bit outside of the city, it was a lengthy drive to the cottage. Her fingers clenching the wheel shook and she had to keep wiping tears out of her eyes so she could see the road.

When she reached the cottage, Livy sat in her car and stared blankly at the small building of two bedrooms, living room and kitchen.

The exterior was wood painted brown to fit into the natural surroundings.

The cabins were spread sporadically around the lake. Some in clusters, this one happened to be set far away from the others and almost completely surrounded by trees.

The lake glistened a blue mirror a hundred yards behind the cabin. Livy took out her cell and dialed a number.

"Lieutenant Colonel Miles," the gruff voice barked through the phone.

She took a deep breath, let it out. "Um, Lieutenant Colonel, this is Livy, uh, that is Elizavetta Stirling."

Sounding slightly surprised, he said, "Miss Stirling, how are you?"

"Um, I'm, well, I need to request some time…off."

He said quickly, "Oh? Is everything all right?"

Coughing to clear the tears clogging her throat then hiccupped a tight catch in her small, somber voice she replied, "I, uh, I just need some time. Please."

The sound of hesitation in his low voice indicated he heard the despair she tried to hide. "Miss Stirling, is there anything I or anyone else can do to help you?"

She was quiet for a few seconds swallowing back the tears. "No, uh, I just, need some time."

He didn't say anything at first, then, "Of course. Whatever you need. How about a week? Two?"

Livy pondered what to do, then, sighed, cleared her throat again. "Um, yes, can I have two weeks without getting into…um trouble?"

"Miss Stirling," Miles was acutely aware of her situation, and he and Bay had been speaking privately about the recent developments. The attack near the bar, her slashed tire, the break-in at her house.

As far as he was concerned, she'd had enough troubles to last ten people a lifetime. But, Bay had sworn him to secrecy so he couldn't offer her comfort or reassurance.

"No, you are certainly not in any trouble. I want you to take all the time you need. I would like you to call me in…" he paused, "two days and tell me how you are doing."

She didn't say anything. Although she tried to hide it, her sniffing came through the cell.

He said gruffly, "Miss Stirling, that is an order."

185

Swallowing her distress, she said in a tiny voice, "Yes sir. Thank you, sir."

Now he cleared his throat and said, "Listen, does Commander DaRocco know that you-"

Livy hung up and gathered her cases and found the key to the cottage under the ceramic frog under the window.

Her life crashing down around her shoulders, Livy lifted heavy legs forcing herself to go inside. She looked around at her refuge.

A plain, log-style like cabin. Wood paneled floors and walls, simple, country-ish with scattered rugs and plaid curtains at the windows. The furniture wasn't expensive yet was still soft and serviceable.

She dropped her bags and plopped down on the couch and just sat staring dismally at the walls.

She must have dozed off. She heard her phone pinging.

Wearily, Livy got up and picked it up off the end table she'd left it on. Looking down at it, her stomach churned.

There were eight messages from Bay.

She didn't bother reading them. Taking the phone, she shut it down completely and took the battery out of it then tossed it on the table.

She lay down on the sofa. She hadn't eaten all day, the crying had exhausted her and gave her a pounding headache. She didn't care about food, she didn't care about anything. And she never would again.

Caring about things, people, only led to disappointment and heartache. Bay broke her heart, and damn if she didn't miss the big honey-haired asshole.

Closing her eyes, Livy was determined to never think of him again. He would be gone on some mission in a week so he would not be there when she returned to the base.

She would ask for a transfer somewhere else, she didn't want to be a laughingstock, and she knew she couldn't bear to see him.

If they wouldn't give her a transfer she would quit. She could flip burgers or clean toilets, anything but have to ever see Commander Bayou DaRocco again.

Chapter Fifteen

Bay had been disappointed and dismayed when he returned and Livy was gone, along with her belongings.

Hell, he had hoped to talk her into staying with him…permanently.

He had called her repeatedly, but she wouldn't pick up and didn't return any of his messages.

Disconcertment gnawing at his gut, he went to the garage, hopped in his truck and drove over to her house.

Parking the truck in the short driveway, he strode up to the front door and knocked. He knew she wasn't there because her car wasn't there. But, something made him wander around the house, and he saw the broken window.

"What the hell?"

He had keys to the house. Unlocking the door, he went inside and wandered around.

Livy had been there, her closet was empty as was the bathroom and everywhere else. Every personal thing of hers was…gone. Livy was gone. She must have broken the window to get inside.

His pulse started hammering, panic rose up his throat closing it, he had to struggle to draw a breath.

Livy was gone.

She'd been there and now she was gone.

He grabbed his phone and called her again, but the call didn't go through, she must have shut off the phone, she didn't want to talk to him. What the hell?

He had to think, something must have happened.

Bay drove back to his place.

The rest of the night he just sat there, rewinding their time together. It was wonderful, sexy, loving. They had laughed and cuddled, she was happy, they were happy, why would she not want to see him, talk to him?

After a sleepless night, Bay drove to the base in the morning.

He ambled around to Livy's classes and found out she wasn't in any of them. Secrecy be damned, he asked every person he came to that knew her, male and female, if they'd seen her, all replied in the negative.

"Bullet, what's up? You weren't in MMA training this morning?" Fitzgerald Willis came up to walk alongside him. He kept the red springy hair cut short, and wore dark sunglasses perched on a stubby freckled nose.

Bay shrugged. "Ah, something came up." He stopped walking, Willis stopped too. "Listen, Fitz, you know that little trainee, Livy Stirling?"

A grin split Fitz's freckled face, he nodded. "Yeah, what red-blooded male doesn't? Seen her a couple times now without the bun and baggy clothes, babe is a fucking knockout. Superfine tits, Bullet, makes a man wanna-"

"Yeah, whatever," Bay cut him off with a scowl. "Have you seen her today?"

Fitz shoved his sunglasses up over his head, revealing his pale blue eyes. The red hair sprung up around the glasses.

189

He thought, then said, "Nope. Haven't seen her. Trust me, if I do I'm hitting that so-"

"Shut up, Fitz, you asshole." Turning on his heel, Bay stalked away from his friend and teammate, leaving the freckled face in surprise, his mouth hanging open.

Two days went by and Bay was about to pull his hair out. Not a word from Livy, no trace of her.

He called her family, they told him they hadn't heard from her in months. His mind couldn't stop racing, thinking about things that could have happened to her.

That bastard that kidnapped her, what if he'd been waiting for her- no, he shook his head. "Stop panicking," he scolded himself. Her things were gone, a kidnapper wouldn't have taken her and them. No, she didn't want to be found.

He strode swiftly across the grounds ignoring people who called out to him and went straight to his lieutenant colonel's office.

"Hey, Trisha," he greeted the pretty woman behind the desk.

Her smile turned wide when she saw him. Primping her short dark curls, the Lieutenant Colonel's admin assistant greeted him. "Bayou DaRocco, I haven't seen you in an age. I sure hope you've come to see me."

She smoothed the white dress with tiny red polka dots down her figure trying to draw his attention to her form. Her lips, nails, and pumps were red to match the dress.

Bay smiled vaguely back at her. "I need to see the lieutenant colonel, is he in?"

Her brows drew down along with the red lips in a pout. "Oh come on, Bay, you could visit with me for a minute-"

Bay strode past her to the lieutenant colonel's door. "It's important, Trisha, please let him know I'm here."

The pout morphed into a frown. Huffing her annoyance, Trisha pushed a button and advised the gruff voice that answered that Commander DaRocco wanted to see him.

Not hiding the irritation in her voice she snipped, "He said go right in."

"Thanks." Bay didn't even look at her as he opened the door.

Lieutenant Colonel Garrett Miles sat at his desk mounded with piles of papers, he was staring at a computer.

In his late fifties, Miles' hair, mostly dark brown but his temples were sifted with grey was cut military short.

His build was large and in excellent shape, he wore an olive and brown uniform. Intelligent hazel eyes looked up at Bay as he entered.

With an authoritative smile, Miles greeted him, "Hey, Commander, what's up?"

Bay sauntered to the desk and sat down on one of the light brown leather chairs in front of the big desk. He crossed an ankle over a knee and steepled his fingers together in his lap.

"Lieutenant Colonel, you know Livy Stirling," he said through stiff lips.

Closing the lid to his laptop, the LC nodded. "Of course. We've talked about her. Poor thing, so much trauma in her young life, and none of it easy to move past." His strong features matched his commanding presence.

Bay mirrored his nod. "Yeah." He said, "The thing is, we got sort of...close."

Miles sat back. Twining thick, roughened fingers together, he set his hands on his desk, and regarded Bay with a slight smile. Crinkles stood out around his greenish-blue eyes in his darkly tanned face.

He could tell Bay was interested in the girl already from their previous discussions about her. "That so? Good. She needs someone strong in support of her, especially with that son-of-a-bitch murderer out and about."

"Uh huh, anyway," Bay sat up straighter, set his hands on the chair arms. He looked down at them then up at Miles. "The thing is, I told you she was staying with me because her house had been broken into and I wanted her safe."

Bay awkwardly cleared his throat then continued, "But ah, Livy and I were hanging out and everything was great. I mean, hanging out like in ah," his lips pulled in.

Miles nodded again with a knowing crooked smile. "I got it. Go on."

Bay cleared his throat again. Talking about his love life was not something he was comfortable doing. Especially since he'd actually never had a love life before, at least not since like seventh grade.

"Yeah, so, she suddenly up and left my place without a word. She's also left her house and hasn't been on base the last two days. I was wondering if you knew-"

His head nodding up and down, Miles told him, "Yes, yes, she called me."

Bay's brows popped. "She did? Can I ask why? Where is she? What did she say?"

Miles' smile deepened seeing how distraught his commander was.

Bay was not known for having any serious relationships.

The smile disappeared at the true worry etched on Bay's hard face. One solidly broad shoulder shrugged, Miles said, "It wasn't a lot. She said she needed some time away. She wouldn't say why. I told her she could have two weeks off. I uh, hell son, I'm sure she was crying. When I mentioned your name, she abruptly hung up."

The hazel eyes narrowed at Bay with some suspicion. "You didn't-"

"No, that's the thing, Lieutenant Colonel, everything was great. We were doing great. Hell, I was going to try to talk her into..." he broke off, his neck turning slightly red.

"That is, I was hoping she would actually, move in with me. Like permanently."

"No fucking kidding?" The LC chuckled, dark brows slivered with grey arched.

"Yes," Bay said pensively with a frown. "That's why, I mean, we had just," his neck turned darker. What was between him and Livy was not fodder for gossip, but the LC had a vested interest in her.

"Ahem, ah, we'd just been very...close. Then, I had to go out for an hour or so for a meet with the men. When I came back, she was gone, lock, stock and barrel. No word, she won't respond to my calls and I can't find her."

"Hmm," the LC's lips pursed, he tapped his fingertips together, brows arched. "And you don't know what happened in that hour you were gone?"

Shaking his head, Bay shoved his hair back off his head in frustration. "No. Did she tell you anything? What happened to set her off? Did she say where she was going? Where she was staying?"

"No. She hung up too quickly. She promised to call in a few days, well, she didn't promise, I ordered her to call me so I can ensure she's all right. When she calls I'll tell her you're looking for her."

Bay's bottom lip pushed out. "I'm sure she already knows that."

He looked up at Miles. Asked hopefully, "Was there anything else she said? Any hint of where she could be hunkered down? Anything at all I can use to track her down?

She obviously pulled the battery from her phone so she can't be tracked."

Miles chuckled. "There's that detective in you, Commander, that's why you make such a good agent." His smile disappeared. "But, no, that was it. It was a very brief conversation."

Bay sat quietly for a minute. "If she calls, shit Man, find out if she's all right. I need to know that fucker doesn't have her." His gaze fell, jaw tightened, he blinked hard before looking back up at his chief.

"Try to find out if I did...or said, something to upset her. I know it's not your business, your place, but, damn, if you can I'd be greatly obliged, sir."

He put his hands on the chair arms and pushed wearily to his feet. "Okay. I hope she calls, I ship out in a few days. I'd fucking hate it if I don't talk to her, or at least know she's safe and okay before I leave."

Miles stood up with him. "Yes, I can understand your concern." He walked with him to the door. "I'll let you know as soon as I speak with her, Commander."

Despondent, Bay mumbled, "Thanks," and walked out the door and out of the office not even hearing Trisha calling his name.

As it turned out, he didn't hear a thing from or about Livy before he was sent overseas on the mission.

Bay called in every favor, exhausted every search, but he couldn't find Livy.

He flew out with his team.

On the plane, he sat off by himself, glum and silent, wallowing in confusion and frustration, longing and worry.

Chapter Sixteen

The DAK opts squad stood in a circle studying the maps on the long table.

They were stationed in temporary, portable modular buildings tucked hidden deep in the forests of the Kackar Mountains of Turkey.

Fitz raked the tips of his fingers through the short red springs on top of his head then wiped the end of his stubby nose. He had just trucked in to the camp with the other latest arrivals.

His hands on his hips, he said, "So, Ejaz Pasåd head of a Türük ultranationalist mafia and his gang, his *sicarioes* are holed up in the cavern inside the mountain?" He nodded to the mountain area on the map that was miles from where they were.

One arm wrapped around his waist, Jules Winstead set his elbow on the arm and scratched the black goatee at his chin, his eyes traveled around the map.

He nodded and said, "Yes. Long ago, Ejaz Pasåd carved out the inside of the mountain and has made it habitable. Rocky walls and all. He has generators for light and heat and refrigeration. The people we've managed to capture and interrogate say that he's got the place done up like a fucking stone palace."

All the men wore black T's and camouflage cargos with iron-toed boots, and they were all armed to the teeth.

His thickly muscled arms crossed over his chest, Roddy had just arrived as well. He gestured to the map. "Why the hell can't we just fucking march up to the entrance with guns blazing, maybe toss in some grenades, bomb 'em to smithereens if they resist."

His eyes on the map, Bay answered, "Because we want to take Pasåd alive if possible. He's the snakehead at the top of the *Canis-aureus*, the Golden Jackals. His men, as they call themselves, *sicarioes* or 'blades' – are cartel hitmen.

"He knows where all the bodies are buried, where other satellite gangs are hiding in other countries. We need that damned information. The *Canis-aureus* has moles inside a ton of police agencies, we need to dig them out and slice them up.

"Besides, that fucker should pay for his crimes of murder, sex trading, arms dealing, extortion with hostages for ransom, and you all know there's so much more shit. We need to know everything to clean up all that crap.

"You obliterate the lead jackal and the others will just go on keeping the business running. We need to find them all."

"Well," Nels 'Irish' O'Connor said, "I agree with Roddy. Let's attack the front, charge in and grab the motherfucker. We have the men and the firepower."

Outside the plastic window other combat personnel patrolled. The DAK team had been brought in because Ejaz Pasåd had proven too difficult for the country's authorities to ferret out of his mountain hidey-hole.

"We can't, everyone else has already tried. Pasåd has made it impregnable. Steel doors feet thick, booby traps all over the front. No one has gotten near to, much less try to get through the entrance," Jules told him.

"We've been spending these past few weeks just getting the camp set up and doing reconnaissance."

They were silent as they all stared at the map.

Von Green proffered, "So, what if we got on top of the entrance, on the mountain and, I don't know, bore down, drilled into the cavern?" He shifted a hand under his scrolled braids and rubbed the back of his neck.

Bay shook his head crossing his arms. "No. We could cause a cave-in and accidentally kill them, and us. Besides, as soon as we started drilling, Pasåd would have his high-powered weapons ready for us the second we broke through."

Shaking his head, Von squinted his crescent eyes at the map and muttered, "Damn rat jackals are armed to the teeth inside their impermeable fortress."

Quiet resumed as the men perused the map.

They'd been there for three weeks setting up camp and doing recon. Studying the maps, the area, the mountain, and Ejaz Pasåd.

Now that the compound was intact and surveys were completed, they had been brainstorming how to get inside the mountain lair to get to the bad guy without getting any of their own men killed in the process.

They threw out ideas, but nothing seemed concretely feasible.

"Okay," Bay sighed. "Let's take a break. There are more troops being brought in daily. A truck just came in."

The first squads arriving had choppered into the closest rural city, others flew in at a private airstrip some distance away and were trucked in along with the parts to the modular camp.

Once on location, the troops had ventured furtively out of the city and into the dense woods to clear the forested land so they could stealthily put down the rest of the choppers under the cover of the thick foliage.

If the helicopters came in too close, they could be seen from the mountain, so they made dirt roads into the thicket and brought trucks through to the hidden camp to nestle closer to the mountain.

Even so, they were tucked away quite a distance from the mountain. The trucks went back and forth picking up more troops and bringing them to the camp.

Pre-fab modules were brought in and put together like puzzle pieces along with temporary barracks.

Everything was done quietly and discreetly, last thing they needed was for Pasåd to know they were there and plotting how to get to him.

Actually, he likely already knew and was laughing his ass off at their impotence to be able to grab him.

Roddy combed his fingers through his wavy red hair and grinned. "I hope they sent in more broads. Hell, there's not even half a dozen here for fuck's sake. The competition's too steep."

"Maybe the bitches just don't like that red hair," Von teased. The Asian eyes his mother blessed him with twinkled against the dark skin inherited from his father.

Roddy eyed Von's braids in neat rows over his head and bound at the base of his neck. "Yeah, well, at least they can run their dainty little fingers through it, it's not all tied up in twists and rubber bands, bro."

"And I resent that comment about redheads you asshole," Fitz joked joining the men.

The group headed out the door teasing and mocking each other leaving Jules and Bay alone.

His arms still crossed, head down, Bay stared at the map.

"Hey, Bullet, let's go get a coffee, you'll burn your brain out, give it a rest. We'll work some more later," Jules said to him.

Bay didn't say anything or change his stance.

Jules moved closer to him. He knew what else troubled his friend. "Come on, she's just a skirt, get her out of your mind so you can properly concentrate on the mission."

"I'm not-" Bay closed his mouth, there was no point in denying his insides were eating out at the thoughts of what was going on with Livy, and why she left him without a word.

At his wit's end trying to figure out what the hell happened, and unable to hold in how fucking wretched he felt, Bay had told Jules everything.

Jules had commiserated with his best friend and commander. He hated seeing the toughest man he knows suffocating under his broken heart.

"Yeah, okay, so come on, let's get some coffee, refuel, and we'll come back to this." Jules headed for the door and waited for Bay to stop glaring at the map and follow him out of the module.

When they got outside, the camp was buzzing.

There were already 40 or 50 men, and a few women on site, but a truck had arrived and was parking.

Half the troops wandered over to see the new arrivals. Check out if they knew any of them, and, check out if any more females were sent.

It was dead boring in the woods with nothing to do but set up the camp, patrol and wait for orders. And as is normal with bored males, their minds turned to sex.

Chatter followed Bay and Jules as they trod towards the module building they used as a mess.

Barracks surrounded the basecamp with smaller mods within the circle. Trucks were parked in groups behind the barracks.

Surrounding the entire area were miles of thick scrubby forests, beyond those were skyscraper mountains.

Just as they were reaching the mess, Von caught up with them. "Damn," he cursed a few words. "I could really use a drink. I'm gonna put away some serious alcohol when this mission is completed."

"I'll second that," Jules laughed. Ahead of him, Bay's boots clomped on the straw rugs put out in front of every building for the people to clean their boots before tracking mud inside.

"Oh- fucking- shit," Von suddenly drawled.

Jules asked, "What?"

"Uh, the truck, man, with the new troops," Von answered, sounding funny.

"Yeah? So what? More men to eat up the shitty food," Jules sneered from behind Bay who had his hand on the door to the mess.

"Chicks, dude, chicks," lewd glee laced Von's deep baritone.

Jules paused and turned around. He was seeing his own little redhead at home, but hell, it doesn't hurt to look. "Oh fuck," he croaked.

Bay was opening the door.

"Bullet, bro, she's here."

Facing the mess, Bay muttered with disinterest, "She who?" and started through the open doorway.

"Her, Bay, Livy Stirling, is here," Jules said in a hushed low voice.

When Bay froze, Jules and Von shared a look.

Bay swung around, and his face paled.

Livy was being helped out of the truck, by at least five men.

The men were grinning, each one trying to be the one to help her.

The blood rushed out of Bay's head and pooled in his feet.

"Hell, bro, she's thinner than ever but still has those killer curves," Von remarked.

All three men stood gawking, watching the other soldiers gather around Livy.

Her face was completely blank, but Bay knew her well enough by now he could see the anxiety in her eyes, her lips pressed together hard to shield against the overwhelming feelings from the unwanted attention.

"What the fuck is she doing here?" Bay muttered under his breath.

A soldier exited a building and strode to the truck with an iPad tucked under his arm. With a curt air, he glared at the men surrounding Livy. They stepped back but didn't disperse.

The six other men that had traveled in the truck with Livy were now grouped with her.

The soldier with the iPad put his hand on Livy's back and started ushering her and the other men across the camp towards an office mod.

Bay strode after them. Jules and Von grinned at each other watching him stalk across the grounds.

His eyes burning a hole in the hand on Livy's back, Bay approached them. He barked in a low voice, "I've got this, soldier."

The group all stopped. The soldier leading them with his hand on Livy's back turned to Bay with a frown.

"Commander, sir, I have orders to take the new people to the O-Mod for orientation, assignment, and barrack designation."

"I will go with you." Bay glared at the soldier's hand that was still on Livy's back.

The soldier's mouth pursed, he dropped his hand.

Livy's anxious ice-blue eyes rounded brilliant and wide at Bay. She was just as surprised to see him. Then, her lids lowered and narrowed at him, her mouth tightened.

What the hell? Bay thought, *she's angry with me?*

"Ah, of course, Commander, everyone, this way," the soldier said him and to the group.

Livy shifted her glare from Bay and hurried to walk beside the soldier. Bay followed with the others.

The soldier held the door to the O-Mod open for the new people to pass through, his eyes lowered when Bay walked by him. Heavy boots tromping on makeshift floors spread in all directions.

Inside were several folding tables and a few makeshift cabinets. Half a dozen people, all dressed in the same camouflage pants and black T's were busy at work studying laptops and other material.

The soldier side-stepped Bay and went up to a table two men were sitting at, their heads together.

"Captain Wright, sir," the soldier announced in a firm level voice, "the latest recruits are here."

The two men looked up.

One had a short, grey buzz-cut and piercing blue eyes surrounded by creases of wrinkles in a darkly tanned, weathered face. He was around 40 with a bulky chest and pure military look about him. Tats covered his arms to his wrists.

He nodded, his gaze flicking over the new people, returning several times to Livy. "Good, good," he said in a deep, gravelly voice filled with lungs that had smoked cigars for years. "Welcome. Sergeant Martes will give you your assignments and sleeping accommodations."

His gaze went back to Livy, hard-carved lips turned up cunningly at one corner. His expression was a combination of annoyance that she, a civilian female, was there, and admiration for her looks.

"Ms. Stirling, unfortunately, there are very few females on this mission. I know you don't have combat training so this may be tough on you. We're in a fuck- uh, treacherous jungle under difficult circumstances, but your Lieutenant Colonel Miles felt that you had some sort of…ah, training or insight or someshit that could possibly be useful in the mission." His expression indicated clearly he didn't agree.

Her voice empty of any inflection, Livy stared steadily at him and said coolly, "Yes, sir."

LC Miles had received glowing reports from her instructors about how intelligent and quick she was, and her out-of-the-box thinking was outstanding.

The captain's gaze rolled down her figure right on the edge of insolence, and back up to her flushed face.

Her hair was pinned back in a ponytail but loose tendrils wisped around the heart-shape of round pink cheeks. A tiny smattering of freckles across her small nose only made her look younger, along with the vivid blue eyes riveting with youth and vitality.

His eyes returned to her bust. She wore the same regulation uniform as everyone else, olive green and beige camouflage cargos and black t-shirt.

Bay made a sound much like a growl.

Captain Wright's brow arched as he shifted his eyes to him. "Commander? Are you here to see me?"

There was no mistaking the flint of warning in Bay's dark green eyes and fixed mouth.

The captain frowned at Bay's hard gaze.

Biting back his rising rage, Bay stated, "I want to know why I wasn't informed that she, a civilian, would be here." It took effort to keep the anger out of his voice and his eyes off Livy. Bay had avoided looking at her since their initial eye contact, and it appeared she was doing the same. *Why the hell is she mad at me?*

Wright's lip curled in a partial sneer. "I guess Miles decided at the last minute, and you were already deployed here. No point in calling you when she was on the way and you would see for yourself soon enough."

Gruff and barely keeping a lid on his fury, Bay said, "She needs to be sent back immediately. She has no training for any of this; she can't even fire a weapon. She is in danger and you damn well know it. You never should have agreed to her-"

Wright stood up and leaned over with his knuckles on the table. He had large rough hands, he was bulkier where Bay was as muscular but the rest of his body was built of leaner, sinewy muscles.

Uncompromising mouth angry in his hard-angled square head, square jaw grinding, Wright blustered, "Listen here, Commander, this is a joint effort of several organizations. Yours does not top them all. The decision was made to send her here, we will meet in the morning to brief her and get her input. I am not going against orders, and since I have control of the trucks, there is nothing you can fucking do about it."

The two men glowered at each other. Steam practically poured out of Bay's ears he was so furious, and, Wright didn't like being questioned or ordered about, a pissing contest was about to ensue.

The other men in the room watched with interest, trying to suppress their grins at the top dogs sparring.

"Sergeant Martes," Livy's soft voice cut through the tension. "You were going to show us our accommodations?" She smiled, and started for the door. The sergeant about stumbled over his own feet rushing after her.

He glanced back at the captain.

Wright's eyes were on Livy's ass, and Bay was still glaring at Wright.

Wright nodded, and the sergeant escorted Livy and the other soldiers out of the mod.

"Listen, Commander-" Wright said, but Bay had turned his back and was going out the door.

He followed the sergeant who took the other men to their mod of barracks and then brought Livy to a small round mod. The pair disappeared inside.

Bay waited outside the door.

The mods were built of aluminum and canvass, easy to put up and then take down and transport.

When the sergeant exited, Bay stepped inside.

The inside was like the one he shared with his team only smaller. Four air mattresses were on the floor and four duffle bags were beside them.

There were only three females besides Livy assigned to the mission and they were currently out in the field.

Bay felt his stomach crimp at the thought of the untrained, inexperienced, *dainty* Livy out here in the wickedly dangerous jungle on an equally dangerous mission. For God's sake, if she was captured by the ferocious Jackals or some other just as vicious rebels-

Livy was staring down at the duffle bag beside the mattress assigned to her.

"Liv," Bay said quietly.

She swung around, her mouth open.

He saw a flash of... pain in her eyes before they hardened.

"What are you doing here, Commander?" she asked stiffly, crossing her arms over her chest.

First thing she needed was to put a jacket on so the other motherfuckers would stop gawking at her tits in the form-fitting black T.

Bay didn't move from the doorway. He couldn't. If he got near her he'd have her in his arms in a heartbeat and his mouth seizing hers.

Clasping his hands behind his back, his legs akimbo, biceps bulging in his tight shirt, he squashed his inner turmoil and said quietly, "We are all here to find a way to get to Ejaz Pasåd and arrest him. Why did Lieutenant Colonel Miles send you here?"

Livy blinked at him. Her gaze fell to his lips before rising to his eyes. Dark green blazing fierce with fury that she was there, and bewilderment at her behavior towards him, all entwined with his raging desire.

She tightened her arms around her body as if she could read his struggle to resist pouncing on her. She shrugged one slender shoulder.

"I…he said I had a…gift, or something, in strategy. The word was that he wanted to send everyone he could think of to brainstorm a way to get this…villain."

"Huh," Bay snorted. "Villain is an understatement. He is head of one of the biggest, most bloodthirsty cartel gangs in the world, the *Canis-aureus*. He is a murderer, a torturer, rapist, drugs, arms and sex-slave dealer, the list goes on and on. And that fucker Miles sent you here smack dab in the middle of his fucking den?"

His voice went shrill at the end, he dragged a furious, shaking hand though his hair.

Dropping his hands to his lean hips, his face a mask of ire, he ordered, "You are getting back on that fucking truck and on that fucking helicopter and going straight back to-"

Her brows shot up then lowered over angry eyes, her hands fell to her curvy hips mirroring his stance. She cut him off, "I will certainly not do that. I was sent here, I have my orders just like you do. You have no right to boss me around. Now, this is the *women's* quarters, you need to leave."

Well over six feet tall with his broad shoulders and thick chest and arms, Bay took up a lot of space in the small room.

With his fierce glowering and commanding posturing, Livy subtly moved back a step from him.

The skin on his neck and face darkened at her defiance, and worse, her fear of him. Then, his mouth softened.

He took a step to her, said gently, "Livy, baby," he held out a hand. "What the hell happened? Why did you leave me? Why did you disappear? Tell me what's going on. What happened to make you disappear?"

Her arms went back up to wrap protectively around herself. She took another step back from him. "I don't have to tell you anything," the vitriol in her voice stung like a slapping scorpion's tail.

207

Brow a low hard ridge, he moved closer. Voice so quiet he almost whispered, he said, "Yes, you do. After what we shared, Livy, yeah, you owe me an explanation, and I am not leaving until you tell me what the fuck happened to cause this chasm between us."

The pair glared at each other. Livy's skin paled while Bay's grew darker with his anger and puzzlement.

He took a step closer, her hands came up protectively and the blue eyes rounded in fear. Her voice trembled as she ordered, "Stay back, Commander."

His face fell. *Great, back to Commander.* "Shit, Livy, you know I would never hurt you," and he inched closer, keeping his arms innocuously at his sides.

"But I swear, I will stand here all night, in front of everyone that comes in here until you tell me what the hell happened."

Her arms tightened, eyes wide and miserable before she lowered them. "Fine," her sigh of resignation did nothing to remove the wretched, mortified shame in her bearing.

After a deep drawn breath, she told him, "When you went to your meeting," she peered up at him, he nodded, his brow knit in confusion. "You didn't bring your cell, it buzzed. I thought it was maybe you calling me so I looked at it to see if it was you."

"It wasn't me, Liv, I told you I was coming right back after the meet."

"No," her sigh was shaky with sadness and shame. "It was one of your guys, Roddy I think. He left a text, said you won the bet."

Her voice grew aching and angry, eyes narrowed, she went on, "He said there was a bet that you couldn't nail me. He called me," tears clogged her throat, she turned away from him. "Frostine the Snow-girl."

Peering briefly back at him, she saw the guilty look on his face. "I see. Your expression confirms it was true. You made a bet, Bay, to see if you could- could have sex with me, the ugly girl-" Her voice broke. "H- how could you?"

"No, no, Livy, it wasn't like that, I swear. I can explain!" His arms out, he moved to her, but she stepped back with her hands up to stop him.

"No. Slapping at a tear, she said, "Don't you dare come near me. I swear I will scream. Get away from me, go away."

Stricken at her pain, his voice rough with the misery she'd endured because of him, his stupid friends, Bay said brusquely, loudly, "No, dammit Livy, I didn't bet."

At her slight jump from his anger, he gentled his tone, "I showed blatant interest the first day I saw you and the guys seeing it said you were, uh, cold and turned everyone down.

"They joked and told me I hadn't a chance of a snowball in hell of getting you to go out with me. I ignored them, Liv. I wasn't paying any attention to their stupid talk. Trust me, I was single-minded that night, I only had intentions on seeing if I could get a date with you."

"Yeah," she sniffed, "to nail me and win your stupid bet. Get out." She ran trembling fingers under her eyes to erase the tears.

Bay pulled out his cell and sifted quickly through his texts, then he saw it. Unread, amongst dozens of others.

His tanned skin blanched when he read it, damn how it must have hurt her.

Dragging his arm across his eyes, his sigh heavy remorse, he said, "Livy, I never saw this. At that time I was only reading texts that were about this mission or that came from you."

His lips pulled in, she hadn't sent him a text or a message or anything that day or since. "I never saw it. If I

209

read it I would have explained. I mean," but she had seen it and fled before he could have explained it to her.

Livy's heart hurt. She had been tricked, shamed, mortified, and betrayed by a man she was strongly growing to like, and wanting to be with.

Tone shallow like speaking through a hollow reed, she sighed, "You won the bet, Commander, jolly for you. You collected your winnings, go buy your friends a drink in celebration with them and leave me alone." Weariness and sadness weighed her soft voice down.

No fucking way he was letting this happen, lose what they have. He wanted a life with her.

Bay moved towards her, anxious and sincere, he needed for her to believe him. He said urgently, "Livy, listen to me, I'm telling you, I wasn't paying any attention to their antics, stupid Punchy and his stupid words.

"He was drunk and saying a lot of stupid stuff that night. I had nothing to do with that bet they were screwing around with, I swear to you, nothing. I wasn't paying any attention to what they were saying."

Bay's face puckered dark and angry, brows down hard like daggers over earnest green eyes. His voice heartfelt and grave with the need to convince her, he said, "I was never involved in any shit-assed bet. My God, Liv, I spent half my time chasing you down.

"I spent the entire weekend with you, I brought you to my home. Fuck, I've never brought another girl there but you. You think I'd do all that for some stupid bet? If so I would have fucked you that night on my couch, you were drunk and very willing."

A blush brightened her cheeks as Livy recalled her wantonness that night.

"And honey, I wanted you so badly, but I didn't fuck you because I didn't want to take advantage of you. I didn't want to chance losing you because of it."

He spoke quickly as she opened her mouth to speak. "If it was only for the stupid bet I would have fucked you and sent you home instead of spending the weekend with you. You think I could have pretended to like you, play with you, eat and just hang and watch TV with you?"

He wiped at his forehead then set his hands back on his hips trying to appear as nonthreatening as possible. "Livy," his lungs expanded with a deep breath, "why would I have called and texted you like mad when you left?"

She stared blankly at him.

"Why would I have searched everywhere for you, asked everyone if they'd seen you? I can prove I went to your house looking for you, you broke the damned window to get in."

His bleak smile wry, he went on, "Why would I be trying so hard right now to convince you of my feelings? Baby," he forked his fingers through the top of his hair, a vein beat at his temple with the strain of trying to prove his genuine interest in her, in them as a couple.

"I had your car fixed and security put in for your house. I did that because I wanted you to be safe because I fucking care about you. A lot."

Livy studied him hard, seriously intent on reading his expression, weighing the honesty of his words, but the hurt still invaded. She'd had a couple of years to have grief dig inside her and catch a strangle hold on her trust.

She had been vulnerable those years to hateful opinions of her, from the courts, the law, the press, the other victims' families, nosy strangers, even from her own family.

"You had other reasons. You wanted to look good in front of your superiors. I was a- a- stray cat, a charity case. You-"

Incredulous that she even came up with that, Bay snapped, "That's bullshit." He spat with a harsh bark, "That's fucking bullshit, Livy."

Her brows drew down. Crossing her arms and lifting her head, she said with haughty anger, "Don't you curse at me, Commander DaRocco."

He looked instantly contrite. Scrubbing his hand down over his mouth, his jaw, he said, "You're right. I'm sorry. I'm not used to being around ladies that much, except my ma who would have washed my mouth out with soap." He tilted his head with a crooked grin because she really would have tried.

"Anyway," he raked his hands through his hair before plunking them back on his hips. "The point is, Livy, I like you. I've wanted you from day one. Not for a goddamn bet, or altruism or any other fucking reason, but because I wanted a relationship with you. I told you that. We talked about it that Monday."

Swiping at the tears that were falling, her voice constrained with the pain she'd felt at his betrayal, she cried in disbelief, "Why? Why would you want a relationship with a plain Jane, damaged woman like me? I don't believe you."

Turning her head from him, her sigh a whimpered whisper, she cried, "Please just go."

Muttering, "Fuck, Liv," he scrubbed his fingers down his face again in exasperation, scraping over his dark five o'clock shadow. "This is ridic-"

Suddenly there were voices behind him, female voices.

"Hey, what's going on here?"

One of them said in a deep feminine voice, "You two gonna fuck it's not gonna be in here."

"Shit," Bay mumbled staring at Livy who refused to look at him. He turned and saw the three female soldiers assigned to the mission.

"Ladies, ah, soldiers, could you give me and Ms. Stirling a moment?"

A woman with short choppy hair and a tough face walked up to him. She glanced at Livy who was swallowing back tears then to Bay.

"I don't think so, Commander DaRocco. Males are not allowed in female barracks and you know that." She stood stolidly flanked by the other two unwavering soldiers.

"Ah, shit." Bay scowled, then said to Livy, "Liv, honey, come outside and talk about this with me. Please."

Her face flaming with embarrassment, Livy looked at the three women stifling their nosy grins and then to Bay. She didn't have the strength to deal with this right now.

She needed to sort out her thoughts and she couldn't do it with his big overpowering body towering over her. "I...will see you...at the meeting tomorrow. Good night, Commander."

"Liv..." the plea in his hunter green eyes hit the closed wall in her blues. His shoulders dropped with a sigh. "Yeah, sure. Tomorrow."

He speared her with a hard promise, "We will, and I mean *we will* talk about this tomorrow, Liv," then spun on his heel and stalked out.

Chapter Seventeen

$\mathcal{B}$ay felt like his guts were turning inside out.

This was why he did not have relationships. Fuck a woman and move on, no strings, no worries, no heartache. Hell, his heart was bleeding at the pain he saw in Livy's hurt expression.

All he wanted was to scoop her up and take her the hell out of there. Out of the jungle, out of danger, out of her murdering stalker's reach, put her somewhere safe where when the fucking mission was over they could spend time, alone, together, get this shit cleared up between them.

He was sitting in the mess hall-mod with his team for breakfast, and he could barely eat. His eyes were glued on the gorgeous woman across the room.

Livy was surrounded by men; they were all hitting on her, including that bastard Captain-fucking-Wright. Bay had seen his interest in Livy yesterday when she'd arrived.

Last night after he left her barracks he went and had words with Wright. He had told the man to back off, but the captain had only smirked at him as he sucked on a long thick cigar and said, "Ain't no ring on that little girl's finger, son, she is fair game."

There were so few females that the ones that were there were crowded by the male soldiers.

Livy's cheeks glowed bright pink, her nervous eyes flit around as the men all talked to her at once.

Wright kept touching her, her hand, her shoulder, her hair. She subtly leaned away from him.

Bay cursed under his breath, "I'm gonna break every fucking bone in that bastard's-"

Book-ending him, Jules and Von laughed out loud.

Jules said, "Shit, Bay, not like you to lose your cool. I've seen you balls deep in gunfire and bombs, and you're letting a little flirting drive you nuts."

"It's really pretty funny." Von chuckled.

"Yeah, funny, shut up you assholes," Bay growled into his coffee.

"What?" Roddy across the table saw Bay's scowl and the others' mirth.

Fitz and Nels looked over with interest.

"Trouble in paradise?" Nels asked. "What can be bothering you bros on a nice day in the middle of the motherfucking humid as a wet rag jungle on a mission that is going nowhere?"

Bay didn't look up from his coffee, and Jules and Von just laughed.

Not everyone needed to know Bay's business. The ribbing would never end if they knew what was going on with him and Livy.

He'd have it out with that idiot Roddy when they were back home. His fists will be in Punchy's face for screwing this up for him. Bay's hands clenched as they were itching to punch the stupidness off his ruddy face.

The guy was a great agent, had your back in the worst of combat, but he was stupid when it came to females and Bay was going to teach him a lesson.

"The meet is in ten, let's head out," Jules said, dropping his napkin on his plate and standing up.

Bay, Von, Roddy, Chuck, Fitz, Nels and a few others got up with them. After tossing their refuse in the trashcans by the door they filed out of the mess.

Bay stared at Livy on the way out. He could see her carefully keeping her lids low so he couldn't catch her attention.

They met back in the O-Mod. It was a large circular mod and was currently filled with the team leaders of all the different divisions sent there, the CIA, FBI, INTERPOL, Evgeny, and others.

The room was thick with murmurings, a smattering of laughter.

No one was in charge, everyone was sent there to work out how to get Ejaz Pasåd out of his mountain and arrested. Only the lead squad teams were present, the rest of the grunts stayed outside patrolling and doing chores.

Bay and Jules stood near the long table with the maps.

Across from them, Captain Wright had come in with Livy in tow and bellied up to the table with her next to him.

Still, she resolutely kept her gaze down, not making eye contact with anyone. She was clearly confused and embarrassed, unsure why she, the only civilian, was there and what good could she offer.

The men started in like they had since yesterday throwing out ideas on how to get to Pasåd.

The majority just wanted to storm the front of the mountain entrance. Others suggested dropping bombs on the lower part of the beginning of the entrance to blow the top and front open.

"Again," Captain Wright's aggravation came out with a growl of impatience, "we've already chewed that dog up and spit him out. If we bomb the motherfucking mountain we chance killing Pasåd. We need him alive. That would be a total last resort and we ain't there yet."

A CIA agent dressed in fatigues added, "There also might be innocents trapped in there and we were instructed to avoid collateral damage."

"Yeah," Wright gruffed. His muscled arms rigid, he placed his big square palms on the table, rounding his shoulders. "Come on, guys, think for fuck's sake, think."

A low murmuring rolled around the mod but no one offered any more suggestions than had previously been tossed out, already dissected for probability of success, and rejected.

Her voice quiet and shy, Livy said softly, "Um, uh, what about the back of the mountain?" Her feminine voice so soft amongst the harsh, arrogant male baritones, every man in the room shut up and looked at her. She was the only female in the mod.

Wright turned to her with a 'please be quiet little lady' look, but another man said, "What do you mean?"

Livy moved closer to the table and pointed at the backside of the mountain.

"Here, what about oh, tunneling or something, going in through the back? I mean, how do they get in and out without going out the front where you can grab them? They have to get supplies and get out to do their dirty deeds."

It was quiet in the mod as the men pondered her words.

Bay said, "You're right, Ms. Stirling, that's how they mostly get in and out. We tracked the *sicarioes* in the first weeks we were here. They already have tunnels through the sloping back with many exits. The problem is, they've booby-trapped the tunnels, and they are so long that we would easily get picked off if we tried to get in through them."

"Yes," Jules added, "we tried. We did recon, found a bunch of the traps, and almost didn't make it out. They can hide guards anywhere along the length of each tunnel and ambush us."

Chuck Houston said, "Yeah, and it would take forever to burrow our own tunnels, and they would see us, hear us coming miles away and be ready for us before we even got within a mile of the interior."

Nodding in agreement, Jules said, "After much study, we could see that if we tried bombing the narrower backend that would likely cause a cave in, they'd be buried. And if not, again, they'd be there waiting for us as we tried to breach the gateway."

Bay was staring at Livy with pride, damn smart little thing, his heartbeat tapped like a keyboard on speed. Alas, even when he spoke directly to her she didn't look at him.

The men threw ideas back and forth for an hour. They were just about to take a break when Livy spoke again.

Some men now looked at her with respect, some still smiled like she was a little girl that should not be there, so she closed her mouth.

"What, Livy?" Bay said quietly, and, praise God, she raised those beautiful glistening blues to him and he wanted to dive right into them.

Her gaze trained on him briefly before dropping to the map, her cheeks flushed with shy embarrassment.

Nonetheless, she emboldened her stance and voice and said, "They have to be getting water from somewhere.

Probably from the lakes here in front," she leaned over the table and pointed at the river lines on the map like spider-legs going beneath the mountain.

"This tributary here goes right through near the entrance and appears not to be too far underground. Easy enough I would guess to get their water supply from."

"So what?" A man with a thick Eastern European accent asked with impatient indulgence.

Livy cocked her head towards him with a vaguely polite smile and replied, "If we block the water supply, they would have to come out and fix it. If it was a big enough blockage, a great many of them would have to come out for repairs."

All eyes were on her, half in confusion as to what she was inferring, the rest in curiosity.

Continuing on, her gaze back on the map, Livy said, "With so much activity, the entrance to the mountain might be um, compromised. Unsecured. Half the men outside, and half inside, it would be easier to grab them."

The room grew still as each man pondered her words.

Wright said, "They would know it was a trap. They would come out like gangbusters, they have really big weapons, hon," his condescending tone came with a patronizing smile. "They would get us before we could get them."

"Hmm," Livy murmured, her eyes on the map. "This is the jungle, and it rains a lot and hard," she picked up an iPad and typed on it.

The men watched her, waiting silently, wondering what she was doing.

"Not the best time to be shoe shopping, sweetheart," Wright said drily, a few men chuckled.

Ignoring them, Livy's eyes dashed back and forth as she read her search.

After a minute, tapping the pad, she said, "There's a storm predicted in two, maybe three days. We can block the river after the storm, but not completely so they aren't suspicious."

She glanced around then looked back to the iPad. "Every day we block it a little more. They will think that the storm knocked down trees or something causing a drainage or flowing problem and would send out a small crew to check it out."

No one spoke or moved.

Livy continued, "If we make it a- a- really big blockage, big fallen trees, uprooted shrubs and mud that appears to have been swept along with the current and into an enormous natural dam, they would have to go back, get more men and equipment, saws and stuff, to clear it."

All attention on her, some shook their heads as if her suggestion was ludicrous, others nodded in agreement, a few just blinked blankly at her.

She went on, "That's when you nab a big group of them while they're away from the mountain. Then, you can grab ones that are sent out to look for them when they don't return, kind of like in horror films where someone goes out and doesn't return and another goes out and so on."

Several men chuckled at the picture she described.

Emboldened, Livy went on, "And, at the same time, you can also storm-rush the entrance while it's open letting them go in and out. It will be a surprise attack, they won't be thinking of guarding because they'll assume there's a nature made problem, not a man made one."

The room grew seriously quiet.

"They'd be thinking it's a natural disaster and might not expect troops waiting in ambush. Your survey maps here," she pointed at one of the front of the mountain, "show cameras at the direct entrance and the back, but none at the far sides.

"If you come in from the sides of the mountain, they couldn't see you approach, and you could do a, what do you call that sudden hard attack?"

"Blitz," Bay said, staring at the map. He plucked at his lips with a thumb and finger contemplating her theory.

Wright rolled his eyes at Bay, stuffed his cigar between his teeth and disputed Livy's stratagem with heavy sarcasm, "Eh, shit, DaRocco, it's a dope idea from a little girl that should learn to do her job which is to just stand there and look pretty, and leave the thinking to us professionals. Those fuckers ain't gonna fall for a-"

"Actually, Wright," his expression stoic, Bay stuffed his hands in his pockets and said, "I think it could work. It's the best, most feasible idea we've come up with. Brilliant actually. Brilliant, Livy," he smiled at her.

She raised her lashes for a shy second up to him then quickly lowered them.

Wright blurted with belligerence, "Wait just a fucking minute, Commander-"

Everyone's eyes bounced from Bay to Wright to Livy and back.

Bay drew his hands out of his pockets and crossed his arms over his brawny chest, eyes narrowed at the captain.

"You don't have to agree with it, you can go frolic off somewhere and try something else. But, the rest of us," he glanced around and saw the majority of the room nodding in agreement with him.

"We're going right out now and start taking down trees and brush and whatever else we can use and get ready to slowly plug that river before the storm hits."

"I'll get crew to get the axes," Jules said. He took a few steps over to Livy and kissed her cheek. "Good going, Livy, brains and beauty." He grinned at Bay's frown and grabbed the rest of their team and left the mod.

Most of the other leaders filed right out behind them without glancing back in Wright's direction.

"Listen here, DaRocco," Wright got in his face blustering, "you ain't in charge here, you can't tell everyone what to do."

Bay didn't flinch, he moved his harsh face close to the Marine's, and returned gruff for gruff. "Didn't say I was. But I am in charge of my team, and if the rest of the troops here agree with the idea and fall in, that's on them. Now, get the fuck out of our way, we have work to do."

He caught Livy's arm before she could blink and pulled her away with him.

"Hey, girlie," Wright barked after them, "you get back here!" He strode quickly across the ground to catch them outside. He moved in front of the pair. "You," he pointed at Livy, "are under my protection, you will stay with me. Let these other fools-"

Moving Livy behind him, Bay held a hand up to Wright. "You stop right there, Captain. Ms. Stirling is part of Evgeny Base, sent by Lieutenant Colonel Garrett Miles, and therefore is under my command."

He half-turned and set a big hand on Livy's back. "She doesn't need two bosses."

He started moving with her, then turned back and snarled in Wright's face. In his quiet, deep voice, he commanded the startled, fuming captain, "Stay the fuck away from her, Wright."

"Or what, big man?" Wright puffed his chest up, flexed his biceps, his hard face grit in a fierce threatening scowl.

Bay glared at him and said coolly, "Just stay away, asshole, or you'll find out," and he led Livy away from him with his hand on her back.

When they were out of sight of the blustering captain, Livy stopped and swung around.

Announcing, "You are not in charge of me, Commander DaRocco," ire sparked at him from her blues. "I will thank you to stop bossing me around. I am going to go work with the other females."

She stalked away from him, leaving him standing with his mouth open. Then his lips closed while he shook his head with a lop-sided grin.

He watched her disappear into a mod then he took off to find his team and get moving on the plan. Livy's plan. His Livy. He'd figure out a way to get her back by his side. Where she belonged.

They couldn't use battery operated saws or anything that would make a lot of noise that might carry for miles, but they were far enough away from the mountain and insulated by the dense jungle that the sound of axes and handsaws couldn't travel to Ejaz Pasåd's lair.

Working around the clock, by the time the storm struck two days later, they were ready.

Near the narrowest fork of the river before most of it dipped below ground, they amassed their debris.

Even while the storm still raged, and it was a mighty monsoon, men continued filling the riverbed with the big trees that would be carried with the raging current to the narrow neck where they would lodge like a beaver's dam.

With no trees to hold back the banks of the river, heavy mud would break down and sludge downstream, to gather and slowly help block the water flow to the mountain.

People worked in shifts due to the tremendous strength of the storm. They tired quickly with the physical work under the pounding deluge.

Two more days passed, the storm was losing its ferocity. Soldiers checked back periodically advising the condition of the blockage, where it was and how much water it was damning.

Chapter Eighteen

Inside the mess where most everyone not working gathered to while away the time with food, card games, darts, and just talking, Livy was huddled in the corner with the other females, all agents from various countries. Her soft lips were pressed in an angry moue.

"Oh Livy," a brunette with toned muscles laughed at her as she threw down a queen of spades. Her British accent melodic as she spoke, "You should be grateful your big-ass commander refused to allow any of us women to be involved with the blocking work. I'm saving on my manicure, girl," she wriggled her red nails at the women.

"Honey," she smiled at Livy, "we don't always have to be in competition with the men. We all have our own strengths that can be used at different times in different ways. Let your commander do what he does best, command us using the best of our abilities at the right times."

"Yah," the German agent beside her agreed. Her body was thick with big curves, she had a round nose and curly blonde hair.

"I'm glad he nixed us having to go out there in that nasty storm. We're inside toasty and dry, honey. Here's my damned ace you pulled out, you bitch," she exclaimed cheerfully to the Brit as she threw her card on the queen.

The wind and rain had battered against the mods threatening to blow them away like Dorothy's tornado. Thanks to the soldiers' diligence in digging them in and securely tying them down, the buildings clung like roots sure to the ground.

The last few hours the whistling wind had died down and the rain had lessened to a slight drizzle.

"True that," Livy said still frowning, "it's nice to not have to do that hard work, but still, we shouldn't be treated like we're babies. We are just as capable as the men-"

"Sugar," the third agent, an American CIA, broke in. "Some of us are just as tough as the guys," she skewed a mocking glance at the German, then ran her gaze down Livy's petite frame.

"But you aren't. Shit, girl, you would have been blown away in the first wind. That storm was brutal. You would be more in the way than of any help, really. No, your commander," she glanced over with admiration at Bay sitting with his team across the room, "is right. You wouldn't have lasted 60 seconds out there. I don't see why you are so acrimonious to him."

The big blonde German, Gretchen agreed. "Yah, that is one fine hunk of meat. He never takes his eyes off you, Liv, and you won't give him the time of day. It's like a game watching you two. He tries to talk to you and you run away leaving him flustered with an angry, and sad face watching you go. What's up with you two?"

Livy shrugged and took two cards. "Nothing. I hardly know the man."

"Yeah, well, I think you're going to get to know him a lot better any minute," the Brit warned with a grin.

Bay was coming straight towards them. He stopped right beside Livy and nodded to the other women, "Agents."

They all smiled with coy invitation at him, but he only had eyes for Livy.

His hand on her chair, she was the only one who didn't acknowledge him. "Liv, we need to talk."

Her bottom lip pushed out, she carefully laid a card on the others on the table without a response to him.

"Liv," the insistence in his voice audible. The other women stopped playing and watched the couple.

Without looking up, Livy said quietly, "We have nothing to talk about, your friend did all your talking for you," then she snapped at the German woman, "you going to throw down or pass?"

"Liv, we are going to talk, right now. I don't want to embarrass you in front of the others, but we need to hash this out."

Her head slanted, she canted her eyes up at him. "Oh? Are you pulling rank, again?"

Bay jerked his fingers through his hair, then set a hand on the back of her chair and pulled it back for her to stand up. "If I have to, yes."

Everyone looked back and forth from one to the other like a tennis match was playing out.

No one moved, Livy faced the table.

"Livy," warning growled in his low voice.

Suddenly, an excited voice burst from the doorway, a soldier rushed in. "Commander!"

The room stopped hustling, grew quiet and everyone gave the soldier their attention.

Bay reluctantly turned from Livy, but kept his hand on her chair.

"Soldier?" he said quietly, his low voice traveled easily to the door.

The soldier hurried over to him. "Sir, the first of 'em, the *sicarioes* have come out looking."

Now Bay fully turned to him, moving his hand. "How many?"

"Looks like just half a dozen, sir. Our spies got 'em located almost to the blockade."

"All right," Bay sighed. "Keep them in sight, no one engages, stay invisible, no one gets seen. We want them to go back and get more help. Let's go." He looked at Livy, then suddenly bent, cupped her chin, and kissed her with such greedy lusting hunger, the other women moaned in envy.

When Bay pulled away, Livy's eyes were clouded, parted lips damp and pink, she blinked at him in a flummoxed haze.

He caressed her cheek with a knuckle. "As soon as this shit is over, we're talking if I have to carry you off somewhere private and tie you down."

He pivoted and strode off with the soldier and some other men following them out the door.

"Carry you off?" The Brit sighed, watching Bay stride away in his cargoes and black T with masculine coolness, strong wide shoulders tapering to a tight ass they were all staring at.

The lighting rolled over his hair accenting the honey tints, the locks had grown long enough in the past weeks to curl over the back of his collar. He swaggered confidently as a leader, the men automatically followed him.

"Tie you down?" Gretchen groaned, waving a hand at her flushing face.

"Girl," she said to Livy, "you can't turn that fine specimen away. He's panty-scorching hot. Damn huge jungle shoulders, powerful build to go with that arrogant manner, insanely good looking even with that hard face and aggression lurking in those searing green eyes."

She inhaled and shivered. "And his hands? Huge and strong, you can see that dick is-"

"Uh, please, uh, excuse me." Lord, they were as bad as the girls back at the base. Mortified, Livy jumped up and hurried out to go hide in the barracks.

By the end of the next day, the river was more clogged, lessening the water flowing through.

By the third day it was almost completely choked, very little water dribbled past. *Sicarioes* or 'blades' the cartel's hitmen darted back and forth from the mountain entrance, checking out the river and reporting back.

When barely any water trickled into the mountain, finally, several large contingents of men warily left the mountain lair to study it.

Bay gave out the orders, and all of the troops obeyed him without question. He had ordered the troops to stealthily surround the area where the river was obstructed and spy on the *sicarioes*.

The troops hid silently within the thicket of brush and trees, remaining silent and camouflaged invisible.

Bay posted more troops to come in from the sides and surround the front part of the mountain, and also had teams covering the exit tunnels out the backside of the mountain to catch rebels fleeing.

Bay had instructed the soldiers to wait until all the *sicarioes* that were going to come out were down by the river, occupied in setting up their equipment to start hauling away the debris.

The big trees that had been felled needed to be cut into smaller pieces before removing them from the river. With generator operated saws, they also brought picks and axes, wheelbarrows, the men worked, cursing, sweating bullets, grousing and muttering for hours.

When they were filthy and exhausted, Pasåd sent more men out to help, leaving the entrance to the cave fairly open for them to come and go.

Intent on clearing the blockage, no one noticed her until she was out in the open.

Down by the river dam where the *sicarioes* worked to clear it, Gretchen, the German agent, sauntered out from the thick scrub in short-shorts that stretched across a big round butt. On the top, a tight blouse exposed much of her large breasts.

Daintily combing her fingers through her shoulder-length blonde curls, she simpered, "Hello boys. I'm kinda lost, maybe one of you could help me?"

The *sicarioes* froze in shock.

Suddenly, completely distracted, a few spontaneously stepped towards her, instant lecherous lust in their eyes. All attention was on Gretchen.

A sharp whistle pealed out and all hell broke loose.

The *salīre* began, the military maneuver of agents and soldiers descended on the *sicarioes* all at once, from all directions, shouting, creating chaos, startling and confusing them.

Slashing and stabbing with knives, machetes, and bare hands, only a few of the gangsters died in the scuffle refusing to surrender.

Bay had ordered no gunfire if possible, he didn't want the rest of the gang in the mountain alerted to the ambush. The river jam was a good distance from the mountain.

Simultaneous to the river ambush, soldiers stampeded into the open front entrance of the mountain hoping to rush in and take everyone over with surprise and, this time shots were abundantly fired.

No one cared if every member of the gang died except for the leader, so they went in with guns engaged, soldiers eager to fire without hesitation at anyone who resisted.

Bay hoped to capture Ejaz Pasåd alive and bring him in to justice. The leader had valuable information that could save many lives, but if he died in the attack, it was better than letting him live to kill and harm forever.

Half his team at the river ambush, Bay, Jules, Von and Nels rushed in with the rest of the troops attacking the cave lair.

Surrounded by harsh rock, and hard packed dirt under their feet, they fought through noise and flying dust and stones shooting up all around them, screams and curses ringing off the stone walls.

A gun in one hand, a knife in his other, slashing throats as he worked his way through the throng of shrieking *sicarioes*, Bay kept his eyes peeled for the head of the cartel octopus, Ejaz Pasåd.

After the narrower, rough-hewn opening, the cavern widened to numerous carved out dwellings, illuminated with gas lanterns and generated lamps.

The rooms were crammed like normal homes, with furniture, appliances, satellite cable and the internet.

Bay had warned his people to watch out for innocent women or children, but was relieved they found only hardened, bloodthirsty criminals.

He slew several *sicarioes* guarding a broad, arched doorway. When he passed through, he ducked just as bullets flew past his head slamming into the rocky walls behind him.

Stones chipping from the rock piercing and ricocheting around him, Bay dropped to his knees on the hard earth and rolled while firing.

Jumping to his feet, Bay hurtled against a rock wall. Staying low, he saw Pasåd, manic, fierce and cursing death threats as he fired frantically spraying gunfire everywhere.

Dressed in a white shirt and trousers like he was on a tropical vacation, his dark face scrunched up, the stocky man with black hair plastered in sweat to his gnarly head was screaming and shooting blindly.

Bay vaulted across the door firing low. He heard Pasåd scream when a bullet hit him in the leg. Pasåd collapsed crying and cursing.

Bay rushed over and kicked the weapon out of the cartel leader's hand and slammed his boot on his neck, crushing him to the ground.

Grinning grimly down at the gangster, Bay gloated, "Ah, finally, this is the first day of the rest of your incarcerated life, you bastard, Pasåd."

Snarling and struggling under Bay's foot, his pained and furious dark face turning red as a beet, sneering with fury, Pasåd screamed, "Who the fuck are you? You're a dead man, you fucker, a dead man!"

Bay bent and jerked Pasåd to his feet, spun him around and handcuffed his wrists behind his back, then shifted him back around.

Bowing his head slightly with ignominious insult, Bay introduced himself. "I am Commander Bayou DaRocco of the DAK Special Opts Squad based out of the black side of Evgeny Surgo-Base.

"And, you, you son of a bitch, are under arrest. Feel free to speak or don't, ask for a lawyer or don't, I don't give a shit. Come on, you fucking killer," he yanked him forward making Pasåd limp on his injured leg.

Ignoring Pasåd's crying and whining between snarling and swearing revenge in several different languages, Bay dragged the cartel leader through the cavern and out the opening of the cave.

A hundred plus people in a gnashing gnarl of shouts and cries amassed outside. A few *sicarioes* were still in the cave, but they were prisoners in plastic cuffs. Soldiers were hauling them out and to the Mods were they would be held prisoner before taken away to reigning authorities to be prosecuted.

Pasåd's white clothes now rumpled, torn and smeared with dirt and blood, his face scratched, bloodied and bruised from Bay's violent take down, still cursed and threatened as Bay dragged him along and then turned him over to Jules and Von's custody.

Relieved of his prisoner, Bay strode around checking on the ambush at the river, and then around the rear of the mountain to see that they were completely successful in their coup.

Soldiers whooped at him in triumph, *sicarioes* cursed and hurled threats of vile vengeance.

Hours later Bay made his way back to the camp.

When he reached the hidden compound, he was greeted by more soldiers.

One of them looked up in glee. "Hey, Commander, check out this haul," he gestured to a stockpile of money, AK's, M4-A4 assault rifles, 50-calibre sniper rifles, heavy machine guns, a ton of ammo, an enormous stockpile of drugs, and more.

"You did it, Commander, you fucking brought down the biggest cartel in history."

Bay smiled. "*We* did it, soldier, all of us, without one loss on our side. And, we wouldn't have gotten this far without the brains of that woman in there."

He clapped the soldier on the back, then tromped through the rest of the camp congratulating and praising others as he went.

Done with the fire and brimstone, the only thing on his mind was seeing Livy and getting the shit between them straightened out.

He went to the mess-Mod first where half the people were gathered, chattering excitedly about the successful mission. He didn't see her there.

Captain Wright was clustered with his closest soldiers. Bay trod over to him.

A cigar clamped in his mouth, Wright greeted him with a bit more respect than earlier in the week. "Hey, Commander, congrats on the mission. We got 'em, eh?" When the soldiers had started felling trees and loading them into the river, Wright had given in and ordered his men to assist.

"Yeah, yeah, where is Livy Stirling?"

"Hell, son, as soon as that first group came out checking on the river jam, I put that little honey in one of the trucks and sent her out of here. She should already be in the air on her way back."

"What the fuck? You sent her away? Why?" Brows arched in angry puzzlement, Bay moved closer to the captain.

Wright shrugged. "She did her part. She's a civilian, like you said, it's too dangerous for her here in this clusterfuck, shouldn't have been sent in the first place."

Still confounded, Bay said, "Yes, but, now-"

"She's no longer needed, I sent her back. I didn't want her caught here if the shit went sideways and the cartel came to fight us here."

Captain Wright casually leaned his bulky body against the wall and imperturbably stuffed an unlit thick cigar in his mouth.

"Ha," a man nearby snickered, "you sent her back because she refused your advances. Heard she slapped you when you got a little too...frisky."

Other men close by laughed at the red that crept up Wright's rough face.

"Ah," rifling his palm across his greying buzz-cut, Wright chomped on his cigar. Spitting on the floor, he growled, "Little bitch doesn't know a real man when she sees one."

Bay snarled, "You fucker," and hauled his fist back and bashed it into Wright's jaw knocking him flat on his ass.

His ass on the ground, humiliated in front of the men, Wright cursed him, "You bastard," he rubbed his jaw. "I'll have you court-martialed for that."

"Sure," Bay snorted, "go ahead and try. I'm not in the military, I'm black-opts, you know I can't be touched. If I'd seen you lay hands on her I would have killed you, you prick. I warned you she was taken. So count yourself lucky you're not going home in a body bag."

He stomped away from the grumbling captain and made his way to the women's Mod. He knocked then went inside.

The mod was empty. He trod over to her air-mattress. It was gone, as was her duffle. "Fuck," he spewed in frustration.

"Hey, Bullet," Von said behind him, "it's good she's gone. It's too dangerous for her here anyway. She wasn't even safe from that asshole captain. The word was he cornered her alone in here. Livy slapped him when he was all over her.

"Wright was pissed and coming at her with his fists raised, at that moment that Brit agent came in and boxed his ears from behind and he split without another word. I only just heard about it now, we were out in the field when it happened. So, seriously, she's safer home than here."

Raking his fingers through his hair, Bay turned to him. "You don't understand, Von, she's no safer at home. There's a fucking escaped psycho killer after her, and I'm stuck here. I have to see to Pasåd's getting back to the authorities, I can't get to her. She has no protection, man."

Von asked, "What the hell happened anyway between you two?"

"Ah, that idiot Punchy was drunk and left a stupid text on my phone congratulating me on winning the bet by nailing Livy."

Von's brows drew together under a furrowed brow. "But you had nothing to do with the bet. You were pissed when he was even joking about it, so you weren't even involved. How did she know anyway?"

"She was at my place. I was in that last meet with you guys when the text came through. She read it, and believed it, and fled into hiding. I couldn't find her to talk to her and she's been avoiding me here. Fuck, I have to get back to her."

He started for the door, then stopped. "Von, you and Jules and the others need to see to Pasåd. I have to get to her, she's in danger."

"Of course, Bullet, we got it handled. There are tons of soldiers here, we got it covered. You go find her, keep her safe." Von clapped Bay on the shoulder.

"Thanks," Bay said with husky gratitude in his voice. "If it wasn't so fucking important I'd never leave an uncompleted mission."

"I know that, bro. The woman's life is at stake, that's more important than delivering a bunch of punk thugs to the authorities. Our job is pretty much done, anyway. We were to capture or kill them. Mission accomplished." Von grinned large, perfect white teeth at Bay.

"I'll get the transporting in action then I'll check back in with you when I'm on home soil," Bay told him. He was itching to get on a jet and get the heck out of Dodge to find Livy.

"All right. Go, man, we've got it covered."

After a grateful fist-bump, Bay rushed out the door to get the extraction organized and moving, but it was still ended up being days before he could leave the camp and start back to the U.S.

There was too much paperwork flowing through that required his signature and certain authorities like the FBI, CIA and others barraged him with questions about the mission.

At the very least he contacted Lieutenant Colonel Miles asking the LC to check on Livy and possibly supply a guard for her.

Chapter Nineteen

On the return flight back, Livy was given a message that she was to stay on the base for a few days and then check in with Lieutenant Colonel Miles upon his return from meetings out of state.

Since many people were out on missions, a bed was open for her to stay in the barracks.

When she was informed he had returned, Livy went to the LC's office and presented herself to his administrative assistant, Trisha Peck.

Dressed in a black skirt and white blouse, Livy stood stiffly in front of the woman's desk waiting for her be acknowledged.

When Trisha did not look up at her arrival, Livy cleared her voice delicately and said politely, "Hello, I am Livy Stirling, I am to meet with Lieutenant Colonel Miles."

Trisha abjectly ignored Livy, letting her stand in front of her desk for several minutes while she calmly searched fashion sites on her computer.

Livy was growing tired of being treated like a useless female. Clearing her throat louder, she said with as much polite assertion as she could muster, "Excuse me, Miss, the lieutenant colonel said I was to report to him as soon as I arrived."

Rolling her eyes, Trish sighed like she was being asked to give up her life's savings. Still, she waited before turning from her computer. When she did, her gaze raked Livy, her lip curling in a sneer as if she found Livy hideous.

"And you are?" Trish drawled even though she was well aware of who Livy was since she had announced her name, and she would certainly be on the appointment log.

Trisha's short, dark curly hair wisped around her face which would be pretty except for the red lips twisted in repulsion. Dark blue eyes studied Livy like she would a bug she want to squash under her foot.

Biting her tongue, Livy said evenly, "Elizavetta Stirling."

Again, Trisha trolled down then up Livy, and, again, her nose wrinkled and lip curled like she found Livy pathetically ugly.

The word had spread that Commander DaRocco had serious interest in the petite young woman with the big haunted eyes.

Most of the females on base took offense that Livy was new to the base and DaRocco had hit on her when he'd never hit on any other more than willing woman stationed there, including Trisha.

Trisha grunted and picked up the phone, pushed a button. "Sir," she said when the line was answered. "Ms. Stirling is here."

She nodded while hanging up the phone. Motioning with her head, she sniffed, "Through that door, there," and turned from Livy back to her computer as if she wasn't even there.

LOUISE FURLEY

Fine with Livy, she'd prefer people paid her no attention. She'd had enough attention to last a lifetime; she just wanted to be left alone.

Trying to ease the remnants of nerves still lingering in her tight shoulders from her experience in Turkey, her exhale was hard-pressed. She knocked softly yet firmly.

When she heard Miles call out "Enter," she drew in another deep breath and went in.

Lieutenant Colonel Miles stood up when Livy came through the door. "Ms. Stirling," he smiled kindly, "please, come in, have a seat."

He motioned to a pair of leather chairs in front of his desk.

The chairs, taupe colored with gold studs running down the front, a table with five matching chairs around it, and a bookcase lined with file folders filled in the rest of the room.

Awards and military photos aligned the walls, behind Miles' back a window let in natural light.

Livy hesitated, then she went over and sat in the chair he indicated. Smoothing the skirt, and nervously tugging on the blouse, her hair was wrapped up in a bun at the back of her head, her black heels gleamed.

As he sat back down, he averted his eyes when she crossed her legs.

"So, Ms. Stirling, I have a report here," he tapped on his computer. "You are to be commended for your intelligence and clarity figuring out a strategic way to get inside that mountain, capture the infidels with little physical risk to all, especially to our people."

His smile professional yet courteous, tinged with respect and admiration, he said, "You've barely started your strategy and air training and already you are a success. Even though you are still in training, you will receive a promotion, and a title."

He folded his hands on the desk, and leaned over slightly. He said gruffly with a slight incline of his head, "I am very proud of you." His brow quirked at her silent stoicism.

Then she murmured demurely, "Thank you, sir."

"Ah," he said, "Commander DaRocco said you weren't an egotist. That you were as smart and clever as you are beautiful."

His mouth stiffened in a slight frown at Livy lowering her eyes, her lips tightening. "Ms. Stirling, you know that I am aware of your...tragic history. I am sorry for the hell you've been through."

Her cheeks staining pink, Livy's eyes rose. "Please, Lieutenant Colonel, I really don't want-"

"Of course, I understand. I just wanted to let you know I know about your ordeal. Oh," he opened a desk drawer and pulled out a box, he pushed it across the table to her.

At her quizzical look, he explained, "Commander DaRocco left that with me before he went to Turkey. It's the keys and codes for the alarm system at your house, and how the alarm and the motion sensors work. He said to let you that that the window that had been broken has been fixed."

She just stared wordless at the box, making no move to take it.

Miles let out a problematic breath and sat back. "Ms. Stirling, I may be out of line, and heaven forbid I get in the middle of my staff's personal business." He sighed hard, then said, "But I'm going to say my piece anyway."

He smiled at the one brow that arched over her blue eye.

"I have known Commander DaRocco for quite a while. He and I have...well," he grunted a laugh, "a professional

241

relationship but we're also friends. He has confided in me his…difficulties with, uh, you."

Both brows arched. "Sir, I don't think-"

Cutting her off, he said, "Ms. Stirling, I am fully aware it's none of my business, and trust me, ever the gentleman Bay certainly gave no details. However," he pushed his chair back and stood up, then came around the side of his desk and leaned a hip against it.

Today he wore the same camouflage cargos and black T everyone else did. Crossing his arms, he nodded down at her.

"Bayou DaRocco is an honorable man. He was hand-picked to lead the DAK squad, a special black opts, because of his skills. He earned the rank of Commander in that specialized unit by his skills, his brains, immense bravery, his amazing strategic prowess, and his integrity. I know about the alleged bet.

"Honey, listen," he held a hand up when she frowned with mortification and opened her mouth.

"There was no bet. Agent Roddy Curtis was fooling with him. DaRocco didn't know you'd read that text and believed it. Trust me, Bay would have had no part in such ignoble behavior. He's tough as iron but a good man, Ms. Stirling, Livy."

He leaned over, setting his palm on the desk. "He is not a liar or a scoundrel, or a coward. Anything he told you would have been the utter truth. Please understand, I know nothing of any intimate details of your and DaRocco's relationship, only about the bet and the resulting outcome of it."

He took an uneasy breath before going on. "And Bay's distress over what happened, how hurt you were. As well as," he sighed with a slight smile, "his own anguish at your leaving him. He cares about you, Livy, sincerely. Uh, a lot." Color was streaking his sharp cheekbones at discussing his soldier's love life.

A tiny smile touched the side of Livy's mouth. "Lieutenant Colonel?"

Leaning against the desk, Miles set a hip on top of it letting one leg dangle. "Yes, Ms. Stirling?" He clasped his hands and rested them on his thigh.

"Why do they call Mr. Curtis, Punchy?"

Surprised at the unexpected question, Miles allowed himself a grin. "During their SERE, the Survival, Escape, Resistance and Evasion course- is part of the training for the special opts in case you're taken prisoner.

"One of the, ah, trainings, is you get punched in the face constantly to toughen you up. The more you could take, the less you got hit. Roddy Curtis couldn't take a punch, so he was hit a lot. Hence, the nickname Punchy. Next time we talk, I'll tell you how Bay got the moniker of Bullet," he said with a conspiratorial wink.

A genuine smile brightened Livy's face. She stood up, and picked up the box. "Thank you, Lieutenant Colonel. May I be excused?"

He nodded with a serious smile. "Of course. Just…"

Already starting for the door, she paused and turned around.

"Give DaRocco a chance, at least listen to him. I've never seen him give a damn about a woman before, you've tipped him on his head," he chuckled, "and I can't wait to see that hard fall he's going to take. Hell, woman, he's already bouncing his head on the ground from worry over you."

"Um," unsure what to say Livy looked down at the box in her hands.

"One other thing, Miss Stirling," he called out as she turned towards the door.

"Sir?" She swung back around.

His voice serious, Miles said, "Bay called me with concern and asked that I put a security detail on you. Unfortunately, there are so many out of the camp right now all I can do is send a detail to drive by your house periodically."

"Oh, okay."

"Just," he paused, raking a hand through his short hair. "Watch your surroundings. Stay on base as much as you can, use the alarm when you're home. Try not to wander about until the law gets this guy. And," he leaned forward, "call me or the base or 911 if you are even in the slightest alarmed or think you see this guy."

"Yes, sir."

"I don't need to tell you to not engage with this guy should he approach?"

Her brow lowered, lips thinned. "Of course not, sir, I of all people know how dangerous he is."

His head bobbed. "Yes, yes, of course. All right," he huffed a deep breath. "Carry on. Just remember to call ASAP if you fear anything at all."

"Thank you, sir." Livy dipped her head once and left his office.

She didn't have to resume her training for a few days so she jumped in her car and left the base aiming straight for home.

She wouldn't have to worry about Bay for now, he was still across the world, and with the alarm system she would be safe at her house.

The sun was setting behind her while she drove. Images of Bay trampled through her tired muddled brain as she hit the main drag. The big man with the hard face stalked her thoughts, she hated to admit it but she missed him.

The way his eyes turned from shamrock green ice to the color of the deep broiling sea when he looked at her. His tough hands on her body, rough and sure, skilled and insanely passionate.

The way he made her feel like she was drowning when he kissed her, so hotly dizzy, so unbelievably turned on. He could make her feel things she-

Livy shook her head dispersing the pictures in her mind of them naked together in his bed, and all around the rest of his place, and pulled into her driveway.

She parked the VW and went around the side of the house. The window she'd broken was repaired. A smile danced across her face, even when she wasn't there he had been taking care of her.

"Darn him," she sighed. When he got back, if he was still interested, she would listen to what he had to say.

Although, after all the time that had passed, and the action they had just gone through and he was still dealing with, she was probably the last thing on his mind.

The man was lusty and robust, he likely had already turned to any of the other various females that had given him blatant invitations, and thoughts of Livy were long gone from his randy brain.

Traipsing back to the VW, she took out the suitcase and brought it to the front door. She had studied the contents of the box the LC gave her while sitting at red lights.

She memorized the alarm code and unlocked the door and pressed the buttons to reset the alarm so the police wouldn't come.

Letting out the breath she held, she set the suitcase down and turned on a lamp. Something was different, a glint caught her eye.

Livy looked across the room and her eyes widened in stunned wonder. Holy cow, there was a television. A brand new flat screen- the box under it indicated there was also now cable.

Gasping, "What on Earth?" she trod over and saw a short quickly scrawled note.

She picked it up and read:

Don't fly into a panic, Livy, the cable is paid for up to a year. You owe me _nothing_, and you are not a charity case. I want you to be happy even if you choose not to be with me.

STAY SAFE.

Bay.

Unbelievable, she smiled setting the note down. What she needed was a nice warm, scented bath.

Shaking her head at Bay's generosity, without him even knowing where he stood with her, she headed for the kitchen.

Pouring a glass of water she brought it, candles, and her cell into the bathroom.

First, she took a quick hot shower to wash her hair, then flipped the plug lever and kept the water running to fill the tub. Drizzling in some bath salts and adding bubbles, she lit the candles.

The scent of vanilla flooded the bathroom. Turning on the cell to her music, she wrapped a towel around her wet hair and set a toe in the churning water.

"Ahh, that is nice."

Music playing softly, she slowly sank into the silky warm water. Laying her head against the rim of the tub, Livy closed her eyes and tuned everything out.

Shutting off her brain, she lay partially floating, letting everything slip away with the floating bubbles.

The track of soft music ended and swept into the music she had programmed for her workouts at the gym.

She hadn't been going to the gym long enough to have a sufficient amount of tunes so the track ran out after only a few songs.

Livy held up a hand and giggled at her wrinkled finger.

"I'm a prune, time to go." She lifted the lever for the tub to drain, stepped out and dried off.

Blowing out the candles which were now puddles of melted vanilla, Livy went into her bedroom to put on jeans and a short-sleeved, thin knit sweater.

It was growing dark but she didn't turn on a light. Yet something glinted, again. She looked over and smiled.

He'd bought her a TV for her bedroom too.

Sighing at his generosity and missing him, she murmured aloud, "What am I to do with that man?"

Her drying hair waving into curls down her back, she wandered back into the kitchen to get something to eat.

Wondering how long it would be before Bay returned to the States and they could talk things out, maybe have that relationship they both seemed to want, she flipped the light switch, and stopped walking.

The lights didn't come on.

She flipped the switch again and again, nothing.

"Darn bulb," she muttered and strode across to the light over the oven and pushed the button.

Again, nothing. Heading to the laundry room to flip the breaker, mumbling, "Must be a power-outage-"

"Elisabella," a deep voice, silky cheerful, yet coarse in its monstrous malevolence sauntered out of the dark shadows.

Spikes of terror rushed up Livy's spine shooting up the hairs on the back of her neck.

She swung around with a cry of disbelief. Shock sucking the air out of her lungs, Livy stumbled back against the counter.

"Kenaz!" she gasped.

The horrific memories slammed back to her like a vicious punch, as evil-personified stood in her kitchen grinning a Joker's deadly leer at her.

Chapter Twenty

"Miss me?" he said with smirk. All 6'3" of him leaned casually against the doorframe, blocking the exit.

Her hands went to her throat, Livy croaked, "How did you get in-"

The smirk slunk into a nauseating smile. "I tried to cut the wires of the alarm but whoever had it installed was smart. It was installed so that any kind of tampering with it whatsoever would set it off. So," he shrugged, "I just got to that transformer there at the end of your street, and, voila, no one has any electric."

He took a step further into the kitchen, grinning as he watched the goose bumps visibly pop up her arms.

"I saw the bathroom lights on, your hair is wet," he sighed with a vulgar groan, his hand went to his crotch. He palmed his erection.

"I just wish I'd gotten in here sooner and caught you while you were in the bathtub, naked, so sweetly vulnerable. I mean, what man could resist that?"

"The- the phone calls," Livy stammered trying to stall, "I knew it was you."

Confusion rippled across his face quickly replaced with his smirk. "Anyway, you got dressed quick. Bet I can get you undressed just as quick, huh?"

His nasty leer turned Livy's stomach in repulsive fear, her hands clutched together trembled.

Blatantly squeezing and pawing his hard-on, he grinned a mix of lust and rage. "You know the cliché of the serial killer who just hates the one that got away. Well," he nodded with an offensive cheerfulness. "Have I got plans for you. For us."

"I, uh," her throat so dry, Livy licked her lips. "My boyfriend is coming any minute...with- with his friends. They are all special opts agents, big, strong," her trembling voice rambled with the words shaking out, but she couldn't help it.

Taking another step into the eerily darkening kitchen, he still smiled. "Please, Elisabella, don't lie to me, we have so much...history together, why, we're practically friends. Ah, I much prefer your real name, Elisabella, not that weird Elizavetta some moron came up with thinking to fool me."

"No- no, I'm not lying, he's coming right now, any second. He carries a gun. A lot of guns. He- he's an ex-marine." She backed away but had nowhere to go, the kitchen counter was already at her back.

Kenaz had a squarish head made up of thick hard ridges. With the long dark eyes he looked like a bloodthirsty yet elegant Russian gangster. Severally sculpted full lips chuckled.

"You have to know, my precious Elisabella, that I have been following, yes, stalking you. Sure, you disappeared a couple of weeks ago. I couldn't find you, thought maybe you were shacked up like the whore that you are.

"But, your friend, Farah, I think her name was, was a fountain of information. She said you hadn't dated since you got to the base, that you are estranged from your parents, and you have a few days or so off so no one will be looking for you. I was actually not prepared to take you so soon. I didn't think it would be so easy to find you and get to you. But, here you are, so-"

"Was?" Stricken with dread, Livy's face drained of what little color it had left. "Please, you didn't hurt Farah?"

While she talked, Livy reached behind her to a black marker she'd left on the counter and wrote *Kenaz* on the tiles. If only she was within reach of a weapon, a knife.

Lips still curved up like the foul Joker's, he shook his head as if regretful, but the obscene smile said not really. "Come, really, Elisabella, we spent enough time together, you know me pretty well. I will say, she was a disappointment. Gave you right up after my very first question."

"And," he frowned, shaking his head, "she died too quickly. She wasn't any fun, not like you, my brave beauty."

He looked up at Livy, the smirky smile returning. "Okay then, enough reminiscing, let's go," he stalked straight to her.

"No!" Livy screamed and lunged for the silverware drawer.

His hyena laugh ringing through the small kitchen, Kenaz pounced on her.

She jerked the drawer open and grabbed a fork and waved it at him.

In a blink he snatched her wrist and wrenched the fork out of her hand, throwing it with a mocking laugh.

His sick psychopathic laughter was the last thing she heard as his fist connected with her jaw knocking her out.

As she started to come to, Livy's head, feeling stuffed full of cotton was pounding, her jaw ached.

Blinking slowly, and carefully shaking her head to clear it, she went to move, and could not. She jerked at her arms, her legs, they wouldn't move.

Her head was hanging forward, hair over her face. Her gut coiling with fright, Livy realized she was sitting in a chair and her wrists and ankles were tied, just like...before.

She didn't want to, but she forced her pained eyes to open fully, and then snapped them shut after one horrifying look.

Her heart plummeted as terror raged through her body, she was back in the cabin.

With her one quick peek she'd seen Kenaz's table of instruments of torture a few feet away. Knives, electrical wires, scalpels, screwdrivers, other things she didn't even know what they were.

Her flesh quivered as if he were there watching her, but her peek had revealed the room was empty. That gave her some reassurance to fully open her eyes and truly see her dire predicament.

Breaths rushing out in ever increasing frantic huffs, twisting her head in all directions only confirmed that she was indeed in the original cabin where he had held her and the other unfortunate victims captive. The tools were there, Kenaz was not.

Looking down, her skin crawled. The floor was still covered with gobby bloodstains. The police must have just sealed the cabin up after investigating it and removing the bodies. The other chairs Kenaz had bound his hapless victims to were askew around the room.

Livy's chest hitched, tears of helplessness stung her eyes.

The monster wasn't even there and he still had the power to torment her, scare her beyond comprehension. Of course, she was restrained, she didn't need Kenaz present to generate fear.

Livy struggled against the ropes, but, as she already knew, it was futile. She had to just sit there like a girl on a platter waiting to be consumed, in prolonged, brain frying, exquisite agony. She wondered why he wasn't there.

Kenaz had calculatingly placed her chair so she wasn't facing the door, thereby ratcheting up the tension and fear by not being able to see him coming at her.

She might have no warning before he…touched her. She was pretty sure she was alone in the building. There was only the one large room in the cabin, she could see the miniature kitchen from where she sat.

Of course the cells in the back where he'd kept the girls before taking them out for torture weren't visible from where she was.

The door to the tiny bathroom stood open, as was the small window in it. She would be able to hear if he was hurting other women in the…cells.

She glanced towards the window, she had been out for hours, dawn was verging. Maybe he went for supplies, he'd said he had caught her sooner than he expected.

"Great," she bemoaned. "I'm so damned easy to capture. What a helpless, careless wuss."

Wait- a shadow passed by the window.

Her stomach gripped in terror. *Oh no, he's back!* She could not prevent the shudder that reeled through her like a current of electricity, and he hadn't even started with his electrical games.

253

Her head already spinning with fear, her entire body quaked with desperation. Gasping like a fish out of water, Livy struggled to not scream in her panicking fright.

Out loud, whispering through lips chattering with tremors of rising hysterical dread, she claimed firmly, to make herself believe it, "I refuse to give in. I refuse to give him the satisfaction that I am scared out of my mind. I will not scream no matter how…much he does, *how bad it gets*," her words ended on a choked hopeless sob.

The step outside the cabin squeaked. He was right outside the door!

Livy couldn't see the door, she couldn't see the knob turn, but she heard it. Then she heard the old rusty door creak open. Her nauseated stomach rose to strangle in her throat, Livy's breaths raced in rapid, silent screaming pants.

Thankfully she hadn't eaten anything or she'd be barfing it up. As it was, it was all she could do to keep her bladder from releasing as the terror grabbed hold of her with grisly fingers, and squeezed.

Footsteps crept painstakingly, torturously across the floor, coming up behind her.

Livy closed her eyes, dropped her head and held her breath but the sobs wracked inside her chest.

Chapter Twenty-One

"Bella?"

Her head flew up, eyes popped open. "Daddy?"

"Oh God, Bella," his voice aching, Livy's father moved to stand in front of her. "My poor baby!" Tears streamed down his face as he clasped his hands in front of his chest as if in prayer.

Mouth dropping aghast, she croaked, "Daddy? What are you doing here? Wait, first, untie me!"

He looked around, saw the table of implements and grabbed up a knife. Quickly, he cut the binds on her wrists then crouched and freed her ankles.

She jumped up and threw herself into his arms, crying, "Daddy!"

The hand that stroked her hair shook as Anthony Blossemia wrapped his arms around his daughter.

They both clung and cried, then Livy pulled back. "Daddy, how did you find me?"

Anthony brushed her hair off the side of her face caught in her tears. "I went to your house. You wrote us about it, but," he smiled sadly, "you haven't invited us to see it. So, I flew out without letting you know ahead of time so you couldn't come up with an excuse not to see me." His sad expression was a mirror of hers, they both held a measure of guilt at their estrangement.

"The lights were off, your car was there, but the kitchen door was wide open. I went inside, looked for you, obviously you weren't there. I noticed the electric was off, that made me suspicious. In the kitchen I saw where you'd marked *Kenaz* on the counter and I knew that deviant had taken you. Again."

The strain of fear for her welfare creased around his mouth tightening it and shrinking his eyes, and was in the tremor of his arms that held her.

"The guilt, Bella, it was eating your mom and me alive, it's why we treated you so damned poorly. It was my fault, if I had only answered my phone…" his deep breath dragged with pain. "You wouldn't have had to go through that horror, and the other girls, maybe…"

"We don't know if things could have been better or worse, Daddy. We all need to move forward." She hugged him hard. Then, "But, here, the cabin? How did you find it?"

Wiping at his wet eyes, sucking in a deep breath, he nodded. "Yes, what's now is what is important. I kept all the paperwork, the trials, everything from the…incident. The location of the cabin was in the papers. So," he shrugged.

"I figured it would be a place to start. I called the police, but as an adult, and since there was no evidence you had been taken against your will, they wouldn't do anything about you until you were missing for 48 hours. So, here I am."

"Oh Daddy, this time you came for me!" Livy cried and hugged her father.

After a brief respite of relief, Livy dabbed at her streaming eyes and stood back from him. "We need to go, right now. He could be back any second, we need to-"

256

"Elisabella, darling, you should have let me know we were expecting company," Kenaz drawled. He stood inside the threshold. So big, he blocked most of the early morning's rising light.

Anthony shoved Livy behind him. He bellowed with rage, "You won't get her in your clutches again you filthy sick bastard!" He raised the knife to hold Kenaz off.

But Jered Kenaz only laughed, hard. "Seriously?" Taking in the slim man in his late forties no taller than 5'9", he laughed some more. On a chuckle, he said, "Mr. Blossemia, I presume?"

Neither Anthony nor Livy said a word. Livy clung to her father's shirt and Anthony planted his feet on the ground holding the knife in the air.

"Elisabella, you should be proud of your daddy coming so bravely to rescue you. I see where you get your courage from. Alas," he bumped one shoulder and pushed the long sleeve of his shirt up to one elbow, then shoved up the other sleeve as if he was about to get to work. Heavy work.

"You clearly have no fighting experience," he mocked, his gaze sneering down Anthony Blossemia's thin frame and glasses over his professor-looking face.

The killer started to move into the room.

"Stay back, I swear I will cut you!" Anthony shouted, waving the knife.

Kenaz burst into gales of laughter. Doubling over, he clutched at his belly while he roared with laughter.

"You- you're insane you psychotic monster!" Unsure how to take the madman's behavior, Anthony stood still with the knife still raised. He ordered the deranged killer, "Get out, get out of here-"

Kenaz straightened up and in one motion, his face withered in disgust and venom, he threw a knife striking Anthony in the chest.

Livy screamed.

Anthony froze in shock for a heartbeat, then he crumpled to the floor.

His face a mask of fury and the promise of death, Kenaz turned his attention to Livy who was still screaming.

Voice rock hard, void of any hint of sympathy, or humanity, Kenaz warned, "Just for that, the pathetic heroics of your father, I will prolong your torture, my Elisabella, even more."

He put his foot on Anthony curled up on the floor and gave him a nudged kick. He didn't move.

Kenaz smiled up at Livy, grinning at the tears streaking down her face. "You were my favorite, you know. I kept you for last. I wanted to savor you, fuck you raw, for however long I wanted to, before starting the cutting on that beautiful face, slicing up that creamy skin. Those amazing tits," his sadistic gaze fell to her chest heaving in terror.

"I wanted to feel them, fuck them, and," he grinned, "fillet them."

The cruel grin drifted into a sicker, fouler smile as he started to advance on her. "And now, my precious, I can finish it. You are mine for as long as I-"

Livy darted for the door leading to the cells.

Running as fast as she could, she could hear his sick, insane laughter following her.

Swallowing the sobs for her injured father, she fled down the corridor, her shoes clacking on the cement. She found the cells, hoping she could lock herself in one.

It would only be a short breather as he would maybe have the keys, maybe not. But he could sit and outwait her. She'd rather die of thirst or starvation then let him at her.

"*Oh no,*" she cried, the doors had all been removed from the cells. His footsteps pounded down the hall behind her.

Quickly, she surveyed the room for anything, even a chair to hurl at him, but the area was completely empty. She jumped behind the open door.

"Elisabella!" Kenaz bellowed from outside as he ran to her. "I will make you pay out of your skin for making me chase you!"

He ran inside the room.

As he passed by, Livy jumped out from behind the door and raced back through the corridor.

Roaring, "Goddammit!" Running back after her, he thundered, "You will be fucking sorry when I get my hands on you, Elisabella! I will peel off every inch of your skin while you scream for mercy!"

Livy ran as fast as she could, bursting hysterically into the main room, but he was right behind her.

Kenaz grabbed her hair and snatched her back against his chest so hard he winded her. His breathing loud and deep, his chest bumped against her back as he caught his breath.

His fist wrapped in her hair, he wound his other arm around her, pinning her arms down along her sides.

Livy's lungs wheezed with her fear and trapped frantic breaths.

His mouth against her ear, he cooed, "Okay my darling, you've had your fun. But this won't be a repeat of last time. This time, you won't get away from me." He licked the side of her face laughing at her grimace and pushed her towards the chair.

"Please, Mr. Kenaz," Livy begged. "You're going to kill me and you've killed my father. Please let me say goodbye to him. Please."

Forehead in a scowl, at first he was going to deny her, then Kenaz considered it and he smiled. "Sure. It will make my torture all that much sweeter watching you slobber all over him. Go ahead. Give him a kiss goodbye then get your ass in that chair."

His gaze greedily eating her up, he licked his lips and said, "As soon as I bind you, those clothes are going. I'll prop dead papa up against the wall so you can stare at him while I defile you, and cut up that gorgeous body."

Anthony Blossemia was still curled on his side, his white shirt already soaking with blood from the knife in his chest.

As Livy knelt sobbing beside her father, Kenaz turned his back to pick up the rope.

When he turned around, she was standing. And she plunged the knife she pulled from her father's body into his heart, and then jumped back with a shriek.

Kenaz's hands went to grasp the knife's handle, his eyes wide with shock and then disbelief, then, they glittered with admiration.

Clutching the knife, he couldn't pull it out because he was already dying. "My Elisabella," his breath heavy, "you are still my favorite-" he tumbled to the floor and lay on his back, blank eyes staring at the ceiling.

One hand covering her mouth, the other on her stomach as Livy suppressed the waves of nausea and terror, she watched him making sure he was dead.

His chest no longer rose with air, his eyes were already turning opaque. She hurried to her father and dropped to her knees.

Livy put her fingers on his neck, his pulse fluttered.

She ran back to Kenaz and ripped his shirt off him then crouched back beside her father and pressed the shirt on his bleeding wound.

Luckily, the knife had been small and Anthony had shifted just as Kenaz stuck him and it hadn't gone in that far, it appeared to have missed anything immediately lethal, although he would likely bleed out if she didn't quickly get help.

She felt his pockets and took out his phone. Turning it on she saw there were no bars. "Oh my, God," she wailed. "There's no satellite in these cruel woods."

Livy got up behind her father and shoved her hands under his armpits and dragged him. She pulled him across the wood floor thankful it wasn't carpet that would make it even harder.

It took forever, she was small, and no matter how thin he was, he was dead weight. She had to drag and rest a second, drag and rest a second.

She got him outside, and she hated to do it, but she had to drag his body down the steps. Cringing with the awareness that she was hurting him, she still had to do it.

Outside, Livy left him to lie on the grass and she ran to Kenaz's vehicle that had parked behind her father's blocking him in. Peering in the window, she saw the keys in the ignition.

"Yes!" she crowed. "Finally some luck." Biting her lip, she hurried back to her father to get him into the car. "Daddy, please, I could use your help," she cried to him, but he was out cold.

Standing behind him, she shoved her hands back under his arms again and dragged him. It seemed to take forever for her to get him to the car.

Suddenly, an arm wrapped around her and jerked her up and off her feet making her drop her father's arms.

Livy screamed and kicked. "What? Let me go!" she shrieked.

A male voice she didn't recognize, the tone unpleasantly sarcastic, snarled, "I think not my little frump."

The man's arm was so tight around her chest she could barely draw a breath.

He set her on her feet, swung her around, grasped both her hands and shoved her back hard against Kenaz's car.

Holding her wrists in one hand, Duke Rashad forced them roughly over her head, bending her spine back over the hood of the car.

Holding her taut, he leaned back enough for her to see his scarred face. "Yeah," he grinned meanly at her horrified gasp, "you remember me."

The man who had accosted her that night at the bar that Bay had beaten to a bloody grisly pulp was there.

How could that be possible?

Was she in a never ending nightmare?

Chapter Twenty-Two

"I don't understand, what are you doing here?" Livy cried breathlessly through a throat quickly fusing with renewed terror.

Duke moved his legs between hers and shoved her feet apart. He forced her to lie on her back arched over the car while he leaned above her keeping her arms over her head pinned against the hood with one huge hand.

Her arms staked, his legs between hers keeping them spread hard apart, she couldn't move, couldn't even lift her head.

Dark hair fell over triumphant dark eyes. His olive skin glistening with sweat, Duke drew a finger down the side of her face.

"Yeah, I gotta tell ya, hon, this whole thing goin' on here shocked the shit out of me. I returned, you see, for revenge of course, and I find you have some crazy killer stalking you."

His shoulders lifted as he glanced over at the open door to the cabin. He could see the fallen Kenaz lying in a spreading pool of blood near the doorway.

"Now that he's eliminated, good job by the way, I'm gonna give you what I wanted to that day before the fucking commander got his ass all involved. Then, I'm gonna kill you and get my revenge on DaRocco watching the fucker suffer for your loss."

Livy's eyes widened at his handsome face seething over her marred with several scars.

Seeing her blanch when she saw the damage, he growled furiously, "Uh huh, your lover's work. I owe that bastard. But it's easier to get to you, I will hurt him through you, bitch.

"It will hurt him more knowing I raped and tortured you, and he was helpless to save you. He will have to live with what I do to you, and with your death, knowing it was all his fault."

"How-" she shoved with all her might, he slammed her back against the car bruising her shoulder blades and banging her head on the hood.

Her arms and back stung and ached from being arched back so far, pressed down so hard, and slammed against the car.

He pulled her up on her toes, making her legs and hips curve and stretch so far she thought she'd snap in half.

Slamming her again with a hard shake, Duke bent his contemptuous face close to hers and taunted, "You aren't going anywhere, bitch, I have plans for you."

A knife suddenly appeared in his hand and with one quick slice he cut her thin sweater down the front, the torn halves fell apart exposing her bra and her panicked chest pitching in fear, flat stomach sucking in with shock and horror.

Mocking her, he snorted, "You wanted to ask how I got here?" Sniggering with mirthless humor, he said, "Hell, it was child's play to find where you lived, and so fucking crazy." He grunted a chuckle.

"You are so fucking popular, I wasn't the only one staking out your house, go figure. I called a couple of times just breathing, yeah, to frighten you, irritate you, but to also trace the line to make sure I had your correct address. Sneaky, huh?"

For every struggle to escape she made, the wider his smile grew, and the harder he squeezed her wrists, and the more brutally he slammed her back against the car.

Her fear seemed to excite him more, Livy fought to slow her breathing. Her chest billowing with her panicked breaths only attracted his attention to her breasts that he was pressing his own thick chest against, and brought a sick lascivious grin to his destroyed face.

He shoved her hands up further over her head, sadistically wrenching her up to the point she was almost completely off her toes, and tears of pain slipped down her face.

Duke set the hand with the knife in it low on her hip, pushing her harder against the cold metal of the car, and intentionally brushed his thumb over her sex.

Laughing when she tried to squirm from his grip, he shoved her legs further apart to immobilize her even more and said, "Yeah, I watched that freak break in and snatch you. I didn't know what he was up to so I followed you guys.

"I read he escaped from prison after raping and killing a bunch of chicks, and you're the one that put him there, like you could have done to me, huh? But I'm no damned freak like him, right?"

Yet, he sounded impressed with the sick antics of the serial killer, Kenaz. "I parked way back and hid for a bit to make sure no one else was coming. Then I started hoofing through the woods to creep up on you guys, but before I got far from my car I heard a vehicle coming. I ran back, hopped in and followed the crazy fucker as he drove outta the woods."

Livy didn't care how he got there, her mind was on how to get away from him.

"The guy only drove to a small bait shop for some shit and returned. Hell, girl, by time I parked again and made my way here you'd done the deadly deed. Tell ya honestly," he winked, "I kinda wanted to watch him do his thing with you."

Livy wasn't listening to his drivel, she was stretched taut like a rubber band about to break over the hood, and Duke nestled his hardened erection between her thighs and against her womanhood so she could feel it.

As he spoke, he crudely rubbed it up and down and back and forth on her cleft over her jeans, roughly dry humping her. His gaze lowered to her breasts rounded over the peach silk bra.

His brows drew down, he held her hands with one of his, the other clutched the knife and he clearly wanted to touch her, but he couldn't grope her while holding her wrists and the knife.

With a grunt of exertion, Livy tried to thrust him off her again and was rewarded with another vicious slam on her back. His boots dug into the graveled driveway as he pressed harder against her, shoving her further up on her toes with his pelvis.

With a slow slice, he cut her bra and stuffed the knife in his belt, he didn't fear her fighting him off, he had a foot and a 100 lbs. on her. Scantly covered by the cut sweater, her bare breasts swung into view, bouncing when he thrust her harder against the hood of the car.

Livy jerked a hand free but he quickly grasped it and slammed it back over her head. Leaning over her, holding both her hands with both of his, a huge unpleasant leer brightened his marred face.

His dark eyes roamed over her face, down her chest and back up, the heat of his breath gusting her skin. A taunting smirk curved up half his scarred face.

"Honey, you ain't no frump now are ya, I was pretty wrong with that. You're actually damned hot, damned fine. I'm gonna fucking eat you up." Duke licked his lips and bent to suck the swell of a breast.

He slathered his tongue over her skin, chuckling with his lips on her plump breast as she tried harder to squirm from him.

Holding her arms rigid to the car, he sucked her flesh viciously hard until she whimpered, then he bit her. Livy couldn't hold back the scream at the sudden pain.

Her struggles, grunting and writhing under him to get free, only made him laugh and lean back to admire the red blotch and teeth marks he left on her soft breast.

"Yeah, that's it, my mark. You're mine now, gorgeous." He covered her mouth with his. Before she could try to bite him, he brutally kissed her then moved to suck on her neck.

"Duke, listen," Livy cried panting, bending her neck to the side trying to get away from his teeth viciously biting her flesh.

"Yeah, babe, I'm listening," he leaned back, and with a grin, ripped her belt open and wrenched the button on her jeans apart.

"I am so fucking hard, babe, I want to take you inside and fuck you in comfort, but I can't wait. I'm gonna have to fuck you here against the car first then we'll go in for more. Does that meet with your approval?"

Snickering, he licked the inside of her ear, and suddenly crushed her breast so hard in his hand with such rough viciousness she cried out.

He grappled at her jeans trying to shove them down, but he couldn't do it with only one hand and his legs between hers. He moved, releasing her hands, and gripped her jeans to tug them down-

Livy jerked her knee up jamming it as hard as she could into his privates.

The air sucked out of Duke's lungs. Eyes bulging, he grabbed his nuts and buckled with a hacking moan, falling to the ground clutching himself, he retched.

Livy ran.

Behind her, she heard him puking, coughing, and croaking curses and threats at her. She didn't think she had time to get in the car and get out without him grabbing her, so she ran around the back of the cabin thinking she could disappear into the woods.

Huffing rapid breaths, her heart pounding in her throat, Livy raced behind the building and came to a sudden stop.

The back only went a few yards and she could see, the land suddenly chopped off. The ground ended in a steep, sharp, sheered gorge with deadly rocks jutting at the jagged foot.

She remembered. The river was below, just a few feet beyond the rocks. She had fallen into it the last time. She was lucky that time, the fisherman had caught her, she wouldn't be so lucky this time.

"Oh God," she begged in a harsh whisper, "help me!" She had no choice but to run back around the other side of the cabin hoping that Duke was looking elsewhere for her if he was on his feet.

Holding her breath, Livy ran as fast as she could, racing blindly around the side of the cabin- and slammed right into him.

He grabbed her with hard fingers digging around her arms.

She screamed and thrashed, kicked-

Chapter Twenty-Three

"Livy, stop, it's me, Bay!"

Déjà vu all over again! His cool, deep, wonderful voice above her head, he pulled her into his chest.

"Oh Bay, oh God," she sobbed, burying her face in his shirt.

"Okay, Liv, everything is-"

"No!" She wrenched back. "He's here, out front, we need to-"

"I know, baby." Bay set his hands on her shoulders and glanced to the front of the building. "Kenaz, I saw what you wrote on the counter, he-"

"No," she fought to get loose of his hold. "Not Kenaz. I killed him, he's dead. It's Duke-"

Thinking she was losing it, Bay spouted, "Rashad? Duke Rashad? What about him? What do you mean you killed Kenaz?"

"Bay, Kenaz took me, he's dead. Duke followed us, he-he- wants to hurt me, us. He's out front. He- he had me, I kicked him, got free and ran. Didn't you see my dad? My dad is hurt, Bay, he's on the grass. You didn't see Duke, that means he's behind us- he'll come after us, we need to get out of here!"

Growling in consternation, "The fuck you say, Liv," his eyes fell to her cut sweater, to the bruising fingerprints and bite marks on her exposed breasts.

A dark scowl defacing his already hard looks, Bay pushed her behind him and started stalking around the cabin to the front yard.

"No, no, please, Bay, he has a knife! I don't know if he has a gun too, please, we need to hide!" She tugged on his shirt to hold him back.

"Stay behind me," he ordered and kept moving. She had to let go or she'd fall on her face.

Bay strode quickly, then slowed as he started around the corner of the cabin.

As he neared the edge, he dragged his fingers, sporadically scraping them along the wood structure, purposely making noise, letting Duke know where he was.

As he stepped around the corner, Duke slashed out at him, but Bay was prepared.

He dodged the knife, clutched his hands together and bashed them down on Duke's arm as he hacked at Bay and lost his balance when he missed him.

Duke bellowed at the pain of his likely broken arm, then switched the knife to his other hand and slashed in rage at Bay's gut.

Bay jerked his stomach in, the knife flashed past him with an inch to spare.

As Duke kept going with the momentum, Bay grabbed at the back of his collar, jerked him around and smashed him in the nose.

Duke howled with agony, dropped the knife and covered his nose with his good hand.

"You hurt my girl? You fucking hurt Livy you sonofabitch-" Bay rammed his fist into Duke's stomach. When Duke doubled over, Bay bashed him in the face again.

Duke stumbled, Bay grabbed his shirt again yanking him to his feet and pounded on him until he crumbled to his knees, and he still beat him.

"Bay, no-" her hands covering her mouth Livy tried to stop him.

"Stay back, Liv," Bay snarled at her and smashed his fist into Duke's ruptured, bleeding face again and again. "I mean it, he won't hurt you again. Ever."

Livy grabbed frantically at his sleeve, crying, "No, Bay, stop, you can't, don't be like him, don't kill him!" she pleaded.

His huge fist in the air, Bay slammed it down on Duke's throat crushing his windpipe. "My code, Liv," Bay grunted in short panting breaths. "He was gonna rape and kill you, I'm only gonna kill him. It's what I do, what I am trained to do."

Wrapping a hand around Duke's crushed neck, he muttered furiously, "Baby, you don't need to suffer through another goddamned trial. Now, stand the fuck back." He held a hand out waving her away.

Stepping back, "No, Bay," Livy whispered, "don't."

On his knees, sitting back on his heels, Bay hesitated, then hit Duke so hard he broke the rest of the bones in his face, and then he let him go.

Duke plopped on the ground, alive, barely, unconscious, his face a bloody pulpy mess.

Wiping his sleeve over the sweat pouring in his eyes, Bay said to Livy, "Baby, you-" she was gone.

"What the fuck Liv-" he jumped up and ran after her.

Out front, Livy was crouching beside her father.

Bay sprinted to her.

"Oh Bay," she sobbed, "he's still alive, but I don't know, there's no phone service out here, I need to get him to a hospital."

She looked up at him, but he was running down the driveway. "Bay! Wait!" she shouted. "Don't leave me!"

In seconds he drove up in his truck and hopped out.

Hurrying over to Livy, he crouched, grabbed Anthony Blossemia's arms and shoved him over his shoulder in a fireman's lift.

"Come on," he said to Livy as he strode to his truck.

He gently laid Anthony in the back seat and climbed behind the wheel as Livy scurried after him and struggled up the high step of the truck.

Laughing, Bay leaned over and caught her arm, pulling her up on the seat. As soon as she closed her door he blasted down the drive and to the street.

Heading to the hospital, Livy turned in her seat to look at her pale father, his chest barely rising with shallow breaths. "Your truck, it wasn't there, how-"

"Yeah." Bay glanced at her with one hand on the wheel. "Duke parked down the tree covered lane so you wouldn't see his car. I saw it, but I thought it was Kenaz's so I parked behind it. I didn't want him to see me coming."

While he drove, his head flicked back and forth from the road to her bouncing jiggling bare breasts, and back and forth. He shrugged out of his shirt.

"Here," he handed it to her, "you need to cover up or we'll get in an accident." His mouth quirked in a regretful grin as she took the shirt and slipped into it effectively covering her breasts.

Buttoning the shirt, she smiled at the big bruiser behind the wheel with gratitude, relief, and affection. "How, I mean, everyone just keeps popping up! How did you find me?"

He grinned at her then turned his attention to the front window. "You're not only one who can think strategically, baby. I saw where you'd written Kenaz's name on the counter. He wasn't so wealthy he could just buy or rent property all over the place. So, I thought, where would be the last place anyone would look for him?"

"The original crime scene, the cabin. You are so smart, Bay," she purred with admiration.

"Yup. Actually, I had the team doing a search, but there was nowhere else we could possibly look. I took a chance and came out here."

"Oh Bay, you came for me!" Livy shuffled close to him and caressed the side of his face. "My black-opts shining knight came to rescue this damsel in distress." Shyly, her shoulder drew up. "Thank you, Bay, thank you."

He smiled, turning his head, he reached for her hand, caught it and kissed it. He twined their fingers and held them.

"Always, baby, I will always come for you, my beautiful ice princess."

Chapter Twenty-Four

$\mathcal{A}$ few days later, Livy stood outside her father's hospital room looking through the window. Her mother was inside with him.

Marielle Blossemia stood beside her husband's bed, bent over and clutching the one hand that didn't have tubes coming out of it.

"Livy, uh, hey," a male voice came up behind her.

When Livy turned, she crossed her arms, cocking her head at the ruddy-skinned man with the auburn waves. "Roddy," she said flatly.

"Uh, yeah, so, how ya doin'? How's your dad?" His sheepish tone and lowered head displayed his shame. He raised his head and grinned lopsided at her shocked gasp.

She was gaping at the big black shiner around his one swollen shut eye.

"Yeah, Bay had a little, *chat*, with me." The grin turned to a serious straight line. He wriggled his shoulders and stretched his neck side-to-side.

"Listen, Livy, we were just kidding around, I was being an ass. Bay had nothing to do with the bet. We, I was drunk, I was just fucking- uh, messing with him. I didn't know

275

you'd see that stupid text. I knew he had a chick in his room, and then I saw your little car in the garage next to his and then I knew…uh, that it was you. Seriously, Livy," his voice shook slightly.

He looked directly at her, the remorse darkening his light green eyes. "I never meant to hurt you, I swear. Please, don't be mad at Bay."

A soft smile curved her pretty lips. "I'm not, Roddy. If I had just stuck around, trusted him, I knew what kind of man he was by then, but," she shrugged.

"I was pretty fragile at that time. Now, I know he would never do anything so…" The side of her mouth tugged up in a grin. "Immature, un-chivalrous, misogynistic, pig-"

"Okay, okay," Roddy held a hand up with a hangdog grin. "I gotcha. Trust me, I learned a lesson. So," he ducked his red head then grinned anxiously at her, "are we good then?"

Uncrossing her arms, smiling, Livy stood on tiptoes and kissed his cheek. "Yeah, we're good."

"Hey, what's going on here? Do we need to have another chat, Punchy?" Bay strolled down the hall towards them. "Your hands need to get off my girl, bro, like yesterday."

Roddy quickly stepped way back from Livy with his palms up. "No, no, no way, Bullet. We were just," he glanced at Livy who was grinning at Bay. "We were just clearing the air, seriously, we-" he trailed off.

They weren't even listening. They only had eyes for each other. Smiling cheerfully, Roddy trod off down the hall giving the couple some privacy.

"Ah, I leave you alone for one second and you're all over one of my men?" Bay teased, his hand skimming across her side then up her back, pulling her into him.

276

"Hmm," Livy smiled, slipping her hands up and around his neck. "I was curious about redheads, you know, does that red hair make a man's kiss any more hot-"

"You're never going to find out, babe," Bay retorted, the hand at her back pulling her closer, the other cradled the back of her head, bringing her in for his kiss.

"I am the only man you're going to be kissing from now on." He lowered his head to capture her mouth in a steamy, hungry kiss.

Ignoring the chuckles from passersby, they continued kissing until the door to Anthony's room opened and Livy's mother came out.

"Livy!" she squawked. "For heaven's sake, you're making a spectacle of yourself!"

Marielle Blossemia scolded her daughter, "We brought you up better than that, kissing in public for crying out loud!" She made tsking sounds while shaking her head.

Her hands still wound around Bay's neck, Livy gave her mother a hazy, happy smile. "No worries, Mom, we were just leaving."

His hand curving under Livy's chin, Bay gazed lovingly into her blue eyes. "Yeah, we're going back to Livy's house to clear out the rest of her things and bring them to my place."

"Oh!" Marielle's face stained red. Her brows slashed down in disapproval. "Living in sin? Livy, I hardly think your father and I-"

"Only for a short time, Mrs. Blossemia," Bay assured her, lowering his honey colored head to Livy again.

Against Livy's lips, he said, "Because we're getting married as quickly as we possibly can. I'm not letting anything or anyone come between us again." He cradled her head and whispered with a grin, "I'm never letting you out of my sight, Frosty."

Marielle's brows flared straight up to her hairline that was the same as Livy's. "What? Oh! Oh my, well, we need to, hey-"

Ignoring her, Bay slid his hands under Livy. Lifting her into his arms, he started down the hall, their eyes connected, unwavering.

Winding her arms around his neck, over his shoulder, Livy called out to her mother, "I'll call you, Mom, later."

His mouth descending on hers, Bay muttered, "Yeah, much later. We have a lot of catching up to do, don't we baby?"

Grinning at him, Livy nodded, letting him suck at her lips. "Yes." She whispered, "I think we may have missed one or two pieces of furniture…in our christening of your place."

Bay crushed her against his chest with a big, lusty smile, "Oh yeah? We need to hurry then, don't we?"

Striding down the hall with his precious bundle, his lips on hers he murmured, "I can't wait to get you home. To our home."

"Can't wait!" she exclaimed against his mouth.

He leaned back, grinning happily at her. "Baby, did I tell you that I love you?"

Livy nodded beaming blissfully. "Yes, about a hundred times on the way back from the cabin, and all week, all the way here, all the-"

He sealed their lips, the grin still on his face.

Their mouths still touching, he said, "Just wanted to make sure you heard me. I'll tell you I love you every day of our lives together. And we'll tell our children we love them every day too."

Her lashes sprang up over widened eyes. "Our children?"

Bay set his forehead against hers and nodded. Smiling broadly, he said, "Oh yeah. Only thing we need to clarify is how many. How many do you want, baby?"

Livy caressed the side of his face. "I never thought about it."

"Well then, we should just get started on creating them. We can decide as we go along. What do you think?"

Lifting her head for more of his kisses, Livy whispered, "I think I love you, Bayou DaRocco, and I always will."

His eyes lit with tenderness, Bay replied, "And I love you forever, Elisabella Blossemia."

The End

Dear Reader, thank you for choosing <u>Bay's Bet!</u>

I know you could have picked any number of books to read, but you chose this story and for that I am extremely grateful.

I hope you enjoyed this novel, and if you did, **please leave a review** *where you acquired it, and look for other exciting titles in my name!*

About the Author

Louise Furley loves writing romance with a huge helping of suspense. Sunny Florida is home where Louise is a graduate of St. Thomas University with a master's degree in Mental Health and lives with Bob, her own hero.

Louise is the author of numerous published novels. When not researching or writing, she is dreaming of unique plots, and discovering fresh ventures she hasn't yet experienced in the world.

Ride along with her as she travels new and thrilling journeys!

If you loved this adventurous romance, please check out the first few chapters of <u>Neco's Rescue</u>

Chapter One

Neco Bardiche let the answering machine pick up the call. He had no desire to talk to anyone. Ever again.

As he passed the landline phone, he heard his brother's voice speaking. "Come on, Nek- pick the fuck up, I know you're there, pick up-"

Neco grabbed up the landline and growled into it, "Why are you bugging me, Josh, you know I want to be left in peace." He cradled the phone between his shoulder and ear while he headed to the kitchen for a beer.

"Nek, give it a rest," his older brother scolded, "you know damned well none of it was your fault, none. You can't let-"

Neco sighed not bothering to hide his irritation. "I don't care anymore, Josh. I'm finally getting back on my feet, you know I don't want to see or talk to anyone." *Least of all my family who keep trying to nurture and comfort me.*

His brother's sigh came through loud and clear. "Yeah, we know. But you can't just blow us off because your heart is aching. Mom is so freaked you won't return her calls. You can't just shut off family because of the tragedy."

1

Neco dragged a hand heavy with annoyance through his hair then sucked down half the beer before saying, "Josh, enough said. You all know I want to be by myself for a while. Just leave me alone."

"Nek, bro, I can hear that tough edge in your voice, you've turned cold. Ice cold. You sound like, I don't know, like a man who has been released after doing ten years of hard time in prison, stone-hard and empty. It's damned scary."

"Yeah, so? I don't fucking care."

Silence. Josh's breathing was so loud it sounded like he was right in the same room as Neco.

Josh kept his voice level, carefully submerging any sounds of reproach, "It's been like forever, bro. First you disappeared for months. We find out you buried yourself out in the damned wilderness somewhere living like a wild bear or something, climbing mountains, hunting your food. What are you Grizzly-fucking-Adams?

"Then you leave the city to go build a house in that rural town, Lark in northern Washington, and hit the bottle. You can't go through the rest of your life regretting, and blaming yourself, and drinking yourself to death. You need to come home."

Pinching between his eyes with his thumb and a finger, Neco's aggravated sigh was harsh, loud, he didn't care. "No. I'm not coming home. I moved way the hell out here in no-where's-ville to get away from people. All people."

"Even your damned family, Nek? You have to punish us along with yourself?"

Dead silence.

Josh waited. Still silence. "Okay, fine. Stay out there in the sticks and nurse your broken heart and your pride. We'll give you some more space, and then we're coming." His voice intense, imposing his will over his younger brother's, he demanded, "You hear me?"

Neco shut the phone off and set it in the cradle. He stared at it for a long time. The longer he stared the colder and harder, and emptier, his heart felt. In fact, he no longer had a heart. A stone had taken its place. He felt nothing.

Maybe down the road he'd care about his family again, but right now, after all the fucking shit that went down, he felt nothing and wanted to see no one. Just leave him alone so he can work and try to get back all he'd lost.

Well, that was never going to happen, you can't bring deceased people back. His stomach stitched with a sudden pang. He shook off the feeling and went to get his only friend now, another beer.

Hysterical with terror, she ran for her life, down one dark street after another. The rain blinding her, the wind shoving her in so many different directions it was a job to keep upright, avoid crashing into something.

Screeching tires squealed behind her even on the slick streets as the car took the corners ruthlessly chasing after her.

She couldn't draw another pained breath. Panting like a building on fire, shallow breaths with tightening wheezes, her lungs felt like cement she'd been running so long.

Her legs heavy with fatigue were slowing down, she couldn't keep this up. But she had to keep going, if they catch her they will kill her like he had-

The car careened in front of her just as she burst out of an alley to the street.

She screamed, tried to stop and back-pedal, but it was too late- Two men jumped out of the car, grabbed her and hustled her into the back seat.

One of the men climbed in after her, the other man hopped in the front passenger seat and the car took off.

The man next to her clutched her neck, the look in his tiny mean eyes brutal. Digging his fingers into her throat he commanded with ferocious fury, "Tell me, where is it? Tell me and I'll let you go."

Trying to catch her breath, she could feel the sweat pouring down her shaking spine. Her eyes wide in horror, he held her so tightly she couldn't move her head.

His dark eyes sparking fiercely, squeezing, jerking her neck hard, he spat with threatening menace, "Goddammit, tell me now or I swear to God you're fucking dead!"

She stayed mute, trying to swallow under his tight clench, her big eyes staring unblinking with terror and hopelessness over his big hand.

He released her then hauled his fist back and socked her.

Then he hit her again and again and again until her world went black.

Chapter Two

Driving back from the store with the raging storm thundering all around him, Neco was still thinking of the earlier phone call with his brother. It got his craw up that they wouldn't just leave him alone.

Josh told Neco that he was wallowing in self-pity and to buck up and get it together, move on. How could a person move on from such devastation?

Neco shook his head, that was never going to happen. Life had changed irreparably, he would never be happy, carefree, or damned trusting ever again.

Cursing a blue streak, it was a job to keep the truck on the road. The storm was fearsome, sleeting wind slammed at the vehicle like a hurricane. The driving rain had been unrelenting torrential for hours and now the drops had turned to golf-ball sized hail.

The hail hit the windows so hard he wondered how long it would be before the glass cracked.

Cursing a blue streak, "Dammit-" he mumbled, jerking the wheel to avoid a flying branch. The rain rushed in thick opaque grey sheets making visibility almost nil.

The truck suddenly went into a wild skid, he scuffled with the wheel trying to pull the truck back into his control.

The side wheels caught the mud on the side of the road making the truck slide even worse, skating sideways until it crashed into a mess of shrubbery in a gulley.

When it came to a sudden hard stop, Neco's head snapped forward. "Great," he grumbled rubbing his neck. "Now I'll have fucking whiplash." He slammed the truck in park to take a moment and regain his bearings.

Peering out the windshield he saw the visibility had only gotten worse. He had turned the radio off when the news alert advised that the river had swollen and pretty much cut off the rural town of Lark from the main city of Sanlura.

The officials advised everyone to stay off the roads until told otherwise, besides accidents, sudden flash floods could be deadly.

"Goddammit," he swore again, slapping his palm on the steering wheel.

Muttering out loud, "All I want is to get home," he jerked the truck into drive. Cranking the wheel to steer back up on the road, he groused on, "Get a beer, plop in front of the fire, and catch the game is all I ask."

He swerved the truck back to the road, half the vehicle was still in the gulley and half on the blacktop. The tires slid, making a nasty grinding noise, but they managed to grab some traction.

Through the obscuring rain something off the road just inside the bushes caught his eye.

"What the hell-" Damn, he wanted to go home but he was drawn to see what the hell had been tossed into the gulley. An uneasy feeling crept into his gut.

As he got closer and struggled to see out the shrouded windows, the hail beat like billiard balls all around the truck, clanging and clacking as they struck hard.

Brows scrunched, Neco muttered, "It looks," he leaned closer squinting out the passenger window as he pulled up, "like a bunch of clothes."

He sat back with a scowl. "Great, some asshole thinks it's okay to toss their trash anywhere, fucking litterbugs." In a huff, he yanked the wheel to pass by it when he thought he saw- a human leg?

"*Shit-*" he wrenched the wheel to get back off the road and shifted the truck in park. Last thing he wanted was to get out in that damned storm, but, a leg? Meant there was a body...

Shoving his ball cap on, he zipped up his jacket. He tugged the collar up around his neck, took a deep breath and got out of the truck. He had to fight the wind to get the door shut behind him.

Jogging to the bundle of clothing with his head down, the hail and rain and wind slapped and beat at him. He was huffing in seconds from his laboring struggle against the hellish storm.

When he reached the clothes, he crouched down and his heart did a summersault.

It was a woman.

She was scrunched up like she'd been thrown out of a moving car and landed hard and rolled.

Neco leaned closer, his stomach clenched. She looked...dead. He'd been in the service; dead bodies didn't freak him out, but a small, slight, torn up woman dying alone on the side of the road?

He shook his head and tried to keep his dinner down. He knelt and felt for her pulse anyway.

Setting two fingers on her cold neck, he barked, "Hell!" and jerked his hand back.

She had a pulse, it was so light he almost missed it, but she was alive. "Holy shit," he ground out. Taking a few seconds to ponder the situation, he made a decision.

Yeah, he should wait for EMT, but they couldn't get through this storm, and sure, he could cause her further damage moving her, but she would surely die if he left her there much longer.

He slid his hands under her and lifted her in his arms as he stood up. The hail pounded them both. She was totally sodden, the wind tossed her hair and clothes, he couldn't see her face, but she didn't weigh much.

He bent over to shield her as best he could with his body and carried her to his truck. He had to maneuver her to lay her over his shoulder to free a hand to get the door open.

The wind fought him at every step, the rain blew under his cap blinding him. He finally wrestled the door open and gingerly laid her across the bench seat with her legs curled on the seat. Slamming the door shut, he hustled around to the driver's side.

Neco didn't spare her a glance as he floored the truck to get it out of the gulley and fishtailed onto the asphalt.

Once he got the vehicle righted and heading down the road, he glanced at her.

Her skin was as pale as a ghost, her lips blue, *damn*, what was he to do with her?

The news alerts said the river was already running over and flooding half the town cutting them off. There was no way he could get to the city to take her to the hospital. He had no choice, he had to take her home.

Like driving in a whirlwind tornado, the truck went airborne several times. It skidded and the wind pushed it sideways, but Neco finally pulled into his driveway and stopped in front of his house.

He shut off the truck, ran to the front door, got it open and then hurried back. He opened the passenger door, she hadn't moved. Her hair covered most of her face.

Taking a deep breath, he reached in and scooped her up. Closing the door with his hip, he strode quickly through the storm and finally into the dry, warm, safety of his home.

It was murky inside. He hadn't left any lights on and the storm made it darker.

Shuffling to the couch, he bent and carefully set her down. First thing he needed to do was get her dry and warm and then see how seriously she was injured.

Leaving her for a second, he hit the lights then ran and got blankets, a flannel shirt and sweatpants, and grabbed up a pair of his wool socks and hurried back to her.

She was still out.

He leaned over and put his ear to her chest. It barely rose, her breaths were so shallow.

"Ah, damn," he muttered in concern. He lifted the top of her, shoved a blanket under her then did her bottom half.

He needed to get her wet clothes off. But he couldn't make himself move.

She was an unconscious, helpless, injured woman and last thing he wanted to do was violate her in any way, and that meant touching her, undressing her.

Taking a deep breath, Neco picked up another blanket and laid it over her. He slipped off her shoes then slid his arm under her back to lift her up.

She was wearing a blouse and skirt. His big fingers fumbled at the tiny buttons on her blouse. It was a struggle to try to get the soaked blouse off and keep the blanket over her to protect her privacy. She could be someone's daughter or wife.

He knew how he'd feel if some strange guy stripped his sister if he had one, and leered at her helpless naked body.

As he undressed her, his stomach lurched with sickness.

Her arms and ribs, even her neck was covered with cuts and huge nasty bruises.

He dropped the blouse on the chair next to him and feeling like a pervert, slipped his hand under her back to unclasp her bra. He'd caught a glimpse of it, dusty pink, silk maybe. He'd seen more but tried to block her breasts mounding over the bra out of his mind.

They were plush and soft and- he shook his head to dispel the picture, chastising himself, "Come on, asshole, you're not some damned perv ogling an unconscious defenseless woman."

Dropping the bra, he covered her top with the blanket then went to work on her skirt. Sure, he was used to undressing women, but this was creepy.

Undoing the skirt, he tugged the wet material down her legs and tossed it on the chair. Bile gagged him as he saw a giant bruise rose over most of her hip and down her thigh, her legs were scraped up, probably from hitting the road. He prayed she didn't have any broken bones or internal damage.

He paused, he couldn't help it, she was small but her legs looked long, maybe because they were so slender with a pretty nice shape- dammit- he shook his head. "Knock it off, creep," he rebuked himself again. The girl was badly hurt and he was perving on her.

Lifting the blanket higher, he noticed that her panties matched the pink silk bra.

It was difficult, but he lowered the blanket and reached under it, grasped the sides of the swathe of sheer material

10

and as quickly as he could, yanked them down and off and threw them at the chair, leaving her totally naked.

Neco tried in his mind to remain analytical, like a doctor examining a patient. It didn't work. Being a normal red-blooded male with his hands all over a finely built naked woman, he was burgeoning wood.

He pushed at his wet jeans cursing himself for getting a hard-on over a woman who was helpless to protect herself against his voyeurism. But, as slim as she was, she had a curvy little body. And worse was yet to come. He had to dress her.

He did the best he could without looking directly at her nudity. Finally he got her into one of his flannel shirts, sweat pants, and wool socks. Everything was huge on her.

He didn't have a bra and panties lying around so she'd have to go commando- *oh great*, his wood turned to iron.

Letting out a hard breath, at least she was no longer naked on his couch. He covered her with another blanket. Now to see to her wounds.

Shaking his head, he stared down at her and asked, "Why the hell did this have to happen to me?"

Looking up to the ceiling, he cried, "Why, God, haven't I been punished enough? I ask to be left alone and you drop an unconscious injured woman on me and make it impossible for me to get her to the hospital."

He held his palms up in supplication. "What next, huh? What else are you going to throw at me?"

The young woman laid there not moving, barely breathing, covered from head to toe in bruises.

Struck with a hint of guilt, he realized it wasn't about him, it was about her. Ashamed of his whiny tirade, Neco knelt beside the couch.

It was hard to see what color her hair was, it was soaked. But it looked maybe like golden-brown, amber? Tawny? Now where did that come from? What man uses the word tawny?

He gently pushed the wet locks off her face and groaned. It was hard to tell what she looked like, her face was swollen, cut up, and a mass of bruises.

His stomach churned, he kept smoothing her hair back, he couldn't make himself stop, like it was a compulsion. His brain was trying to protect him from comprehending the grisly job someone had done on her face.

The damage was no way from a tumble out of a car, no matter how fast it was going and how hard she landed and rolled. Some fucker had beaten her to a pulp. There were fucking fingerprints around her throat. Neco thought he was going to puke.

He forced himself to stop clawing at her hair, and got up and went to get a towel.

Carefully, he tried to dry the long wet mess with the towel. The locks had to go at least halfway down her back. Part of her was muddy and some cuts were bleeding, he needed to get her cleaned up.

Hurrying to his bathroom, he came back with washcloths, another towel, and a first aid kit.

He bathed her face, neck, back, her arms and legs, feet. Then he set about cleaning her cuts and putting antibiotic and bandages on the best he could. He wouldn't know about broken bones or a concussion until she woke up. If she ever did.

No, he wouldn't let himself think like that. No one was dying on his watch. "Huh, like it wouldn't be the first time. Crap," he snorted sarcastically, mentally beating himself up.

Anguish sucked at the pit of his stomach, memories could be a vicious enemy. He pulled his thoughts back to the present, again reminding himself that it wasn't about him right now.

When he'd done all he could, he sat back on his heels and stared at her.

She looked from what he could tell, young, maybe late teens early twenties. She had a heart-shaped face, small nose and pointy chin. Her lips, he bit back a sigh, were what they called 'pouty' in the magazines.

Her mouth was small but puffy, even battered it made a man want to stop what he was doing and suck on it. His dick had settled down somewhat and now the stupid thing was back at attention.

Studying her face, he couldn't tell what she looked like, she had too many bruises. Her eyes were purple and swollen shut, the pouty mouth had a split on the side.

Rage fired in his belly and burned up his chest. How the fuck could anyone strike this- girl, much less beat the shit out of her and throw her out of a moving car?

Maybe she threw herself out trying to get away from the bastard who was beating her. Yeah, he smiled bleakly, that little chin looked defiant. She probably gave her boyfriends, or whatever, husband maybe, a run for their money.

He tucked a pillow under her head and stood up. There wasn't much else he could do for her. He was soaking wet and cold, he needed a shower himself and dry clothes.

Leaving her tucked in, he kicked off his boots and padded down the hall to the bathroom.

Chapter Three

"What do you mean she got away?" the man snarled, glowering at the three men standing in front of him struggling not to cower.

"Explain, and fast, Harry." He was so furious he almost shattered the glass of cognac he held. If he got liquor all over his Dolce suit someone would pay with their neck.

His ebony hair was shellacked back, each strand straight and gleaming. A scowl crimped his strong face with a domineering nose and equally forceful chin. Neat winged black brows with only the faint touch of grey at his temples pointed to his age at low-forties.

"Sir, Mr. Pryce, I was, uh, trying to get the information out of her. She wouldn't talk so I uh, beat her." Thickset Harry glanced at his boss to see if that was okay, the boss nodded without changing expression.

Harry was big and hulking as hired thugs go, heavy shoulders and barrel-chested, short buzzed hair, dark round eyes and thick lips.

Harry went on awkwardly, "So, uh, somehow, I mean, she just wouldn't tell me where it was, so I beat her until she passed out. We were in a freakin' shit assed storm, couldn't see a hand in front of us, right Don?" He glanced nervously at the man who had driven the car, a tall, narrow yet muscular man who nodded nervously without looking at him.

Mr. Pryce fastidiously smoothed his silk tie in an effort to maintain his composure, but his rage was already boiling over.

His tone deliberately menacing, a snarl curling his full lip, Pryce sneered, "Yeah, so what. You let a little fucking rain stop you from getting what I want from that young woman? She's practically a child for God's sake you assholes. You better not have killed her. Besides the pictures, you know I want that bitch in my bed. How the hell did she get away if she was knocked out?"

Harry stammered, "Well, um, well," he looked at the other man with his brows lifted asking for help. "You tell him Don, tell him how bad the storm was!"

His austerely cut, doyen face scrunching into a gnarl of wrath, Pryce bellowed, "I don't give a shit how bad the fucking storm was you pussies!" His words thrust out with spittle at the three men. "It was rain goddammit, not bullets. I said tell me how a slip of a female got away from you three burly fuckers. Now!"

Don and the third man stared at Harry with their mouths clamped shut. They hoped Pryce's wrath would stay on Harry.

Harry's heavy bumpy face paled, his big Adam's apple bobbed in his thick neck with rapid hard swallows. "Well-uh, we were driving down some freakin' rural back road and I kind of nodded off. She uh, must have woken up, I guess, and before we knew it, she had opened the door and flung herself out!"

"Yeah," Don finally jumped in. If Pryce didn't believe Harry, then he and Landers, the third guy were just as dead as Harry.

Don resisted the urge to rake his long knobby fingers through his short blond hair and stuck them in his pockets instead. Shiftily glancing from Harry to Pryce, he sniffed and worked his shoulders to get his gumption up.

"Speak, you idiot!" Pryce thundered. He normally had zero patience and now he was about to pull out his gun and shoot the lot of them. These types of thugs were a dime a dozen. He could replace them with a click of his fingers.

"Yeah, yeah, okay." Don swiped at the sweat beading over his eyeballs making his lashes damp and heavy.

He explained, "I stopped the car as soon as I could, but it was dark and you couldn't see shit in the storm. We drove around, back and forth. Hell, there were hills and gullies and ravines and shit, and woods, she could have tumbled down a hill to another road or into the woods."

"We," he glanced at his compatriots who were staring at the floor, "we just couldn't find her. It was dark," he repeated.

The three men stood nervously waiting for the boss to speak.

Wandering over to stare out the window, Pryce took genteel sips at his drink.

Watching the rain still pelting the glass, he looked blankly out the window, not seeing the gloom, the thunderclouds, the streaks of lightning flashing in the black clouds.

Without turning around, his voice calm and cold as a snake's, he ordered, "Find her."